a MOVEABLE FAMINE

a MOVEABLE FAMINE

John Skoyles

THE PERMANENT PRESS
Sag Harbor, NY 11963

A Moveable Famine is an autobiographical novel. While the narrative follows the timeline of my life, it is not an exact record of events. I have collapsed several characters into composites, and have created others from my imagination. Where I have related stories concerning known persons, I have used their real names because the incidents described are as I recall them.

For information, address:
    The Permanent Press
    4170 Noyac Road
    Sag Harbor, NY 11963
    www.thepermanentpress.com

Library of Congress Cataloging-in-Publication Data

Skoyles, John.
    A moveable famine / John Skoyles.
        pages; cm
    ISBN 978-1-57962-358-6
        1. Authorship—Fiction. 2. Identity (Philosophical concept)—
Fiction. I. Title.

PS3569.K6564M68 2014
813'.54—dc23   2014006118

Printed in the United States of America

PREFACE

We were hell-bent to become poets and all poets stood in our way. We had been outcasts in high school, stars in college and had graduated from finishing school in the art of verse. We drank and smoked and fucked as much as we could while bemoaning our middle-class upbringing and the wasted lives of everyone who did not see the world through the lens of poetry, a lens cloudy with the jizm of jerking off in furnished rooms, which we called suffering.

We contemplated suicide when our thoughts were ineffable. We contemplated suicide when we transformed our thoughts into bitter poems. We contemplated suicide when the world ignored our poems, and we committed suicide when we were ignored by the world of poetry.

With women, we were sensitive, bearing the burden of witnessing our nation's militarism, the savage effect of the

Dow Jones on the poor, the illusion of the comfort offered by religion. We pitied our parents, our siblings' scrounging existences and two-week vacations. We pitied their ignorance of the human heart and their refusal to rake the bottom depths of the soul.

And in those depths, we forged friendships with poets who loved our poetry. Poets with whom we would tap, knock, bang, and finally demolish the doors of poetry's academies, societies and foundations.

We were hell-bent to become poets and all poets stood in our way.

CHAPTER ONE

POEM IN THE BATHTUB—WORD POWER—
GREENWICH VILLAGE—FRANK O'HARA—
MATER CHRISTI—THE CHIEF
PROSECUTOR OF GALILEO

⚮

My mother recited the same poem every night when
she gave me a bath—the ballad Oscar Wilde wrote
while imprisoned for sodomy, a poem in which he envies
a fellow inmate, a murderer sentenced to hang, for having
the passion to commit a real crime. Part of the long narrative of "The Ballad of Reading Gaol" goes like this:

> Yet each man kills the thing he loves
>   By each let this be heard,
> Some do it with a bitter look,
>   Some with a flattering word,
> The coward does it with a kiss,
>   The brave man with a sword!
>
> Some kill their love when they are young,
>   And some when they are old;

Some strangle with the hands of Lust,
Some with the hands of Gold:
The kindest use a knife, because
The dead so soon grow cold.

The bells of the Good Humor truck, children shouting and occasional police sirens drifted into our Queens railroad flat. By the end of each week, I learned a new stanza. Although I didn't understand it, it intrigued me. There were knives and wine and blood, just as in our church, Saint Bartholomew's, named for the martyr who had been flayed alive. Led by nuns, we paraded single file under a statue of that saint who held a blade in one hand and his skin over his arm like a suit. My mother, Olga Bertolotti, grew up in that same neighborhood in a large Italian family. Her sisters became nurses and secretaries and her brothers joined the transit authority and fire department. The men on our block prized close haircuts and shaves; their wives wore heavy foundation garments. Every sofa and armchair was fitted with a plastic cover. My mother graduated from Newtown High, whose most famous alumnus was Don Rickles, where she won a contest for putting the words of the school anthem, "Sing with a Will for Newtown," to the tune of "Glow little glowworm." The prize was a poetry anthology, *A Quarto of Modern Verse*.

The summer I was twelve, I found that book on the knick-knack shelf next to Hummel figurines of girls swinging baskets of daisies, but ignored it in favor of my father's paperbacks, *Increase Your Word Power* and *Thirty Days to a More Powerful Vocabulary*. My father didn't finish eighth grade, but had gotten a job as an envelope salesman and wanted to keep it. The office manager gave him these books and told him to read the *New York Times*. He became the sole white-collar worker on a block of policemen, longshoremen and steamfitters. His story imbued the books with a magical promise—they had *power* in the title, the power to transform a man.

When I did pick up the quarto, I found the words of Wilde I'd memorized, the poem printed across from a photograph of the flamboyant poet with cape and cane. Kipling held a pipe under his brush mustache. Poe scowled next to the outlawish Stephen Crane. I hid the surname of dapper John Masefield with my pinkie and imagined my own name there. If I read a poem twice, I had it memorized.

It never occurred to me that poetry was still being written until one afternoon, sitting in front of the TV eating chocolate snaps, I watched Art Linkletter hold a microphone to Big Eric, a bearded beatnik tapping a bongo drum and reciting in a Greenwich Village coffee house. Women with straight hair and black leotards clicked their fingers in applause. I asked my parents to take me to Bleecker Street. Surrounded by Le Figaro Café's dark mahogany, men smoked pipes and played chess. I ordered a Himbersaft for the strangeness of the name. It turned out to be a simple raspberry soda, but I savored it because a Himbersaft in Le Figaro Café was different from a Coke at Woolworth's.

Most weekends I sat on the lip of the fountain in Washington Square Park listening to folksingers. On Eighth Street I bought a print of wide-eyed children behind a torn chicken-wire fence. I associated these waifs of Walter Keane with the Beats simply because they showed emotion. I listened to anyone who wore a beard and swayed under a tree declaiming from a sheaf, and one afternoon I stood before a toothless old man who lisped a long litany, every line of which began, "Hear my heart." I found a discarded *Village Voice* on the Number 7 train to high school. The front page printed a poem by Frank O'Hara called "To the Harbormaster," and I placed it in the frame of my bedroom mirror. Searching for more of his work, I learned he died that week in 1966, the poem surrounded by a black border of mourning. Poet Ed Sanders ran the Peace Eye Bookstore, a former kosher butcher shop, with hand-printed signs on the shelves that called for the legalization of pot and cunnilingus. On my first visit I left with a mandrake root and a copy of *Fuck You: A Magazine of the Arts*.

I saw poems by O'Hara in an issue of the *Evergreen Review* at my neighborhood newsstand, Admiration Cigar. The cover showed a naked woman jogging through the autumn woods. I paid the dollar and eased it into my book bag, walking home carrying a forest where girls ran nude.

Mater Christi, my high school, three stories tall, was shaped like a horseshoe and divided down the middle into male and female. The genders mingled only in the center of each floor: gym, cafeteria, and the library, where my two desires fused—books and girls. Leafing through magazines, I watched the plaid skirts, knee socks and blouses tied at the neck by bows, and met no one. In the stacks I found *The New American Poetry*, with Kerouac's dizzying line, "Love's multitudinous boneyard of decay." Jack Spicer's biography said to write him at THE PLACE in San Francisco. I sent a letter, waited months, and then I learned he was dead. I revered a photograph of Ezra Pound's lined cheeks and pointed goatee. I stared at his ancient face and imitated "The Cantos," asking the gods of poetry to send Pound's ghost, the powerful voice of antiquity, into my soul. Then I learned he was alive.

Many of the poets met friends and lovers at college. Gary Snyder roomed with Lew Welch and Philip Whalen, so college became a path to poetry. No one in my family had gone beyond high school, and my investigations discovered poet Richard Wilbur at Wesleyan. Bard College interested me because the cover of its literary magazine showed a biker on a Harley kissing a bikini-clad girl in a jungle. My application essay, cribbed from *How to Be Accepted by the College of your Choice*, began, "Our small family has always been a happy one." I took a guidance counselor's advice to apply to the all-male Jesuit college he called a safe bet. I enrolled at Fairfield University of Saint Robert Bellarmine, whose mascot was the stag and whose namesake was the chief prosecutor of Galileo.

Four years later, I entered the master's program in English at the University of Iowa, which I found in the college rankings of *U.S. News & World Report*. My parents had the same response as everyone in my apartment building: "Couldn't you get in anywhere around here?" My Aunt Linda called to congratulate me, but before she hung up, she said, "By the way, John, I think it's pronounced *Ohio*."

CHAPTER TWO

ADVISING APPOINTMENT—THE GANGBANGER
OF IOWA CITY—MEETING McPEAK—
SMOKE RINGS—ALLEN GINSBERG—"RIBBLE"—
PAYMENT IN THE LOW TWO FIGURES

I drove a ten-year-old Mercury Comet to Iowa City. The four-story Iowa Bank and Trust building, the tallest in town, flashed the temperature: 101 degrees. In the *Daily Iowan* classifieds I found a cheap furnished basement apartment with a wall so thin I woke to my neighbor's spoon scraping her cereal bowl. I lived on money from a summer job at the Associated Press, and had a budget of twenty dollars a month for food. I ate mostly hot dogs and drank powdered milk from the Royal Market where the aisles were stacked with products still in their cartons.

The packet of information I received in New York told me to see my advisor, Serge Andreyev, editor of the *Ethical Literary Review*. I walked to his office in EPB, the English Philosophy Building. The Old Capitol, with its gold dome, presided over university buildings known as the Pentacrest. Sandwich shops and barbershops stretched out before it, along with hardware stores and department stores whose windows displayed cracked mannequins in floral housedresses. Two Epstein's Bookstores were a block apart: one used, one new, run by twin brothers, Harry James Epstein and Glenn Miller Epstein. Farmers in overalls walked among sorority girls, hippies, frat boys, school children and tweedy professors. There were bars on every block: The Airliner, Donnelly's, The Deadwood, The Mill and The Vine. George's, The Brown Bottle and Magoo's. Each with its own clientele and some with a particular literary aesthetic.

Andreyev waved me in just as his phone rang. The building was cool, but sunlight entered his office and warmed the spines of the *Ethical Literary Reviews* with the smell of burnt toast. A heavy, bald man with a red face, he kept repeating into the receiver, "I'm on my way. I'm leaving now." When he hung up, he said, "That was my wife. We had ham last night and now she has stomach pains. She's sure it's trichinosis, but it's guilt. I'm taking the bone for testing."

I asked if he would help me choose my courses.

"I really don't know what to suggest," he said. "You can't go wrong. And I have to be off, as you heard." He lifted his briefcase, which contained, I guessed, the ham bone. On the way out, I stopped at a framed print of men touching torches to tree branches and snaring birds with nets.

"Batfowling," he said. "And over here." He pointed to other prints, "Pike fishing and otter hunting. Pursuits of the nineteenth-century common man."

We took the elevator together in silence and, when we got out, he said, "Don't worry. The worst you can do is take a wrong step in the right direction."

I went back to my apartment and opened the course list while my neighbor's voice came clearly through the wall as she phoned friends, telling them that her married boyfriend was cheating on her with a high school girl. She spoke with a twang, and said she was going to call her rival's parents and reveal their daughter's affair.

I chose Seminar: American Transcendentalism.

My neighbor's friends counseled against her plan, but she insisted she could convince the girl's parents to keep her home. As she dialed, I found Poetry Workshop.

"Hello, sir," she said. "You don't know me, and I don't know you, but I want to tell you, sir, that your daughter is going out with a married man." The father's response encouraged her. "Yes, I thought you would like to know." They talked for a while, my neighbor upholding family values, but adding at one point, "And, sir, I hope I can be frank and tell you your daughter is known as 'The Gang Banger of Iowa City.'" Even this did not put off the father and they talked for another minute while I added "Chaucer" to my list. At four A.M. I woke to the roar of a motorcycle, followed by bone-shaking thumps on my neighbor's door. After the visitor drove off, the girl ran to the window, lifted the metal venetian blinds, and moaned a long wavering moan.

In American Transcendentalism, I met the Thompson twins, Mandy and Sandy, from the tiny town of Longleaf, Georgia. Sandy, rotund and blonde, full of giggles and good cheer, was the opposite of her sister whose high cheekbones and dark hair, parted in the middle, gave her a somber look. Elderly Alexander Kern held the class in his living room on Mayflower Heights, a promontory overlooking the city. Deer nosed at feeders outside his glassed-in balcony. Twelve of us sat in a row of folding chairs, six on a side. Kern, an elfin man at Iowa for forty years, sank into an armchair at one end and blew smoke rings from his cigar down the center as he lectured. Twelve heads followed each circle of smoke. On occasion, he reached the farthest student.

The Art of Poetry was taught by Frank Ridge, a second-year MFA candidate in the writers' workshop. Ridge's handsome but slightly pudgy face loomed above a football player's body. He shuffled through the halls, dragging his Wellingtons. We had Catholic, working-class backgrounds in common and became friends.

I thought Chaucer would be a festival of lewd stories, but Dr. Stabile believed Chaucer a religious man who wrote bawdy tales to mock sinners. Stabile rode a girl's thick Schwinn to campus, his long red pony tail trailing down the back of the poplin suit he wore every day. Doctoral students, marked by jackets and ties and the thermoses they carried to the library, comprised the entire class, except for me and a member of the writers' workshop, Mike McPeak, who smelled of beer and missed every other class. Stabile flew into rages at contemporary moral misconduct, condemning the workshop in particular for lecherous behavior. One day McPeak muttered that it was no worse than any other department and I agreed. Stabile crowned his argument against us by pointing his finger toward the ceiling and pronouncing, "May I let it be known that when Philip Roth was here, he seduced the wife of our most prominent faculty member!" After class, McPeak bought me a beer at The Deadwood, a bar with a western theme, where workshop students gathered. Wanted posters of outlaws covered the pine paneling. A gnarled piece of driftwood loomed over the bottles. Frank Ridge joined us and tried to guess the cuckold's identity. McPeak said the answer rested on whether "most prominent" meant the English department or the entire university. "If it's the whole school," he said, "then it's clearly Van Allen of the Van Allen belt."

From then on, McPeak pronounced words in Stabile's class as double-entendres, saying, "Really, do you think Chaucer wrote that scene just to save *our souls*?" But he drew out the last two syllables, so it sounded like, *assholes*. In his research paper, he quoted a character's standard for a successful tale—"Mirth is All," and wrote, "Chaucer puts his *dictum* into Harry Bailey's mouth."

He tried to get me to join in, but I had already been through that at Fairfield with Father Rogers, a sadistic priest who wiped the sweat from his forehead with his index finger and flung it into our faces as we entered his class on Victorian prose. In his role as prefect in the Loyola dorm, he forced students to strip publicly and take cold showers while he doused them with buckets of water. Rogers seemed more comfortable with students like Monk Lawrence who hung by his legs for hours from an isometric bar, and Tim "No Mind" Garahan, who died diving headfirst into a rock in the Connecticut River. My roommate and I consulted Frank Harris's *My Life and Loves*, for its bizarre accounts of famous nineteenth-century writers. He pointed out Tennyson's "preferring dogs to niggers," and that when a physician examined Thomas Carlyle's wife after twenty-five years of marriage, the doctor reported that she was a "virgo intacta." Rogers hotly insisted that biography was extraneous. My roommate's climactic moment was noting that John Ruskin became forever impotent on his wedding night, quoting Harris: "This art historian who rhapsodized over the beauties of marble nymphs was shocked at the sight of a real woman's pubic hair." At this remark, Rogers became so flustered he lost his place and kept licking his finger as he whipped through *English Prose of the Victorian Era*, our two-thousand-page tome of tissue-thin paper. I searched Harris for writers' deaths, selecting the most absurd. I noted that Matthew Arnold died jumping over a fence, and that only five people attended John Stuart Mill's funeral. After a while, I stopped consulting Harris altogether and simply invented things. When Robert Browning died of a heart attack, it was after being chased across a field by a goose. Christina Rossetti's cancer was hastened by her shame at being glimpsed on the toilet when an outhouse collapsed around her.

In college I had embraced the zing and pop of New York
School poetry, thanks to the thoughtfulness of Allen Ginsberg. Stirred by *Howl*, I had read all of Kerouac's novels,
seeking him out in the guises of Irwin Garden, Carlo Marx
and Alvah Goldbrook. I took the train from Fairfield one
night to see him read in New York. He wore jeans and a
flannel shirt and not the saint's robe or sorcerer's gown I
imagined. He sang the poems of William Blake and played
the harmonium. A band performed afterward and, when
Ginsberg joined the dancers, I introduced myself. He took
me by the hand and swung me through the crowd of swirling tie-dyed shirts and kaleidoscopic body paint. A week
later, I regretted not talking with him. I had met Ginsberg's
friend, Tuli Kupferberg of the Fugs, at the Peace Eye when
I bought his book, *1001 Ways to Beat the Draft*. I called
him and he gave me Ginsberg's address in Cherry Valley,
New York. I wrote a letter that began, "I write to you with
the same sincerity you once wrote to William Carlos Williams." He answered with a postcard.

> Dear John S –
> Yes, can't write – gone north, hundreds of
> letters in a pile – in NY check out Wednesday
> nite readings at St. Marks in Bowerie Church
> & there poetess Anne Waldman & others
> come weekly for company and reading – see
> Village Voice listings – Tom Veitch young poet
> is good – and spontaneous – Yes, I still follow
> movements of my own mind & keep notebook
> for Musings. Only raw mind creates surprises,
> not deliberate calculation – What's unknown
> more poetic than conscious known –
> Allen Ginsberg

Anne Waldman wore silver bangles on her wrists
and a full-length loose blue dress that somehow seemed

revealing. I faced her on the altar and felt as if I should genuflect as she told me about the free poetry workshops and mentioned a poet I should meet. His name was Merrill, and she tried to spot him in the audience.

"James Merrill?" I asked.

"No," she said, vigorously shaking her head and looking beyond me. "That's a much more famous poet."

"Merrill Moore?" I had found a book of his sonnets in the library.

"No," she said. "Merrill Gilfillan." I had lost the Merrill guessing game, and she stopped trying to find him, pointing me to the schedule of classes posted in the sacristy. I signed up for Dick Gallup, whose speech had an Oklahoman tinge which grew more pronounced when he used phrases like "out to lunch." Members of Andy Warhol's Factory attended and, at the critique of my first poem, Gerard Malanga, star of the fifty-minute film of a kiss, changed my phrase, "day into dark," to "daylight into darkness," and as he said it, he curved his hand through the air like a breaking wave, making it splendid. One evening everyone was late and Gallup and I sat alone in the room. I asked him about the word "rrible" in his line, "In the quiet air of the rrible morning." He said he takes lines from poems that don't work, cuts them out with a scissors, and puts these phrases into a cigar box. When he gets stuck in the middle of a poem, he reaches in and grabs a scrap. He said, "rrible" must have been part of "terrible," or "horrible." I started calling my poems "works" because that's what Gallup called them, saying, "We have some interesting works to read tonight" and "I've been reading some of Ted's latest works." One poet, Ray, called his poems "shirts." This struck me as especially odd because he never wore a shirt, just a vest with nothing under it. He'd distribute his pages, saying, "I'd like to hear what you think of my new shirts," as a large gold ankh banged against his chest. Gallup pronounced the poems that pleased him "totally great." My poems began to incorporate brand names such as Pepsi, and the precise time of day, like "8:17," and they were not totally great, but suddenly they were totally contemporary.

Anne Waldman accepted three of my works for the *World*, the mimeographed magazine published by the Poetry Project. They appeared next to Lou Reed's "Andy Warhol's Chest," which he recorded with the Velvet Underground. One of my poems began, "Those horses ate my lunch." Another ended, "The genitals are the faucets of the soul."

In The Art of Poetry, Ridge criticized my work for lacking emotion. He quoted Pound—"Only emotion endures"—and introduced me to Robert Lowell, Sylvia Plath and John Berryman who I admired. I could see what Ridge meant, yet some workshop poets wore their hearts on their sleeves in ways I wanted to avoid. I returned to John Wieners's *Hotel Wentley Poems* for mysterious lines like "We ride them/and Tingle-Tangle in the afternoon." When I mentioned his name in The Deadwood, he was disparaged as a lunatic, and a minor lunatic at that. After classes one afternoon, I went to Epstein's where I saw a poster for a reading by poets who called themselves the actualists, poets whose literary extravaganzas included writing mile-long poems; poems of words without vowels, like pygmy and rhythm; and typing poems blindfolded. They had invited Robert Bly to town. Bly had called the writers' workshop stagnant and "arthritic" in his magazine, *The Seventies,* mainly because 90 percent of the current students had been taught at their colleges by Iowa graduates.

Ridge said that Bly, an Iowa MFA himself, had come to his first workshop carrying a bag of snakes and combing his hair with a fork. The reading was to take place in the basement of the Unitarian church and I was curious, as the student poets in The Deadwood both praised and damned Bly.

The Thompson twins invited me to their party for graduate students and Mandy made me promise I'd come. Mild and childlike, she wore homemade clothes and brought baskets of pickles and buttered cornbread to our seminar in transcendentalism. The party was the same night as Bly's reading, but I accepted Mandy's invitation out of loneliness.

After several rounds of charades, we played "Killer," a game in which the anonymous killer's job is to wink covertly, sending the others to their deaths. I was murdered early by George, a handsome older fellow in a sweater-vest who had been writing his dissertation on Blake's theosophy for five years, and which he called "unmined territory." Relieved to be dead, I went to a corner of the room and sat at Mandy's desk where I saw her résumé. Under "Previous Employment," she listed:

Chicken Neck Puller	Longleaf Chicken Factory
Egg Candler	Longleaf Chicken Factory
Chicken Plucker	Longleaf Chicken Factory

When I realized I could have been hearing Bly read his translations of Neruda, Lorca and Tranströmer, which I had admired in his magazine, I asked myself how serious I was about poetry. Mandy fell victim to a wink and joined me. I hinted that these positions might not be suitable for an academic vita, and she was impressed with my worldliness. We faced the living room where the killer was still squinting discreetly, cross-legged on the floor. Mandy moved her hand to mine and invited me to go on a Saturday morning jaunt to collect fallen leaves to staple to her Emily Dickinson paper. I was afraid to discourage her, especially after having criticized her résumé.

When "Killer" ended, the room got into an argument about whether Shakespeare was an age or a man. Mandy hugged me at the door, saying she would call about our foray under the oaks and maples. After that night I decided to apply to the MFA program, and planned my days around meeting Ridge at The Deadwood. *Rolling Stone* paid ten dollars for the tiny poems in its back pages, and we wrote dozens of them over beer and bourbon. I received a ten-dollar check for "In Van Gogh's Room." It was on the basis of that poem, Ridge said, that I was admitted to the writers' workshop, and in particular for one alcohol-driven line, "Crisp flowers show their teeth."

CHAPTER THREE

POI-EMS—THE GREAT CRAFTSMAN—
BARKHAUSEN—WHO'S HARVEY?—
FIRST POETRY WORKSHOP—LOUDMOUTH—
YELLOW SUBMARINE—MY FAULT

We were hell-bent to become poets, but we were students. Those who taught us were hell-bent to become poets, but they were teachers. We were all hell-bent to become poets and all poets stood in our way.

The writers' workshop consisted of a hall of six faculty offices, a bulletin board, and a tiny lounge with a couch, encouraging the hundred and twenty students to go elsewhere, and that elsewhere was usually a bar. The director, novelist John Leggett, came from the New York publishing world. Educated at Andover and Yale, his sharp gray suit matched his silver hair and silver tie tack in the shape of a martini glass. A former navy lieutenant, he marched crisply past the scruffy students in bell-bottoms, some of whom walked barefoot, looking them over, and then disappearing.

On my first day, I read the board's flyers soliciting submissions to little magazines, applications for fellowships, and ads selling books, clothing and furniture and met another new student, David Pryor. Small, bearded and nervous, he kept licking his lips, hoping to catch a glimpse of our teachers. Mitchell Lawson, the elder statesman of the poetry faculty, darted past. His bowl-shaped haircut and the bangs across his forehead made him look like an actor in a movie about the Holy Roman Empire. I had been introduced to him at The Deadwood when I was in the MA program. He said, "Oh yes, I've read some of your poems." He was referring to my application manuscript, and he pronounced "poems" as "poi-ems." He had snapped at the waitress because the wet table stained the suede elbow patch on his corduroy jacket.

When Pryor saw Lawson, he did a double take, and said that before he left his hometown of Syracuse, he had decided to look him up, as Lawson lived there as well, and also was heading to Iowa. He found his address in the phone book and, when he arrived, a man was watering his lawn. Pryor asked for Mitchell Lawson. The man told him that Lawson had packed everything and moved to Florida. "And now," Pryor said, "I see it was him!"

A few moments later, Lawson walked by again, and Pryor confronted him. Lawson's face reddened, and he denied it, returning to his office and slamming the door. Pryor swore his story was true. Then Lawson reappeared and said, "If I was rude, I'm sorry!"

Other new students joined us and I learned that the undergraduate mentors of my classmates were also workshop graduates. Archibald Silver came from Montana's Richard Hugo. David St. John was out of Fresno by Philip Levine. I did have one thing in common with them—each of us had edited our undergraduate magazine and I was consoled that their journals, *Montage* and *Collage*, carried names as silly as mine, *New Frontiers*.

Ridge and McPeak came down the hall and introduced themselves to the others. Pryor pointed to a poster, advertising an upcoming reading by Charles Pless, who had visited his college. Another said that he had Pless's new book, and a third said that the dedication of Lawson's new poem, *to CP*, was to Pless. I had the same displaced feeling as when I moved as a child from Bayside to a block in Elmhurst with the forbidding name of Judge Street. The day we arrived, my mother handed me a bag of cowboys and Indians while she and my father unpacked. Kids sprawled at the roots of an oak tree, and from their prone positions, I could tell they were setting up and flicking down their men. I opened my paper bag and they scorned my braves and cowpokes, saying it was soldier season. Did I have any infantrymen? How about tanks? A cannon?

Pryor asked where I had gone to school. The name Fairfield was met with silence. Ridge interrupted. "Who cares where we came from?" he said. "Where are we *going*?"

McPeak straightened himself at Ridge's wisdom, put his arm around me, and said, "The Deadwood."

Workshop orientation included a party for new MFA poetry students at The Mill, where we hoped to mingle with Lawson and meet Harvey Clay, the other permanent member of the poetry faculty. I had seen Harvey only once, wearing a turtleneck, flipping a quarter into the air and performing magic tricks with a kerchief in front of the bulletin board. He wore a goatee and was as garrulous as Lawson was removed, as stocky as Lawson was thin. Lawson had been Harvey's teacher and had published two slender books of poems in rhyme and meter, a lean output that added to his stature as a perfectionist. Students revered him as a "great craftsman" who dissected their work with his razor intelligence. A telling difference between the two men was how students referred to them. Everyone called Harvey by his first name. Lawson was Lawson. No one called him Mitchell, and few called him Mitch.

The day of the party, cold currents layered the afternoon breeze, and by evening it was frigid. My old Comet took a long time warming up, and I paged through the book of Shakespeare quotations Ridge left in the glove compartment for me to read while waiting. I drove the icy streets and parked across from The Mill. Lawson walked in, hands in both pockets, clearly a duty.

Pryor leaned against the bar and waved. His five-foot frame was diminished further by his taller wife, Wendy, a pretty, freckled redhead. A rock band played, the singer exhorting people to dance. Pryor said they had just arrived, but it was enough time for him to have torn several cocktail napkins into heaps of confetti. The band's name, The Sad Tantamounts, was scrawled in magic marker on a pizza box. I studied the bass player—a brown leather vest over a bright white T-shirt, a dark head of hair. It looked like Artie Barkhausen from the master's program. I had met him at the Thompson party and remembered wondering if he was joking for calling Pound's great work "The Santos."

"I know that guy playing bass," I said to Wendy.

"Is he a poet too?"

The "too" surprised me. It was a title I didn't give myself, but in Pryor's household he was known as a poet.

"I'm not sure," I said. The bass player's head hung down, hair in front of his eyes, his whole body vibrating like one of the thick strings.

Lawson held a glass of Scotch and went from student to student, introducing himself, but the students were more interested in playing darts with Harvey, who was throwing with great accuracy from behind his back and in other contorted positions. I was surprised to see Ridge enter this party for newcomers. He went straight for the prettiest girl in the room.

Lawson retreated to the bar, detached and wan. A drunk, sweet-faced student wearing a skimpy top grabbed his arm and tried to get him to dance. He pulled away, but she persisted. Two of her girlfriends tried to distract her, but she kept leaping onto Lawson's back, palms on his shoulders. He turned and smiled, patting the next stool. Soon they pulled dollar bills lengthwise, playing liar's poker.

Pryor's wife danced and danced. I stood next to him at the bar as he tore napkins and matchbooks. He said his latest project was a sonnet sequence about lightning.

"Ever hear of ball lightning?" he asked.

"Lucille *Ball* lightning?" It was Barkhausen. The band was taking a break.

"Who's this asshole?" Pryor asked me as Barkhausen laughed.

I put out my hand. "Artie," I said.

"I'm starting the workshop," he said. "Like the name of the band? I just invented it."

A faculty member with shoulder-length hair and a long mustache climbed on stage and banged the drums like a windup monkey. Lawson watched and shook his head sadly. The bartender poured him another Dewar's, and something for the girl whose eyes seemed to melt like snowflakes.

"I didn't know you wrote poems," I said.

"I didn't know you wrote poems either," he said. "I couldn't take the dissertation idea, so I threw in the talc and joined the workshop."

I wondered if I'd misheard Barkhausen amid the clanging cymbals. He said he was filling in for the bass player who was late. He jumped on stage, complimenting the flailing, long-haired drummer who Pryor told me was Dan Cook, the novelist. I said I thought this was a party for the poets.

"It is," he said, "but I hear he comes to everything just for the girls even though he's married. A real gash hound."

Wendy talked with a student who told her he had edited his college literary magazine, *Quill*. She grabbed the poet/editor and kissed him sloppily. Surprised and embarrassed, he put her at arm's length, but she just smiled and whispered, "Listen, Bub, I'm not a happily married woman." He moved away and sifted through the crowd. As Wendy stared after him, Pryor reached over, expressionless, and splashed a bit of beer down the back of her party dress. She didn't move.

"It's a natural phenomenon," Pryor continued. "I saw it in England."

"What is?" I asked.

"Ball lightning!"

Wendy screamed, her drunkenness had anesthetized her for a few seconds, but then she felt the cold liquid and spun around bewildered, hoping to catch the culprit.

"I've got twelve sonnets so far," Pryor continued. "Hey, babe," he called to Wendy. He ordered coffee and pushed a stool under her. She gazed dumbly into the crowd.

"Something spilled down my back," she said.

"It's your imagination," Pryor said. "Drink this." He handed her the cup.

"Am I wet?" she said, turning and showing me the stain.

"A little," I said, "but not too bad."

"It feels bad," she said.

I patted her freckled skin with a napkin, and she looked at me sideways, saying, "At least I didn't fall into the pool!"

"There is no pool, you airhead," Pryor said, building the wet napkins into a pyramid.

"I meant like last time," Wendy said. "Back home, at the Aqua Cave." She turned to me again. "Someone pushed me, and it was the deep end!" She began to cry, and Pryor put his arm around her. I excused myself when the bass player arrived and Barkhausen joined us.

"Let's see Lawson!" he said, clapping his hands.

We stood behind Lawson and the drunk girl as they continued their game. Lawson folded dollar after dollar into the breast pocket of his shirt. Barkhausen reached between them, grabbed a bill from the girl and slapped it to the bar.

"She's drunk!" he yelled into Lawson's face.

"He took all my money," the girl said, pouting.

Lawson said, "It's not serious."

Barkhausen shook out a Marlboro and lit it. "How much did you lose?" He spoke with the cigarette between his lips.

"I don't know," she said sadly. "But a lot of money has changed hands!" She sat upright, listed to one side, and Lawson pulled eight or so bills from his pocket and tossed them onto the bar.

"What's wrong with you?" he said to Artie. "I wouldn't think of taking her money." He walked out of The Mill, bumping into Ridge who was leaving with the pretty girl.

A reading by W. H. Auden was scheduled to conclude orientation week. I was looking forward to it as I had seen only one famous poet—Robert Penn Warren. When he came to Fairfield, he wore a suit and tie, which shocked me. I thought all poets were beatniks. The next day, my English teacher reprimanded us for talking during the reading, for the beer bottle that rolled under the seats until it clunked into the foot of the podium, and especially for my wearing sandals, saying, "Poetry is a formal occasion." This was a surprise. I thought poetry was a protest against society.

Auden never arrived. He died that same week and was replaced by Stephen Spender. Spender, another poet in a suit and tie, robust and ruddy, read from Auden's first book, which he had hand printed in 1928. There was something wonderful in the way he clutched Auden's humble pamphlet, with its unassuming title, *Poems*, and its modest number, twenty, the initial step in a great career, the fragile collection almost within our reach.

He read the poems with true tenderness and, when the applause ended, Leggett took the microphone and invited workshop poets to meet Spender in EPB. We rushed over and took our seats. Harvey and Spender entered the classroom. Harvey wore brown jeans, a vest and a paisley shirt, his head reaching just above the breast pocket of Spender's luminous blue suit. They sat on folding chairs and Spender took questions. He believed a poem is a verbal construct and a kind of word game. He equated Beat poetry with abstract art, which he said looked like the palette a painter would use if he knew how to paint. A beautiful blonde said, "I enjoy abstract poets like Wallace Stevens, but Harvey says poetry must be concrete. What do you think?"

"Who's that?" I asked Ridge.

"Belinda Schaeffer," he whispered. "I'll tell you later." As Spender answered, the room filled with laughter and, in that way you can hear something after it was said because you were half listening, I realized that a puzzled Spender had asked, "Who's Harvey?"

"Harvey Clay," she said, equally puzzled. She lifted a pale hand in his direction. "Next to you."

"Of course, of course," Spender said, touching Harvey's shoulder. Harvey grew red, and Spender flushed further. "I agree with Harvey completely," he said, but it was too late. Someone in the back of the room couldn't help repeating, "Who's Harvey?" and voices cackled. It was all the more painful because we worried who we were ourselves, whether we would become anyone and, to derail that awful doubt about our own identities, the words, "Who's Harvey?" appeared scrawled in the workshop men's room, on the bulletin board, and across the walls of bars around town.

A week later, I stumbled on the fiction of Cesare Pavese in the library. The only way I learned was by stumbling, and I stumbled often. I was taken with his world-weary yet stalwart tone: "Maturity is realizing that telling one's

~ 29 ~

troubles doesn't make anything better." In one passage, the "Who's Harvey?" question rebounded to me when the protagonist, a writer, is told by his sister that she wants her little son to be *someone*. "Like you," she says. He replies that she doesn't know what she is talking about, "that to be *someone* you have to live alone, have neither lover nor friend, and then, after a life of isolation, then, after you die, and after you are dead many years, only then, if you are lucky, do you become *someone!*"

I sat in my basement apartment as I read, prepared to live the life of Pavese's character. I looked around and decided that, yes, if that was the prescription, I was on my way—powdered milk, instant coffee, high school sport coat, no girlfriend. I returned to the book, to the sister's response. She said, "Oh, you make everything impossible just so you can feel sorry for yourself."

Barkhausen wound up in Lawson's workshop, the only newcomer to do so. The rest of us had Harvey. His research assistant printed our poems on a Thermo-Fax machine and placed them in a cubby hole near the lounge in advance of our class which met from two to five each Monday. At our first meeting, I sat between Ridge and a former priest who was always laughing and joking except when he was crying. Harvey asked "Bear," a student nicknamed for his size and bristling facial hair, to read his poem, which was written in the "you" voice. The poem was a list of his older brother's cruelties. The final lines read:

> You resented him when he refused
> to lend you his id,
> and you watched him from the window
> frolicking prettily with pretty girls.
> He left you alone
> with his birthday dog
> who bit both your ears.
> You bear the scars today.

Bear read with such feeling that his cheeks shook under his full beard along with the fringe on his buckskin jacket. He paused for dramatic effect after what he thought were his best lines but, due to his heft, it seemed instead that he had run out of breath. He was gasping as he pronounced the final words, overcome by their truth. Yet his reading had the opposite effect. It was like watching someone at a bathroom mirror rehearsing a speech, or overhearing an earnest basso profundo in the shower.

Charlotte Spencer, whose spare poems Harvey would soon flirtatiously describe as *svelte*, stared across the table at her boyfriend and raised her eyebrows happily. Every bad poem made the rest of us better. Charlotte pointed out that the speaker wanted his brother's ID, not his "id," and this comment set the tone. A firefighter from Brooklyn, who quit his job for poetry, wanted to know where on the ear the speaker was bitten.

"The lobe? The helix?"

"The *what?*" several asked.

"The helix," the firefighter explained, grabbing the top of his ear. "The tip."

"Don't complain, Bear," Pryor said. "You got your ears pierced for free!"

Bear's forced grin did not mask his anger, and he gritted his dark, stubby teeth. After twenty minutes of chuckling, we were hushed by Harvey who pointed out that while the poem's emotion overwhelmed its writing, he admired the adverb/adjective combination—"frolicking prettily with pretty girls." I hadn't considered the language, just Bear's performance, and I looked appreciatively at the highlighted phrase.

"Isn't that a bit euphemistic?" someone asked. "How about 'fucking prettily with pretty girls?' Isn't that what it means?"

"How do you 'fuck prettily'?" another said.

"Charlotte, do you think you can 'fuck prettily'?" The question was posed by Todd Trotta, a heavy second-year student.

"Some can and some can't," Charlotte said, looking right at him.

Charlotte's boyfriend, dressed in a tan cashmere sweater and matching sport coat, said, "Fucking is a private matter."

Harvey said, "Poetry is a private matter made public."

"I think you missed the point," Bear said. "It's not about me, it's about my brother." He slapped both palms on the table for emphasis and the hair on the back of his hands quivered.

"Still," Harvey said. "It's about *you* when you put *your name* in the last line."

Bear's eyes, as well as everyone's in the class, leapt to the final words of his poem, "I bear the scars today." Bear squinted deeply. None of us had caught the coincidence, but one student piped up, "I noticed that, but I didn't want to embarrass Bear."

Harvey said, "Opposition is true friendship. Okay?"

The next poem, a tiny thing of six lines, described each leg of a spider.

"Spiders have eight legs," Charlotte said.

Unfazed, the author said. "Then I'll add a couple lines."

When the class and Harvey criticized the poem, the poet turned his page face down and said, "I'm not surprised. I just tossed it off."

We all admired Charlotte's poem about the magical properties of antler velvet and when it was her turn to speak, she was giddy with the reception. "I'm surprised because I just tossed it off," she said. I looked hard at her, to see if she was parodying the previous student but there was no trace of irony. This was a step toward my learning the code. If your poem was a failure in the eyes of the class, and you just tossed it off, you were blameless.

If it was a success and you just tossed it off, you were a genius.

At the break, Harvey and Charlotte talked in the hall, their backs against the wall, facing the same direction. Ridge said we had to be at The Deadwood at five o'clock because the beer distributors delivered kegs and bought everyone a beer. He was anxious for class to end early. Charlotte's boyfriend's poem started the second half and he broke the rule and spoke before discussion ended. The edict of silence imposed upon an author was intended to prevent refuting objections or clarifying murky passages. His poem was a scramble of images and, when someone expressed sympathy for the loss of the speaker's dog, everyone chimed in about how hard it was to lose a pet. The ex-priest said, "I just want to praise the poem for its courage in risking such sentimentality." Charlotte's boyfriend stood and yelled, "It wasn't my dog who died, it was my father!" He gathered his papers and left. We sat in the echo of the slammed door, the ex-priest softly weeping, his face in his hands. Charlotte pushed her chair from the table and followed.

"If it looks like a dog, barks like a dog and wags . . ." Harvey said.

Ridge said, "Bow Wow," and we all relaxed.

Before Monique read her "Poem about the Moon," she said, "In case anyone missed it, this poem is about the moon." She paused and deepened its meaning by adding, "And yet it's not about the moon." Monique had a way of breaking authorial silence. She nodded her head at every comment that supported the poem's intention and rolled her eyes at negative remarks. I looked to see if Harvey would suppress these pantomimes, but he did nothing. Monique's nodding accelerated as a student said that comparing the full moon to a communion wafer was not only original, but sacramental. His comment was seconded by another who felt the poem touched on the significant female presence in the universe. Monique's eyes widened and her chin vibrated as if hitched to a pneumatic drill. The workshop devolved into two games: charades, and trying to find a hidden object—each time we unearthed her intentions, we were "getting warmer," and when we strayed, she gazed at the ceiling, frowned, and we knew we were as cold as we could get.

My piece was last. I had written about the day I was born, and in my quest for a fresh approach, I wrote that I was born as a balloon, "my body swelling with helium." Everyone hated it but Harvey spared a few kind words.

"Aristotle said the sign of a poet is the ability to make metaphors," he said. "However, the weakest writing is at the end, so I'd take the last four lines, cut them and dream your way back."

Ridge said, "Great edit! And a great note to end the class on!"

Harvey looked at his watch. It was four forty-five and we had spent only ten minutes on my poem, but he was just as glad to be through. As we streamed out, Charlotte and her boyfriend were at the door. The boyfriend, obviously under orders from Charlotte, apologized to Harvey who just tapped him on the shoulder and kept going. The gesture had the feeling of someone pitying a lost cause, not granting absolution, and the boyfriend looked at Charlotte as if he could kill her.

As Ridge predicted, we drank a free Budweiser, and then a free Hamm's, courtesy of the drivers. They were brought to us by Brandy, the tiny, cherubic waitress. Her full cheeks and lips were framed by luxurious shoulder-length amber curls, and she spoke only in baby talk. "Dis one for you," she said to me, placing the draft on the table. "And dis one for dis nice man." She gave us free packs of Beer Nuts. Trotta was already there, an empty glass in front of him.

"You know how to move when beer is around," Ridge said.

"Your friend's diction is a bit *inflated*, don't you think?" Trotta said, referring to my poem.

"Cool it," Ridge said.

"You never told me about Belinda Schaeffer," I said. "You know, the one . . ."

"I know!" Ridge said. "The most beautiful and smartest woman in the workshop, that's all! PhD in French from Yale."

"She seems nice," I said.

"Her poetry has a long way to go," he said, and I was grateful for this single flaw.

"By the way," he continued. "Don't let one metaphor dominate a poem, especially if it's a bad metaphor. You just got in deeper and deeper with that balloon trope until you were floating above the Macy's Day Parade."

I agreed that it was ludicrous, and I felt ludicrous. I opened the nuts and poured a pile in the middle of the table while I made a mental note to look up *trope*.

"I noticed you paused today when you spoke about the spider poem, I think you were about to say *terrible*, which it was. When you don't like something, try *mannered* or even *inchoate*."

I said I would.

"Everyone will understand you meant *terrible*. And speaking of terrible, your first line, 'In the neighborhood where I was born,' sounds exactly like the first line of 'Yellow Submarine.'"

I could immediately hear the Beatles singing, "In the town where I was born . . ."

"But failures are stepping stones to success," Ridge said. "What did you think about Harvey's assignment to write our first memories?"

"I'm going to have a hard time writing about opening a refrigerator and having a tray of deviled eggs fall on my head."

Ridge chewed the foam on his beer. "Don't tie the poem so literally to biography."

"No?"

"Recall a scene from childhood and invent something."

"That's a good idea," I said.

I was thinking this over when Harvey slid into our booth. He liked Ridge. Brandy followed him, but Harvey ordered nothing.

"Who's that new guy with the mustache, from California?" Ridge asked Harvey.

"Larry Levis, Phil Levine's student," Harvey said. "The job market is so bad that even though he has a book, he's getting his MFA."

"Another Levine student?" Ridge said. "That makes five."

"Six," Harvey said. "Where did you go to school?" he asked.

"Fairfield."

"Never heard of it." Harvey turned to Ridge. "Charlotte's pretty, isn't she? And a good poet. She studied with Lamont at Goddard. They had an affair. I don't know what she sees in that twerp who left class today."

"He studied with Levine," Ridge said.

Harvey shook his head. "I remember Phil's letter," he said. "He wasn't that wild about him."

In a booth across the aisle, Lawson sat in front of a glass of white wine with members of the English Department. We overheard him saying, "In creative writing, the verb 'to teach,' means to chide clichés, satirize pomposities, and dull the blades of the overly competitive." Harvey left to join them.

"He'd die if he knew I fucked Charlotte," Ridge said, and then he reached across the table and pinched the cuff of my green and white checked flannel shirt. "No one in the workshop dresses like this. There's a thrift store next to the hospital, a lot of us go there." Ridge gave his advice so frankly that we were both laughing, and I looked at him as I hadn't before: a black turtle neck scribbled with lint. On the way out I winced at my flannel reflection in the window and felt the need for a higher power, a North Star, a feeling I had once at Fairfield when I walked into a dorm room just as one of my friends was saying to his roommate, "He's a pathetic empathy of Allen Ginsberg." When he saw me, he turned red and his roommate hunched over his desk. They were talking about me. I didn't know what an "empathy" was, but I could gauge his intent. I was a poor copy. Later, when I looked it up, I found it was not a noun the way they used it, but I still took the remark to heart. I did love Ginsberg. Was it showing too much? Was I drifting into a parody of the literary figures I worshipped? In desperation, I went to Sunday mass in the chapel, kneeling among my fellow students who had fallen into a deep solemnity, with bowed heads and folded hands, their focus straight at the altar. When the priest called for a response, they struck their chests, vowing with the rest, "Through my Fault! Through my Fault!" More than fifty fists and fifty exclamations underscored the final expiation, "Through my Most Grievous Fault!" A baritone passion filled the chapel accompanied by the scent from votive candles like a surfeit of bouquets at a wake, a warm, choking wave. When I walked out early, a few students looked at me with sympathetic eyes, as passengers on a ship steam away from a man overboard, and I felt the same sensation as I left The Deadwood.

CHAPTER FOUR

SRI CHINMOY—BEER BY BEER—
THE ANTI-JINGLE BELLS—A TOUPEE IN THE
SUBWAY—LA HUERTA—WORKSHOP JARGON—
RAS, TAS AND TWFS

∽⧟∼

Harvey told us he addressed all his poems to his dead
father and, in Problems in Modern Poetry, he played
a record of Judy Collins singing "My Father" to inspire us
to do the same. A student who came from an abusive alco-
holic background wrote:

> We called him *Dad* because we couldn't call him
> an asshole and have any teeth left.

When Harvey insisted that the father must have had some
good qualities, the poet opened his mouth and pulled out
a bridge where his front teeth had been.

Everyone's work was more advanced than mine, their
poems formed in the workshop style. My New York School
influences still gave me a tingle but interested no one. I listened intently to Harvey, and spent evenings in the library's

poetry section. Leaving there one night I passed a room where Sri Chinmoy was getting ready to speak, and I went in. Pound's Confucian cantos intrigued me, and I felt, too, that the East might offer spiritual comfort. A professor introduced him, saying the guru slept only ninety minutes a day, had the strength to pick up cement mixers and had lifted many heads of state off the ground. Chinmoy spoke for thirty minutes about the need for world peace. When he took questions, someone asked him the meaning of life. I was so struck by the simplicity of the question that I missed the answer. I overcame my shyness and asked if there was any relationship between atman, meaning breath or soul, and the soulful jazz of musicians playing wind instruments, which came from breath. I was so struck by the convolution of my question that I missed that answer too.

Many workshop students enrolled in The Hand-Printed Book, publishing their own poems in tiny editions. Others studied photography and Chinese painting. Everyone studied drinking, and full-time instructors included Raymond Carver and John Cheever. After every workshop, I went to The Deadwood with Ridge, Pryor, and McPeak. McPeak lived across the Mississippi, in Moline, Illinois, where he taught high school. He was born there, married his childhood sweetheart and had two small daughters. Now, at thirty, he took one workshop each semester, hanging out in bars, moving toward his degree credit by credit, beer by beer. Wearing polyester pants and rayon ties, keeping his curly red hair and beard trimmed, he seemed a conventional suburbanite, which he was, except for his mania about poetry, jazz, alcohol and women.

McPeak had a crush on Brandy and asked her to go to the movies. She put her finger to her lips and said, "I don't tink-toe." When she left, Pryor said that the bartender, a 300-pound biker named Fenster, was her boyfriend. Ridge urged McPeak to expand his quest. He nodded at a table of female students, saying, "Each one guaranteed to have a cunt."

Going from my parents' apartment in Queens to an all-male college, I had scant sexual experience. I had met one girl at a Fairfield mixer, Holly Proper, pronounced, she said, *Pro*-per, from Marymount. A hippie flower child, she invited me to her midtown apartment when her parents were away over Christmas. We met at the information booth at Grand Central but, before she arrived, I found myself staring at the beautiful women, gawking, really, my eyes following a girl in a short dress. A rough voice interrupted my fantasy, saying, "You wouldn't know what to do with it, boy!" I turned to see a smiling, unshaven man in rags sitting on a bag of rags, with a rag on his head.

Holly and I walked down Fifth Avenue, past Lord & Taylor's windows where mechanical elves hammered toys in Santa's workshop. Her long bellbottom jeans, torn at the heels, scraped the cement. A rattling sound surrounded her every step, like a shaking tin of coins. She hiked her frayed cuff, revealing a string of brass discs tied to her ankle by a purple cord. "Anti-jingle bells," she said.

At her parents' place, she showed me her collection of Richard Brautigan books. I thought his work childlike, but since she was deep into the west coast underground, I guessed I had missed something. She sat cross-legged on a couch in the living room and read:

> Fuck me like fried potatoes
> on the most beautifully hungry
> morning of my God-damn life.

She unzipped my fly. She got on her knees and it didn't take a moment, which surprised her. She tugged off her jeans and panties, sat on the couch and spread her legs, guiding my head there. I kissed her thick pubic hair, but the vagrant's words at Grand Central came back to me. I realized he was right and, a few minutes later, so did she. She took off her top and pushed my lips against her large nipples as she masturbated, jingling the anti-jingle bells.

On the train to Queens I sat near the open door between cars, miserable about my sexual performance. A man in a blue Dickies work shirt and pants dozed across the aisle, undisturbed by the slamming chain handrails and wheels clanging beneath the metal coupler. He was coming home from his shift, his newspaper and lunch box beside him. He leaned farther and farther forward, nodding off, then tossing his head upright, never opening his eyes. I was reading *The Portable Blake*, and the passenger's fatigued shoulders and unshaven face bobbed at the margins of the songs of innocence. As the train lurched, he lurched with it and a toupee dropped from the crown of his head. The now bald man continued to bend over what looked like half a hollowed-out grapefruit, with four pieces of doubled-sided tape stuck to the inside. The train shifted and rattled, the half sphere inching toward the open space between cars. I debated retrieving it for him, but hesitated each time his head snapped back. The hairpiece nudged the metal grid next to the door, about to be sucked away, and I grabbed it. As I was about to place it next to his lunch box, he opened his eyes and saw me holding his secret, a badly kept secret, and now an open secret.

"You dropped this," I said.

"Like hell I did," he said, snatching it and checking the seat for his lunch box. "I'm calling a cop." He popped it on his head with the sound of a thwacked tennis ball, shook his shoulders to recover his dignity, pulled himself erect, and walked off as if peering over a crowd. I felt that if I had let it drift away, it would have been a sin, wrong to let the man lose his disguise. My Catholic guilt had gotten me in trouble. I realized, too, that my poking fun at Ruskin had come back to haunt me, and I suddenly sympathized with him. What a better time I would have had if Holly were bald as a statue.

Barkhausen stood by our table at The Deadwood and said, "I hear Belinda Schaeffer shaves her pubes." Pulling up a chair, he lit a cigarette and ordered a shot of rye, saying to Brandy, "And make it a good, healthy shot, too." It was the first time she seemed annoyed. Barkhausen wore a heavy motorcycle jacket with zippers and studs.

"What are you talking about?" Ridge asked.

"Someone in the workshop wrote a poem about her, that's all I'll say for now."

"How's Lawson's class?" Pryor asked. Pryor was smarting from Barkhausen getting in.

"Great," Barkhausen said, exhaling toward a poster of Jesse James. "But he doesn't like much. He shoots everyone down." He made his hand into a pistol and aimed his index finger at Pryor.

"That's what I've heard," McPeak said.

"Does he like your work, Ridge?" Barkhausen asked.

"I think so," Ridge said, taken slightly aback. "He's been supportive."

"I'm disappointed in the lit courses," Barkhausen said. "I wanted to study the Russians, not just English."

"Like who?" Pryor asked.

"Mandelstam. Pasternak. Pushpin."

When we laughed, Barkhausen looked puzzled. He pulled magazines out of his leather satchel, and gave us copies of the journal he published, *La Huerta*. When I opened it, I saw he was the featured poet, with a special section excerpted from his series, "The Devil's Dance."

"What does the *la huerta* mean?" I asked.

"The whorehouse."

"Not really," Ridge said. "It means the *orchard*."

Barkhausen tapped the tip of his Marlboro toward the ashtray, sending cinders into Pryor's drink. "If you get in a taxi in Mexico City and say *la huerta*, the driver will take you to a woman."

Ridge laughed. "If you say *la huerta*, the driver will take you to an orchard."

Every song playing on the jukebox was by Elton John. After hearing "Tiny Dancer" and "Rocket Man" three times, Ridge gave a few quarters to Brandy, and we heard "Brandy (You're a Fine Girl)," and Scott Joplin's theme from the movie, "The Sting."

"This is almost worse," Ridge said.

"I hate ragtime," McPeak said. "My father played that shit when I was a kid, and here it is again."

Barkhausen disagreed. "I like Scotch Opera," he said. Ridge looked at me, and mouthed, *Scott Joplin?*

Pryor said he just framed a broadside by his former teacher, the English poet, Malcolm Gee. He quoted the first line: "Your pathetic isolation dwindles me."

"Sounds like a bad translation," Ridge said. "And it's self-pitying."

Barkhausen cut in, "And a bit sedimental. Did you hear that Rimbaud drank absinthe before he wrote? He disengaged his senses."

"You wish you could write like Gee," Pryor said, huddling defensively over his beer.

No one seemed to notice Barkhausen's opinion.

"Gee snorts baby chick fluff before he writes," Ridge said.

"Remember when Stanley Elkin was here?" McPeak asked. "He met with a student and said, 'You are the god of boredom.' That's how I feel about Gee."

I didn't know who Gee was, so I ordered another beer.

Pryor's feelings were hurt, but Barkhausen, off in his own world, asked, "If Lawson were a baseball player, what position would he play?"

"Relief pitcher," Ridge said. "He'd throw strikes for a few innings, that's it. Could never go the distance." He ordered more beer, and said that in one class there had been a debate over the difference between "gray" and "grey." Pryor said that "gray" has a more metallic sheen. McPeak cornered Brandy under a holster holding two six-guns and asked her opinion.

Ridge had encouraged me to send my poems out and, when the others left, I showed him acceptance letters from *Chicago Review* and *Poetry Northwest.* He smiled, not unkindly, but in a way that made me feel I was displaying silly trophies. I needed the physical proof for myself. Everything else about poetry was invisible—it wafted around us and sometimes through us. So seeing a concrete thing, even a slip of paper I'd toss to the wind on my way home, and even if that paper clung to the base of a litter basket, it was no longer an idea or a feeling, but something real.

I adjusted to workshop life, and continued long days in the library. Someone in class mentioned the poets Dickey and Wright, but by the time I arrived at the stacks, I found many Dickeys and many Wrights. James, Charles, and Jay. I confused James, Ralph and R. P. Dickey, but I read them all.

I had also come to understand the jargon of the workshop, the phrases that said one thing but meant another:

> I admire the poem's ambition.
> *It sucks.*

> I see what it's trying to do.
> *But it doesn't do it.*

> I like the even tone.
> *It's boring.*

> A tour de force.
> *It sucks.*

Send it to the *New Yorker* immediately.
You don't listen to anyone, so why not get a professional opinion?

Have you read X?
You stole from X!

Have you tried writing in form?
You have nothing to lose.

Don't listen to what anyone says.
You're hopeless anyway.

Toward the end of that first term, I found Ridge and Pryor in deep discussion at The Deadwood. McPeak, indifferent to their talk, looked over his shoulder and called to other tables. I guessed the subject was writing or teaching and it was both. Two students who had received fellowships were graduating. The debate was over who would get their funding.

"Dane Hill could get the TWF," Pryor said, ripping a napkin neatly into quarters.

"Not after he read with the actualists," Ridge said.

"Think they'll consider me?" Pryor said, peering up from his bowed head as if asking for mercy.

"You have an outside shot," Ridge said. "You're a good poet and they like you."

Ridge looked at me. "We're talking about aid," he said. He turned to Pryor. "But there are other things to consider, like Anne Graff . . ."

"Don't tell me that, Ridge!" Pryor said. "Things better not work that way." His lower teeth jutted out from his beard when he spoke, looking more like a wolf than a man, a wolf about to tear into the carcass of Anne Graff.

"It could happen, that's all I'm saying," Ridge said. "And if one of the faculty's girlfriends gets it, think of how John would feel. He's got nothing."

"I know," Pryor said, calmer. "What matters is the in-state tuition."

"I could use that," I said.

"These appointments will go to those who already have aid," Ridge said.

"But John could get a research thing if one of the teaching assistants got a fellowship," Pryor said. "Now that he's published."

"I don't know how it works," I said.

"And you and I never will," McPeak said, getting up and corralling a girl by the pinball machine.

"There's Research Assistants and Teaching Assistants," Ridge said. "And Teaching Writing Fellows. RAs, TAs and TWFs," Ridge said. He pronounced TWF as *Twif*.

"Ridge's a TWF," Pryor said. "I'm a TA."

Ridge said. "TAs teach comp and TWFs teach Creative Writing. The RAs do clerical work for the profs."

"The TWFs get the most money," Pryor said.

"The RAs want to become TAs and the TAs TWFs," Ridge said.

"But an RA will never be a TWF," Pryor said.

"I don't know," Ridge said. "Gus Dessler went from RA to TWF, didn't he?"

"He was a TA one summer."

"That's right," Ridge said. "But it's rare. Most TWFs come in as TWFs."

"You could get an RA," Pryor said. "Now that you're published."

"And you're smart. If a spot opens, you could be a TA," Ridge said.

"I hope they think I'm worth the TWF," Pryor said, stammering. "I'm as good as Harvey. I mean, I'm as good as Harvey was. I mean, when he was my age."

McPeak held Brandy's hips as she stood on a footstool, straightening photos of the Dalton gang.

"They better not make that bimbo Anne Graff a TWF!" Pryor said. "It would make a mockery of the system!"

I passed Pryor in the hall when January classes started, and he shook his head negatively on his way to Lawson's office. I stopped by to see Ridge and he told me that Pryor didn't get the TWF. He was not the only one disappointed. The TWF and the TA could have gone to Anne Graff, a faculty favorite, or Roy Napoli, whose minute, curtailed couplets of no more than four words imitated not Lawson, but Lawson's translations of the French poet, Guillevic, which everyone thought was a clever, sideways form of flattery. The disappointed students were upset because the appointments were indisputable. The TWF went to Denis Johnson who had published his first book, and wrote a short story that appeared in the *Atlantic*. On that basis, he had a contract for a novel. Denis had a true insouciance, was a dedicated habitué of the most dissolute bar in town, The Vine, and coursed through the halls barefoot. Sam Silva got the TA, a quiet student with a poem in the *New Yorker*. Pryor raged, but it was only with himself he could argue, and his complaints flared behind Lawson's closed door. We could even catch sentences about his having a wife to support.

Chapter Five

READING ASHBERY TO MY MOTHER—DAPPER DAN COOK—BARKHAUSEN AND WENDY'S TÊTE-À-TÊTE—DRINKING TO CONCENTRATE, DRINKING TO FORGET—LOUDMOUTH GETS SOAKED—MODIFIED LAWSON

∼∞∼

When Lawson brought a poet to campus for a reading, he made it clear that only those who attended were welcome at the after-party. He was grateful to Pryor and his wife, Wendy, for hosting Henri Coulette, his former Iowa classmate from Los Angeles. Suspecting Coulette might not be a big draw, Lawson left a reminder of this policy on the bulletin board. His messages were unmistakable. He typed them on rough yellow paper, and signed them simply *ML*. By the paper alone, the author's identity stood out like the sun. Each visit by a star graduate turned the workshop into a version of Bede's banquet hall, but instead of a sparrow flying in one end and out the other, the visiting poet, hatched here like us, circled above our heads, shielded in flight by a bevy of faculty friends.

The audience was thin; the party packed. Ridge and I brought quart bottles of Pickett's of Dubuque. Wendy placed a Van Morrison record on the turntable and bowls of popcorn around the living room. I was happy to be with friends after a reading, so unlike my solitary forays around the village and to Saint Mark's where I once saw my favorite poet John Ashbery read and had no one to discuss it with afterward. Ashbery's clean-shaven face shone among the stubbled and long-haired. He wore a houndstooth jacket with a tie and moved through the crowd surrounded by a few well-dressed friends who formed an elegant uptown aura around him. Ashbery's arrival was like the coming of an ambassador from a wealthier nation, revered for his sympathy to upstart colonies. He took the lectern and said he'd be reading only one poem. The church went silent. He said it was a long one. He added that he had forgotten to bring the last page. After a pause, he said it didn't make any difference. Everyone laughed. We loved the man who dismissed the linear narrative. The next morning, I sat in my bedroom paging through *Some Trees*. I was bursting to share his poems with someone, with anyone, so I approached my mother who was washing the breakfast dishes. While she soaped an eggy plate, I read her the ending of "Le Livre Est Sur La Table":

> Are there
> Collisions, communications on the shore
>
> Or did all secrets vanish when
>
> The woman left? Is the bird mentioned
> In the waves' minutes, or did the land advance?

Without turning from the sink, my mother placed a saucer onto the wire drainer, lifted a cup from the sudsy water and said, "The land advanced."

Lawson leaned against the refrigerator door, speaking softly with Coulette. Pryor stared up at the taller men and asked what they thought about pseudonyms. Coulette looked over Pryor's head and out the window, saying to Lawson, "Things have changed. What's the defunct restaurant chain you miss the most?"

Barkhausen charged into the kitchen imitating the strumming of a guitar player in the living room. He told Coulette how much he admired his poems, especially "The Telephone Club," about a bar with a phone on each table. He mentioned the line, "The blonde has all our numbers." The poet was pleased and so was Lawson, who pointed at Ridge and me and asked if we were at the reading. We said we were. Feeling defensive, I said, "I liked the lines about the friend 'who turned to games/and made a game of boredom.'" Lawson looked stricken and I realized the poem was about him. Ridge rescued me by asking Coulette what poem influenced him the most. Lawson was still staring at me as Barkhausen interrupted, "Easy for me. 'Give Me a Hoax by the Side of the Road.'" Coulette burst into laughter and held out his hand.

"Yours too?" Barkhausen asked as they shook.

"No," Coulette said. "I like your parody." Lawson continued to lean against the refrigerator, blockading the beer. "Mine would be, I think, 'Lycidas,'" Coulette said. He bent over, sniffed the tiny window box on the sill, and said, "Have you ever thought of growing your own parsley, Mitch?"

Maggie Boyer began a conversation with Ridge. Everyone flattered her because her Magpie Press printed nationally known poets. Her black hair looked dyed, and she had plucked her eyebrows and redrawn them badly, as if she had done so on a bumpy bus ride. She had published a few TWFs, in pages as fragile as butterfly wings with beautiful, swirling covers. She already had a reputation as a fine bookmaker, her art entirely opposed to her appearance.

McPeak arrived from Illinois and his red face showed he had been drinking all the way. His forearms dangled in front of him as he walked, his brain telling his body to reach for a glass of something, anything, and all the better if two glasses were available. I heard him loudly pushing past Lawson's block on the refrigerator, and then Lawson asking if he'd been to the reading. I leaned into the kitchen as McPeak, annoyed, grabbed two beers, faced Lawson, and said, "What?"

Lawson stiffened. "Henri came a long way to be with us," he said.

"I don't care for French poetry," McPeak said, and buzzed out.

Ridge admired Maggie's books, and told her how much he liked her latest edition. Maggie said, "Don't try to be nice to me, Ridge, just so I'll publish you."

"I wouldn't insult you like that, Maggie," Ridge said. "And please don't insult me by thinking I would want my first book to come out with a small press."

She went off to find her husband. Ridge made more than the usual noise with his Wellingtons when he walked past Trotta. We had just workshopped Ridge's mournful poem whose closing line was, "The years add up to one long lack." Trotta said to his friends, "Here comes our Chinese poet, *One Long Lack!*" Whenever a female passed, he'd pretend to end his sentence, with "Period!", "Colon!" or "*Cunt*-tact!"

Ridge muttered to me that he had fucked Maggie once and she was mad that it was only once. I was shocked because she was married.

"And there's always a wrinkle," he said, sipping his Pickett's.

When I asked what he meant, he said that when Maggie was aroused, she exhaled through puckered lips. "Like's she's cooling soup," he said. I went to the kitchen for another beer, feeling ready to be eaten by the world.

Dan Cook arrived with his wife, Nora. The other fiction faculty members were at least twenty years older, so students, especially women, flocked to Cook. He had been raised in Manhattan and taught by an English governess, so his real accent seemed false. In The Deadwood, his luxuriant hair and broad mustache made him look like a living wanted poster. Ridge said Nora had been Cook's student at his last teaching job out west. She had suffered from a bad case of chicken pox in her youth, which plastic surgeons attempted to smooth, but they had made her cheeks and forehead uniformly rough. She was extremely pretty despite her skin, especially when she smiled, and she was smiling.

Barkhausen helped Wendy shake more popcorn. He ransacked the spice rack, tossing oregano, paprika and basil into the pot while Wendy giggled. After they served the bowls, they walked onto the porch and I saw their silhouetted faces almost touching. Pryor swigged from a bottle of Ouzo and smacked his lips. He told everyone he had been reading Greek poetry. McPeak and Bear were locked in an arm wrestling match on the wobbly dining room table, which shook, sending popcorn and a vase of dried flowers to the rug.

Cook bent a female student backward over the couch, lifting her blouse and placing a can of cold beer on her bare stomach, yelling, "Let's initiate the new girl!" A few others joined in applying the freezing metal as she squealed. This was one of the pitfalls of being pretty and arriving for the spring term. When Dan returned to Nora, she turned away. He tried to kiss her neck, but she gave him a good push and he stumbled. Dan took a look around and walked out, slamming the door. The slamming door was entrée for the ex-priest, who didn't know who Nora was, and he took her to the couch where the new girl had endured the cold cans.

I sat on the stairs to the second floor, moving aside occasionally for those using the bathroom. Kim Costigan, a sexy blonde, went past me, followed a few minutes later by the loudmouth Trotta. I heard the bathroom door creak open as Kim left, then Trotta's voice, "The problem with you is you pee out your pussy." Kim said over her shoulder, "And the problem with you is you come out your pee-hole."

Cook returned and tried talking to Nora again. Ignoring him, she asked the ex-priest to get her a beer, and Dan stormed out, slamming the door with even less effect.

Pryor sat next to me, offering a sip of Ouzo.

"It's great that you're published," he said. He was happy. He wanted his friends to succeed. He had a vision of each of us sailing on separate ships, off to establish poetry colonies around the world, emissaries to the hinterlands, who would visit each other, bringing their work to the great unschooled, just as his former teachers and their classmates had done. "It's ridiculous you don't have aid," he said, shaking his head.

"I'm getting by," I said. "You have a piece of popcorn in your beard." I flicked it away.

Belinda Schaeffer told Coulette she had discovered some famous stories by Maupassant that were not written by him. Coulette said that Maupassant hated the Eiffel Tower so much he ate there frequently because it was the one place he didn't have to see it.

"I feel that way about my face," Nora said.

Lawson heard her and ran over, saying, "You're a very pretty woman!" He shook his jowls as he spoke, seriously concerned.

"It's okay, Mitch," she said and touched his arm.

"I mean it, Nora. You have classic looks."

Everyone agreed that Nora was beautiful and her face turned red, except for a dozen white dots impervious to blood flow. At that, everyone stared, and she ran into Pryor's study where she inspected the bookcases.

McPeak had lost the wrestling match to Bear and took a bill out of his wallet. A girl who liked him walked to the table and whispered in his ear.

"I drink to concentrate," McPeak roared, "and then I drink to forget what I'm concentrating on!" He laughed and looked at us. She placed her small hand on his wide red-haired wrist and whispered again.

"I drink to turn the people I'm with into the people I wish I was with! Where'd that French poet go, by the way?" The girl returned to her friends.

Pryor said, "Harvey's out of town tonight, but when he comes back, make it a point to know him. Believe me, you'll get aid next fall."

"I'd feel funny about that," I said.

"Don't be stupid," he said. "Tell him his last book reminds you of Merwin. I mean it, just say that and you'll be golden."

"But it's nothing like Merwin," I said.

"So what?" His bloodshot eyes pleaded with me.

Wendy and Barkhausen flipped through the records. Wendy grabbed her earlobe and said to Barkhausen, "Oh, I lost my earring!" She got an impish look on her face and said, "Probably on the porch." They left the living room, as Barkhausen said, "I think I've lost some of my hearing too."

Dan Cook returned, talked to Nora again, and left again, again slamming the door. By now it had all the drama of a toilet flushing. She stood with some female poets who discussed the difference between *kitty-corner* and *catty-corner*. Loudmouth Trotta listened from his place on the floor among a fleet of empty bottles and yelled, "I prefer *pussy-corner!*" Nora walked over and poured her full glass of beer onto his head. It seemed to flow from the rim in slow motion as the loudmouth unsuccessfully scrambled to haul his quivering mass from the rug, drunkenly sprawling and sliding in the suds. Nora grabbed her purse, yelled thank you to Wendy and, as she opened the door to leave, her husband entered. She kept going and so did he, straight for Havana Jones, the only black girl at the party.

Coulette and Lawson said good night, and when they reached the door, Barkhausen, drunk, screamed, "The locusts have no king!"

"You have a nut on your hands," Coulette said to Lawson.

"Maybe and maybe not," Lawson said.

"The locusts have no king!"

"What the hell does that mean?" McPeak asked Barkhausen. "What the fuck are you talking about?"

"He's full of arcane quotes," Lawson said to Coulette. He looked at McPeak and explained, "It's from the bible. The locusts have no king, and yet they go forward in ranks. It means we are equals, all here to write poi-ems."

"There are no greatest in the kingdom of heaven," Coulette said, quoting Blake.

McPeak shook his curly red head.

"Mitch, I miss Iowa City," Coulette said, as Lawson held the door for him. "Do you know where I can get a rubber stamp of an ear of corn?"

Squealing and laughing came from a corner where Havana stood topless and Cook faced the room, pretending to auction off her breasts.

"Gimme one dollar, two dollar, three dollar, four dollar . . ." he sang, strumming his lips with his finger so it sounded like an astronomically rising sum. Havana's friends were yelling, "Do me! Auction me next!"

Ridge and I decided to go for coffee in the donut shop of the all-night Kroger supermarket. On our way out, Ridge paused at an end table, frowning as he lifted a stack of envelopes Pryor had addressed to known poets. Wendy stood at the window, looking onto Governor Street. When we got outside, Barkhausen was talking to Lawson about leather jackets. Coulette's mind was elsewhere and maybe he was also feeling the liquor, because he interrupted and said, "What do you think is the most used letter of the alphabet, Mitch?" Lawson ignored this question as he had the others. He knew Barkhausen's father was a furrier and complained to Barkhausen that his suede jacket was losing its shape. Barkhausen asked the cost and when Lawson told him, Artie said, "That's why!" Coulette couldn't contain his laughter and even Lawson smiled. I said to Ridge that "e" must be the most used letter, but Ridge thought it was "i."

"Did anyone there really know who I am?" Coulette asked Lawson. Barkhausen put his arm around both their shoulders and started to walk between them, but Lawson turned and said something about not needing an escort. They crossed the dark street and Coulette stepped over something, a dead cat, hit by a car. Everyone was silent until Barkhausen yelled, "Me-ouch!"

"That kid's a riot," Coulette said as they walked away.

McPeak stood on the porch with his arm around the new girl. "To think Coulette came all the way from France," he said.

"He's from California," the girl said.

"Lawson told me he came from France. That's what he said, 'all the way from France,'" and he took a long drink.

At Kroger's, Ridge brought the coffees to our table and told me how he thought Lawson was a real poet in spite of his finicky personality. As he talked, I noticed a girl in the fiction workshop pushing a grocery cart. Ridge saw me staring, and said, "Forget it. It's like sticking a pin into a marshmallow." He went back to Lawson, saying that Lawson wrote too conservatively, too carefully, too timidly to be great. "Everything about him is modified," he said. "Everything about him is *ly*."

CHAPTER SIX

OPEN MARRIAGE—ESSENTIAL FEMINISM—
A SECRET LONGING—FAKE MONIQUE—
THE DUGOUT—LAWSON COMES TO HAMBURG
INN NO. 3—BUBBLE OF NEGLECT

The front window of Iowa Book & Supply displayed dozens of copies of *Open Marriage: A New Lifestyle for Couples*, a best seller disputing the virtues of fidelity. The showcase next to it contained *Feminism: The Essential Historical Writings*. This reflected the tone for what went on in the classroom and beyond. Teachers dated students and a TA had intercourse with his girlfriend on the desk in front of his freshmen class to illustrate a point, which no one could recall. At the same time, feminism was on the rise and a female student complained about Harvey teaching Roethke's "The Geranium" because the poem described the maid who threw out the speaker's beloved plant as "that presumptuous hag." In this climate where sexual liberation and women's liberation crossed, I tried to find a girlfriend.

McPeak's forays from Illinois into the arms of any willing woman and Ridge's ability to pick up girls at random affected me the same way as good poems in the workshop—I tried to learn from them. Ridge had a sixth sense. In pizza parlors and luncheonettes, he would conclude that a waitress who had stood at our table for no more than thirty seconds wanted to go to bed with him. By the time the bill arrived, he'd be meeting her after work.

I had walked under the trees along the Iowa River with Mandy Thompson, gathering autumn leaves for her Dickinson essay, but my lack of enthusiasm for the project put her off. Now it was spring, and dry leaf gathering had been my only Iowa date.

One afternoon by the bulletin board, Jen Thacker and I laughed at the notice by Falcon Namiki, a dashing Japanese poet in the international workshop who was also an MFA student. It said, "Sign up below for my lecture on Karate/Writing." She laughed harder when I pointed out McPeak's posting next to it, "Sign up below for my lecture on Good Old Fashioned Punch-in-the-Nose/Writing." Jen seldom spoke in workshop, but when she did, she reduced long-winded discussions to the very nub of the matter. Otherwise, she kept to herself, smirking the workshop hours away, a plain figure, limp hair in a Buster Brown cut. She suggested we get a cup of coffee and, in a half hour at The Hamburg Inn No. 2, she told me she was divorced, with two young children. Her schedule was difficult: kids, school, part-time job with UPS, and AA meetings. She had to steal time to write, and her children knew not to disturb her when she sat at the kitchen table wearing a tall paper cone on her head. "Like a dunce cap," she said.

"Think of it as a wizard's hat," I said.

The next morning there was a knock on my door, something that never happened. It was Jen. She brisked right in, brushing me roughly with her elbow. I had been trying to write and my desk was covered with books and pages.

"Working?" she asked.

"No," I said.

She sat at the kitchen table. I made her a cup of instant coffee. She said she had just dropped her kids at school. We talked about the frigid weather, hoping it would get warmer. She said she came over to ask me if I was serious about what I had said the day before. I asked her what she meant.

"When you said that people who love art should be together, that we're different from the rest."

"I'm not sure what you mean."

"It's what *you* mean!" she said. "Did you mean what I think you meant?"

"I just meant community's important," I said. I looked at her closely, at the tiny pimples flecking her chin, the dark hair along her upper lip, her weary eyes. She gave me her workshop smirk and said nothing. I said, "I meant, in a world where art is neglected, artists have to support each other."

She said, "I'd be just another easy lay for you, wouldn't I?"

"No," I said. "I mean, what are you talking about?"

"I'm finished talking," she said, pushing her chair from the table. "You're just like the rest." She ran out and left the door open behind her.

I told Ridge the next day, and he offered to fix me up with one of his ex-girlfriends, but I declined. I nursed my crush on Belinda Schaeffer. Not only was she a TWF, but with a PhD, and in French, and from Yale. In workshop, she was thoughtful and kind, untouched by jealousy or need, and passed through us like a fragrance. Only those at the top of the workshop hierarchy approached her— the teachers and her fellow TWFs. The rest of us looked at her like groundbirds admiring the flight of an eagle.

One of the workshop's stars, Jonathan Reynolds, although married, had an affair with Belinda. When it ended, he wrote a poem called "The Cunt," that he submitted to class, but he was afraid to title it that so he typed an *e* over the *u*, so it could be read as "The Cent." His first book came out a month later and included a long love poem entitled, "Letter to X," which Barkhausen had seen in draft. Since Belinda was the subject, I rushed to buy it. The poem described nipples as big as ginger snaps as well as her trimmed pubic hair. Reynolds couldn't resist associating himself with the magic of her name, and the acknowledgments at the back of the book included the note, "*Letter to X* is for Belinda Schaeffer." There were also two poems "to *B*."

I was ashamed to tell anyone, even Ridge, of my longing for Belinda, since it was so passionate and so common. Instead, I asked Monique of the charades and pantomimes for a beer. She was also blonde, with a master's in French. Unlike the rest of the class, she wore tailored clothes and simple strands of pearls. I guessed she was rich. I had overheard her saying that her father invented the twist tie. On occasion, she affected an accent, and it was in full force the afternoon I brought her to The Deadwood. Ridge asked her if she was born in France.

"No." She paused. "Conceived in France."

After a second beer, Monique's accent disappeared. Aware of its vanishing, she began tossing French phrases into her sentences to evoke Parisian charm. A third beer brought it back with a vengeance, and when she repeated, "How you say?" for the fourth time, McPeak barked at her to knock it off.

Talk turned to fathers, initiated by McPeak's poem about his father, which we had just discussed in class. A brakeman on the Rock Island Line, he lost a bet on the Cubs and almost choked to death trying to swallow his pocket watch. My father was an envelope salesman for a company in Harlem and he hoped I'd take over his accounts. Monique said her father invented the flat-bottom

~ 60 ~

paper bag, but by now no one believed anything she said. Ridge didn't say a word about his father, who died when he was in high school.

"What about your father, Ridge?" Monique asked, but he just stared at the table and shook his head.

"His father drank himself to death," I whispered.

"Don't be so *efféminé*, Ridge," she said. "Whose father *hasn't?*" She laughed and lifted her glass. Then she looked at me and said, "My father wrote the slogan, *With a name like Smuckers, it has to be good.* Did you know that, John?"

We left for a poetry reading by fellow workshop students. McPeak nudged me as I slipped out of the booth, nodding at Monique and making a big frown. As we passed Epstein's, a sign announced that the actualists would be writing poems of "beastly English," using nouns that had become verbs like "crow and "sponge." Outside the room for the reading, Monique flirted with Falcon Namiki whose retro Carnaby Street dress caused McPeak to dub him an outlandish pansy. I told Monique I was going to sit with my friends and she was fine with that as I could tell she was ready for a night of karate/writing.

The first reader was a brooding solitary farm boy whose mystifying work entranced us all. He read only a few poems and ended with "Darkness Begins with the Dark," the last two lines of which were:

> wavering like a moist nun,
> like a sad placenta.

Ridge said he admired the double simile. The featured poet, an overweight woman with a following of overweight women, read a poem called "Twenty Lovers": twenty sections which described in detail twenty rotten sexual encounters with twenty rotten men. Her audience knew the poem, and cheered favorite passages. She got the biggest hand when she reached Number Twelve, a one-liner she recited in a smashing tone:

You miserable little bastard!

McPeak started dating Taryn, a stripper who worked at The Dugout. He begged us to go with him to see her, and finally one night Pryor, Ridge and I agreed. We met McPeak on the ground floor of EPB, where the university hospital was conducting a blood drive, cots and tables of cookies and punch filling the lobby. Ridge began speaking intimately to one of the nurses and a moment later told us to go without him. Barkhausen got off the elevator and joined us. McPeak swung by Black's Gaslight Village so Barkhausen could change his clothes. McPeak knew the complex, which had been crazily rigged together by Mr. Black, an eccentric who retrieved his morning paper from his front yard in the nude and who spoke in a falsetto when he spoke to women. On the drive over, McPeak said he had gone out with a girl who lived in the Chinese room which Black had furnished entirely in bamboo and silk and which contained an indoor waterfall pouring from a huge tea pot. Barkhausen's place was on the second floor, which you could get to by stairs, or climbing a tree in the lobby that leaned toward a balcony. Artie put on a starched white shirt and jeans with pressed creases. He pomaded his hair with Yardley's Brilliantine, its lavender scent causing Pryor to sneeze repeatedly.

The Dugout had a bar on each side of the room and a round stage in the middle. Taryn waved to McPeak, and we joined her at a table. I was surprised to learn she was an undergraduate English major. Her freckles and dyed hair matched her orange blouse. Drunken men in T-shirts hollered at a woman in a bikini who danced to "Teach Me Tiger," deftly manipulating her theatre in the round, blowing kisses and whispering to those in front. Taryn told us it was a night of novelty acts and praised her friend's charms as the girl flung her bra to the crowd. Arms flailed for it, and the winner pressed it to his nose. Barkhausen beamed at an Asian woman in a top hat and green velvet three-piece suit who contorted herself across a green velvet couch. Her last number was accompanied by the theme from *Exodus*. At the final crescendo, the dancer, naked except for pasties and a G-string, tipped her hat, and long, straight, beautiful black hair fell down the length of her back and almost to the floor.

When Taryn appeared, we were amazed. She had painted more freckles onto her cheeks, large ones, and had braided her orange hair into pigtails. She wore a white bonnet and a white dress, a dress for a lawn party, and twirled around the stage to "Chicago," her many petticoats lifting, revealing her thighs, hinting at the flesh above, and then lowering the whirling white slips which spun like discs, higher then lower, until for the last five seconds, she spun very fast, raising the petticoats and revealing her perfect buttocks and ruby G-string.

Two businessmen took the table next to us with two women. One said to the other about his date, "Don't ever come to my room again with a piece of shit like this."

"Come on," his friend said. "She's not so bad."

Barkhausen turned to them and said, "You watch out how you talk about the lady!" With his youthful face and ironed clothes, Barkhausen hardly seemed imposing, but he spoke so fiercely the men shut up. A few moments later, one of them rested his shoe on the table, in the middle of his party's drinks.

"The floor's for your feet, so keep them there!" Barkhausen yelled, and the man sheepishly removed his loafer.

I told Artie he should just enjoy the show, but he said he couldn't stand a lack of manners. When he went to the men's room, Pryor asked me, "What's with him?"

I said I had no idea.

"I kind of admire him," Pryor said, shrugging.

Taryn returned to our table. McPeak praised her grace and imagination as he petted away the freckles on her face with a napkin dipped in beer.

Pryor told everyone about Barkhausen and, in his telling and retelling, Artie became known as a great defender of female honor. Pryor visited Harvey and Lawson in their offices, spreading Barkhausen's fame, a little rubbing off on him by association.

Black Tuesday, the day of financial aid decisions, was approaching. The RAs might become TAs, and the TAs, TWFs. Those like me hoped for anything. The stipends were small, but each appointment came with in-state tuition, worth thousands of dollars. I had received mild praise from teachers and had stopped straining for surreal effects. Ridge said that one of the graduating TWFs had insisted to Harvey that I had shed my New York School influences and should be recognized. At The Deadwood one afternoon, Pryor said that he had gone to both Harvey and Lawson to make a case for me, bringing a copy of my poem, "Blue," which was a list of blue things. Pryor said Lawson liked it and called it "an exercise in syntax," which was news to me. Barkhausen joined the table and said his stomach was upset and asked Brandy for "a cup of teat." Ridge squinted at me, but we really couldn't be sure if we heard right. I glanced over at laughter coming from the two women at a table across from us, both pregnant, and each with a cup of tea. This made me wonder further about Barkhausen. He seemed to absorb things around him, and spit them out in a cockeyed way.

"I might go see Lawson myself about giving you aid," Barkhausen said.

Ridge said, "Soon, the guy mopping the floor around Lawson's desk will be whispering over Mitch's shoulder about you."

"It's embarrassing," I said.

"Just wait," Ridge said. "You might get something."

The next morning I couldn't open my left eye. I went to the drug store and the pharmacist said I had either "reader's eye" or "drinker's eye" and gave me a bottle of artificial tears. I worried about my vision because my health care had always been poor. My family doctor worked out of his house with no staff, opening his wallet to make change. When forms had to be completed for admission to Fairfield, he signed the papers, saying, "If anyone asks if I gave you these shots, tell them I did." My tonsils were removed in his office without anesthesia while I was sitting on my hands to keep me from knocking the scalpel away. The optometrist said my eyesight was twenty-twenty. After college, I was drafted, and an army doctor told me I was nearly blind in my left eye. Now I had only myself to blame, for drinking and reading, reading and drinking.

Pryor's marriage was failing and McPeak broke up with Taryn, saying that having sex with her was like playing Chutes and Ladders. He dated an almost catatonic girl from the northwest, and another who hid her voluptuous body under heavy woolen ponchos before he found Maud Deering, a Boston debutante who mocked his Chevy Nova when he offered her a ride after class. He cashed his high school teachers' pension to buy an MG he garaged in Iowa City, then raced along the Coralville strip with Maud's scarf snapping in the wind. Meanwhile, Wendy flirted with everyone, and Pryor escorted his drunken wife from party to party, leaving a wake of torn paper.

Ridge was studying for his doctoral exam, and sat in an armchair surrounded by books, broken toothpicks and stained coffee cups. One evening I visited him after he had read *Middlemarch* in a day. He couldn't remember the main character's name.

"I've reached a point of diminishing returns," he said. "Let's get something to eat." We left for Hamburg Inn No. 3.

Pryor sat at a table by himself, inviting us over, his red eyes showing another fight with Wendy. Our banter couldn't shake the sadness from his face. We all ordered the meatloaf special. While we waited, a shadowy ecto-morph appeared at the open door, hesitant, stepping in and stepping out, as if the floor were a burning pan. Shield-ing his eyes, though it was not bright, he charged inside.

"Mitch!" Pryor called.

Ridge asked, "What is Lawson doing at Hamburg Inn No. 3?"

Lawson, dressed in a silver houndstooth coat with epaulets and a belt around the back, approached our table, all smiles for a change. He asked if he could join us, saying his wife was out of town visiting her mother. Pryor told him about the special and he ordered it, asking the waitress to pour the gravy on top of his fries. The three of us locked eyes at this first instance of inelegance. He looked around in wonder, as uncomfortable with the Inn as it was with him, as we were with him, as he seemed with us, and with his life, a night in an uncomfortable inn, Hamburg Inn No. 3.

Ridge got him on the subject of his hobby, gambling. He told us of a board game, "Win, Place & Show," which he called the greatest game ever. He said that when Mark Strand visited, it stayed on his dining room table for days. We all wanted a good marriage, a longtime poet-friend, a dining room table, and a leisurely pastime. We ate quickly, hungrily, while Lawson fiddled with his plate, handling his fork like a pen. He lined the canned peas into rows, mash-ing some of them with a loud tick. When he had taken a few bites of the meatloaf and eaten most of the sopped fries, he looked at his watch, said goodbye and settled with the cashier.

As soon as he left, Pryor pointed to his plate. "Did you see that? He smashed one out of three peas!"

Ridge and I looked at the row of dots.

"He did!" Pryor pulled Lawson's plate toward him. "He crushed every third pea. Two unstressed, one stressed. Dactyls!"

When we asked for the check, we found Lawson had paid.

Dan Cook parked in front of the restaurant and came toward us, head down, the leather heels of his black boots clicking. He lifted his chin from his ascot and took Ridge aside, his arm circling the shoulder of Ridge's peacoat, which was dappled with cat hair. Ridge turned to us, said that they were going to meet a couple of girls, and they drove off.

So we spent our days, literally scanning the plate of our teacher in Hamburg Inn No. 3, seeing the world madly in stresses and unstresses.

On Black Tuesday, Ridge came to my door to tell me I was again passed over.

"I hate to tell you, but they gave Barkhausen a TA."

"You're kidding," I said.

"They think he's original."

"He is that," I said.

"I tried to point out that his stuff is word salad, but Harvey and Lawson really like it."

"Did you see that new poem of his, where he puts a 'chug of wine' on the table?" I said.

"I know," Ridge said. "And there was one in the manuscript about fucking a woman outside a strip club, in the 'porking lot.' Lawson wrote in the margin, *Streetwise wordplay.*"

Ridge leaned against the doorframe and said he dropped by so I wouldn't learn the bad news around town. I said I would meet him later that night.

After he left, I imagined Barkhausen misusing words in his class. He had recently complimented Pryor on his rigorous writing schedule, praising his "wheel power." I was not as good a writer as many of the others, and Barkhausen did have a rough glamour. I understood the decision and, in some ways, I was relieved to be outside this laying on of hands. I felt the latitude of enjoying that freedom, but a few hours later, I realized I could be laboring in a simple bubble of neglect.

CHAPTER SEVEN

THE IDIOT SAVANT—LIKE A MAN—
MOVING IN WITH KIM—McPEAK FALLS IN LOVE—
A MECHANICAL CANARY—RUDDY JOHN
CHEEVER—RAYMOND CARVER IS MISSING

Unlike most of his explosive Iowa City romances, McPeak's affair with the feminist Stavrula Pallas seemed like it might endure. He had broken up with Maud Deering and sold his sports car. He said that having sex with her was like building a geodesic dome. Stavrula was his age, thirty, with a faculty appointment in both sociology and art. She was a conceptual artist who wrote about the reception of her work among various social classes. They met when he parked at EPB and noticed a party in the adjacent field among haystacks and bundles of corn. He got in line for a cup of hot cider, which he intended to spike with his flask. Stavrula approached him, thinking he was a new, older student, possibly lost. When he told her he was a poet, she was charmed, and inquired about his interest in sociology. He quoted Auden, "Thou shalt not sit with statisticians, nor commit a social science." She saw his trip from the parking lot as a social act, an opinion solidified by his supplementing her own glass of cider with a splash of bourbon.

We went from watching Taryn dance to hearing Stavrula lecture. McPeak basked in her cutting-edge conceptualism the night she gave a talk describing how the patrons of the Detroit Institute of Arts appreciated her piece where she sat in a booth and invited confessions. As I was leaving the auditorium, a tall blonde nudged me, saying, "When was the last time *you* went to confession?" I recognized Kim Costigan who had made that sharp comeback to loudmouth Trotta at the Coulette party, and who had dated almost everyone in the workshop, both poetry and fiction. She wore a short skirt and her large breasts pushed against her blouse.

"Admit it," she said, smiling. "You were staring at me!"

I confessed. I passed the time of Stavrula's talk watching Kim cross and uncross her legs. Here I was in Iowa, the hotbed of hotbeds and still a paralyzed voyeur, like Dickie, the janitor's helper at Fairfield, an idiot savant who swabbed the cafeteria floor and could name the day you were born if you told him the date. Whenever a woman entered, Dickie pushed his broom in her direction. One night I sat with my favorite teacher, the Joyce scholar Lou Berrone, and Nina, his teenage daughter, in the campus snack bar, and Dickie swept his way toward us. Lou gave him her date of birth.

"June 9, 1953," Lou said again and again, but Dickie just stared, fixed on Nina's thighs as he pressed the broom. "Dickie!" Lou said.

Dickie's eyes focused on the nylon stockings, the bristles moving closer and closer until he touched Nina's toe.

"What day was she born?" I asked, but he continued to push, a little white spittle at the edge of his mouth.

"Daddy!" Nina whispered, covering the side of her reddening face with her hand. Lou took Dickie by the arm, escorting him to an empty table by the window where Dickie returned to his routine.

Berrone said, "It's my fault. I didn't realize he'd get like that. And maybe I somehow forgot that he's a man." I could have stared at Nina all day myself. Being marooned on a few acres with only men had turned us all slightly mad. The insistent broom, the helpless, ignited eyes of the idiot savant losing his slender hold on the world, and Berrone's apologetic words, brought back phrases from my reading:

> He is a man, therefore nothing human is alien to him
> Take it like a man
> As a man, therefore he came to all these sufferings
> A Man's a Man for all that

Lou might have forgotten that Dickie was a man, but I never doubted it, or that I was a man, or Lou—but I didn't know it could mean to become hypnotized, to forget everything, to repeat yourself fruitlessly in the face of beauty. And now that beauty was nudging me as we walked out of a lecture hall.

Ridge had told me that Kim had recently won a hundred dollars at The Dugout's Amateur Striptease Night.

"Congratulations on the prize," I said.

"I knew I'd win if I just flashed my beaver at the jukebox a few times," she said.

"Want to get a beer?"

Two weeks later, we decided to move in together, and interviewed for an apartment over a garage owned by an elderly couple, Mr. and Mrs. Alva Yoder. Pretending we were married, we sat in their living room with Mr. Yoder in his honest overalls, and Mrs. Yoder, who sewed a quilt draped across her lap. As I looked at Kim, wearing her shortest skirt yet, I felt less married by the minute. After half an hour of conversation, homemade donuts and buttermilk, they let us have the apartment. Mrs. Yoder said a lot of students had been interested, but she preferred a man and wife.

Mr. Yoder handed me the keys and said, "We've been married fifty years. I still remember the day. It was raining. They say that when it rains on your wedding day, you'll have good luck. And we had good luck." He paused for a moment and added, "And we had bad luck too."

Kim and I were happy in our little place. Our desks in front of a picture window overlooked the gravel driveway. Because I kept a photo of Neruda's studio on the Pacific taped to the wall, Ridge started calling me, "the poor man's Neruda," and confirmed the wisdom of my move with Kim. "You got the best deal in town," he said, letting me know he had gone out with her too. To pay the higher rent and the upkeep of Kim's aged car, I took a job as lunchtime supervisor at Iowa City High School, patrolling the halls with the retired county sheriff who wore a greasy double-breasted blue raincoat. We pushed our way through the crowd, stopping kids from hurling clots of wet toilet paper or aiming jelly donuts at each other. I cornered a boy who rode a unicycle down the main hall, but he simply spun around me and zipped to the other end, as I plodded behind him amid laughter. Lacking all authority, I realized it was probably best I was not given charge of a freshman class.

At the end of the two-hour shift, I retrieved my jacket from the faculty room, spending a few minutes with the sheriff who was always there first, sweating heavily into his wilted coat. He said he couldn't work weekends anymore and I took his place as fire marshal, standing at the rear exit of the auditorium and watching *Our Town* and *The Music Man*. I was glad for the ten dollars a night because Kim had been fired from several jobs. At the Lark Supper Club, she clanged a tray of corn chowder into the temple of Mr. Lark himself as he leaned back in his chair.

She worked as a nurse's aide at the university hospital, but one night at dinner she told me she had forgotten to remove a rectal thermometer from a toddler.

McPeak brought Stavrula to The Deadwood for her birthday, joining Ridge and me in a booth. After a pitcher of beer, he took out a small wooden crate, and from a bed of straw, lifted a lifelike yellow canary. He placed it on the table, touching its breast so the head bobbed as it trilled sweet notes that soared and dipped. We marveled at this strange mechanical creation. Stavrula kissed him and kissed him. McPeak pressed it again and we listened again to its beautiful tune.

"It's an American Singer. The shape, the feathers, it's exact in every way," he said. "An artist in Moline does one a month."

Loudmouth Trotta left his barstool and seemed captivated by the bird, the first time he showed any quality besides scorn and vulgarity. "That's a great song," he said.

"I'm calling it Maria, after Maria Callas," Stavrula said.

"Only the males sing," I said. "You need a male name."

"Oh, come on," Ridge said. "It's not real. What's the difference?"

"No, John's right," Stavrula said. "I'll call him 'Caruso.'"

Trotta asked if he could see the bird. He turned it over, blew on its tail feathers, and said, "Yes, it's definitely a male." He took a seat in a nearby booth.

Stavrula asked him to make the bird sing again, and McPeak touched the switch. Ridge left to have a manuscript conference with Abe Gubegna, an Ethiopian novelist attending the international workshop whose book he was translating. Ridge said that Abe always embraced him when they met and he could feel the writer's .45, which he carried everywhere, fearing assassination by Haile Selassie's men. McPeak and Stavrula went to play pinball. I sat at the table with the American Singer. I ordered another pitcher.

Then I couldn't help myself—I lifted Caruso. I turned him over and blew on the feathers. It was neither male nor was it female. I returned it to its place near Stavrula's drink with all the dignity I could muster, but Loudmouth across the way was giggling and shaking his head at my having fallen for his joke.

Ridge introduced me to Tracy Kidder who was in John Cheever's workshop. He invited me to dinner at his house with Cheever, Raymond Carver and Dick Florsheim, a star fiction student who imitated Nabokov. Tracy wrote short stories, but was working on a nonfiction book about Juan Corona, the mass murderer of migrant workers in California, and had published part of it in the *Atlantic*. A former second lieutenant in Vietnam, he had gone from Harvard to the army, to the arms of Fran, his beautiful wife. He rated workshop stories by the number of laughs. "This story has twenty laughs," he'd say enthusiastically.

On the night of the dinner, Cheever arrived by cab, the way he got around everywhere, except for when he rode in Carver's car with the bullet hole in the windshield. Cheever was sixty-four, ruddy but grim, frail and thin. He wore a three-piece suit and exuded a strong fragrance—as if he had been "slapped with cologne," was how Ridge put it. He handed Fran a bouquet of dwarf roses. Florsheim was already there, in puttees and a white sailor hat, going through Tracy's records, trying to find a replacement for Pachelbel's *Canon in D*, which he detested.

While we waited for Ray, Cheever had a martini he insisted on mixing himself. He recounted going to an American literature professor's house the night before where he was served a black martini, called a "Nevermore," after Poe's raven. "He put a drop of ink in it," he said. "Ghastly! And the professor's little daughter was named Daisy, after Daisy Miller." He gave a fake shudder with his narrow shoulders.

Tracy and Fran were from Long Island's Oyster Bay, and talk turned to summers in the Hamptons. Cheever used the expression "on island," referring to Nantucket. Florsheim said he preferred Paris for outdoor activities like playing dominoes in the sidewalk cafes. I mentioned going fishing on a party boat with my father, out of Sheepshead Bay. For some reason, Cheever thought I meant Cape Cod and asked if I had summered there. Tracy answered for me, "He didn't even *two-week* in Rockaway!"

"Tweak?" Cheever said. "Tweak?"

Fran filled glasses with burgundy. Cheever was on his third martini but accepted the wine. He ranted against the other fiction writers on the faculty as "flat tires." He asked for some big-band music and then embraced Fran and they twirled around the room. At the end of the song, Cheever removed his coat and danced alone to the next cut. Our eyes widened when he put his hand over his heart, but he marched back and forth in the same place on the rug until the music stopped.

When Ray failed to appear, Tracy called Joe Cleary, Ray's friend. Cleary said Ray was in California, teaching at USC. He held simultaneous appointments and neither university knew. United Airlines provided him with twelve roundtrips, on the promise of an article for their in-flight magazine, *Mainliner*, which Ray never wrote.

After dinner, Cheever complained about his bad luck with Iowa women. I could guess why. Sitting in The Deadwood one Monday night, I noticed a female graduate student at his table who had an obvious crush on him. Talk turned to football and Cheever wondered if the Giants were winning. Since The Deadwood had no television, Cheever loudly asked her to go to George's to get the score. She never returned.

Florsheim gave Cheever a ride home, and I stopped at The Deadwood. Ridge and McPeak were there and I described the night. McPeak said, "The most famous guy to come to Iowa City and he can't get laid!" As he said this, Belinda Schaeffer walked in on the arm of a middle-aged man decked out in a double-breasted blue blazer with brass buttons and white linen pants. With her was a faculty member in fiction, Fred Exley, and another attractive girl.

"Jesus," Ridge said, "look at Belinda with the old guy."

I muffled my sorrow as McPeak continued about Cheever. "You know Beth?" he asked. "Beth of the bee-stung lips?" We knew.

"She went back to Cheever's room at the Iowa House the other night. They had a drink and he sat on the bed and stared at the wall. He started a monologue about wallpaper, that wallpaper ruined his marriage. Finally, he propped a pillow against the headboard and asked her to sit next to him. When she did, he said, 'Would you like to lie down?' She said she didn't think so, and then he went back to the issue of wallpaper and started singing a song from his childhood, but he could only remember the first two lines, 'When father papered the parlor, you couldn't tell Pa from paste.' Beth said he sang it again and again, trying to jog his memory. Giving up, he patted the bed and said, 'Are you sure you wouldn't like to lie down?' She again said no. He sang the lines over and over until he nodded off, humming. The next day she got the lyrics from a reference librarian:

> When Father papered the parlor
> You couldn't tell Pa from paste
> Dabbing it here and dabbing it there!
> Paste and paper everywhere
> Mother was stuck to the ceiling
> The kids were stuck to the floor
> You never saw such a family so stuck up before.

"Three drunken girls sang it for Cheever in The Deadwood, arms locked and legs kicking. Cheever was puzzled
but pleased," McPeak told us. He said Cheever became
wistful, and said, "That's a song from my youth that I
thought was long forgotten."

The next morning the front page of the *Daily Iowan*
had a photo of the man in The Deadwood with Belinda
Schaeffer, and the caption, "Celebrated Writer William
Styron to Give Reading."

CHAPTER EIGHT

JOHN BERRYMAN JUMPS—DINNER WITH
CARVER—SMALL BEER—POOR EVERYONE—
AN AFTERNOON WITH BELINDA SCHAEFFER—
FATHER IGNATIUS—THE MAID-RITE

⚬━⚬

When John Berryman leapt from a bridge in Minneapolis, Pryor was the first of us to hear. Malcolm Gee had sent him a telegram that Pryor carried from office to faculty office, unfolding it, reading it aloud and returning it to its envelope. It said:

"The high ones die. He chose the frozen Mississippi."

A former Iowa faculty member, Berryman had taught Lawson and Coulette. Ridge told me the first sentence was a quote from the *Dream Songs*. He said there was something proprietary, melodramatic, pious and finally pathetically peripheral about Gee's note. It firmly established a hierarchy—the high ones—and pitched the life of poetry as a competitive sport. This made Pryor, he said, a messenger from the gods.

Harvey and Pryor walked around Iowa City together, went to movies together and Pryor sometimes met visiting poets at the Cedar Rapids airport and brought them to their hotels, joining the poet and Harvey for dinner. He applied for jobs by the dozen. I ran into him one day as he walked to the post office carrying applications to renowned Ivies as well as to Mountain Empire Community College and Marion Military Institute. He fanned them out for me, also showing letters to the poets he continued to write, complimenting their poems.

"Why are you writing to Lucien Stryk?" I asked.

"To thank him for his book."

"He sent you his book?"

"No, to thank him for writing it," he said, twitching the corner of his mouth, as if I were really stupid.

Ridge advised me not to bother applying, as I had no book. He said to wait until I had a chance at a good job instead of a lousy one.

I mentioned this to Pryor who said, "I have to. I have a wife."

I walked into The Deadwood with Ridge as Joe Cleary roared out for another drink. "Beam ditch!" Jim Beam and water. Cleary, who resembled a toothsome bulldog, introduced me to Ray Carver. Ray furrowed his brow and made sure to get my name and what I did. This was one of his qualities people loved. He and Cleary were arguing about Wallace Stegner, Carver's teacher at Stanford. When Ray liked a writer, he called him "a dandy," and when Cleary scoffed at Stegner, Ray moved on to Lawrence Durrell, another of his favorites. He quoted, "The sea is high again today, with a thrilling flush of wind," saying, "That line sings, it sings!" Cleary said, "It stinks, it stinks!" I couldn't reconcile Ray's love for high rhetoric with his own spare style.

When the bars closed, I often rode with Ray in his old car, empty bottles rattling on the floor. One morning, he called to ask if we had hit anything the night before. I said we hadn't, and he said, "I don't know what could have happened, but the whole side of my car is smashed." Then he chuckled, saying, "This morning, it was all Cheever and I could do to hail a cab to the liquor store."

Ray asked me to have dinner with him at the restaurant faculty went to for special occasions, the Hoover House in West Branch, named for Herbert Hoover, Iowa's only president. We were served by girls in black dresses with white aprons and hats. Our waitress told us that we should be sure to come back in summer for Hooverfest, a day of singing, fireworks and softball. Ray expressed sincere interest, and then ordered two house concoctions made with coconut that Lawson had recommended. When we finished, the waitress asked if we were ready to order. Ray said we wanted to have a drink first, and she said, "You just had a drink."

"That was a drink?" Ray said.

We began many rounds of Jack Daniel's while Ray told stories of bad restaurants. He particularly hated a place in Oregon. After he and his friend had each ordered a whole chicken, the friend pulled out a bottle of George Dickel and filled their glasses. The waitress said they had to get their whiskey from the bar. She told them again when she brought their dinners. She finally called the manager who stood next to the table and told them to put the bottle away and order from the waitress. Ray said that his friend got angry and threw his chicken right onto the manager's shoes. The man walked away, and Ray ended his story with the words, "You know, the chicken stayed on the rug all night. That's the kind of place it was."

Ray said he was flush from beating Lawson at poker. "Drink up! Drink up," he said, lifting glass after glass to his glowing face. We had the specialty of the house, grilled turkey legs, and our plates were piled with tiny long bones, like games of pick-up sticks. After coffee and several cognacs, the check arrived and Ray made a grave expression, saying, "John, looks like we'll have to walk this one." Then his face contorted with drunken laughter, his eyes disappearing into folds of skin. "You go to the men's room and wait a few minutes. By that time I'll be in the car." Before I had a chance to respond, Ray was gone. For a big man, he moved fast. I had a sick feeling as I went to the restroom and read the front page of the *West Branch Times* pinned above the urinal, a story about a man named John Doe who hung himself in the home he shared with his sister on Avenue Street. When I finished, I peered into the bar as if looking for someone, then slithered out the door. Ray pulled away with that serious face, as if he were escaping a great wrong. I felt, crazily, that if we were caught, he could give a credible excuse to the police, the manager, or anyone in authority, a feeling that being with Ray imparted, a feeling helped considerably by enormous amounts of alcohol.

One afternoon, I found the thrift shop Ridge mentioned and bought a black shirt for fifty cents. I put it on and tossed my old flannel into the bin for donations. The shiny cloth gave me a new feeling, a feeling of being almost cool. Passing Donnelly's, a dark bar in the center of downtown, I stopped in. I asked for an Olympia beer. It had just arrived from the northwest and ads for *Oly*, as it was called, constantly floated out of radios, accompanied by the sound of gushing Washington state rivers. Two farm hands at the bar heard my order, and one said to the other, "Oly, Oly, Oly. I say just set a glass of water in front of him and he won't know the difference."

Charlie, the bartender, called out, "One democrat!" and Harold Donnelly poured. That was their name for a regular beer. They called short beers republicans.

As he placed the glass down, Charlie said, "Hippies and heebs, hippies and heebs. That's all we get anymore. Here come two now."

Two professorial-looking men took stools near me. One had shoulder-length hair and tiny, rectangular glasses. A scanty goatee wisped around the other's chin.

"Two small beers."

"What did I tell you?" Charlie whispered to me before calling for two republicans.

I was starting to realize why no one from the workshop came there, when a truck driver my age sat next to me and ordered a vodka tonic. He had come from York, Pennsylvania, the barbell capital of the world, and his payload held tons of weightlifting equipment. He asked me what kind of work I did. I said I was in school. He asked what I was studying. I said poetry. He asked why, a smile on his lips. I said I wanted to learn to write it. He asked a good question—then what? I said that if I were lucky I might be able to publish a book. I had O'Hara's *Lunch Poems* in my pocket and showed it to him. He held it as if it were the Rosetta stone and a poem I had been working on fell out.

"'Blank Street Murmur,'" he said. "Is this a real poem, or did you just make it up?"

I said I made it up and it was a real poem, but maybe not a good one.

"If it's real, why didn't you use a real street name?"

Another good question. I had poeticized the title to a fare-thee-well. "I'm not sure," I said.

"I don't see how you can get this," and he held the white page, "into this," and he bounced the book in the air.

"I know," I said. "It does seem impossible."

A voice from behind me said, "I know you're in the workshop, but we haven't met." I turned to see Belinda Schaeffer holding a couple of books to her chest like a schoolgirl. I put out my hand and introduced myself.

"Mind if I join you?"

The truck driver stared at my good luck.

She said, "I liked the poem about your neighborhood. Especially the title, 'Poor Everyone.'" She sat next to me, indifferently placing her books on the puddles and wet streaks along the bar.

"Thank you," I said. "Ridge thinks I should make it my thesis title."

The two professors began laughing hysterically. The bearded one said, "How about *Suicide Pact*?" I spun toward them.

The other said, "That's great! What do you think of *End It All*?"

"*Puddle-Jumper*!" the bearded one yelled.

Belinda said, "Those morons. Always inventing names for cocktails. And they hardly drink." I recovered from thinking they were mocking my thesis title.

Charlie knew Belinda and, in a courtly manner, he put a glass of white wine before her.

"Thank you, Charlie," she said, and she said it delicately. Everything she did was refined, calm and graceful, but the careless way she placed her books on the bar, almost recklessly, gave me hope that perfection was not something she demanded from others. She might tolerate someone like me, common as well as harmless, like a water stain.

Charlie beamed at Belinda and hovered across the bar for a few seconds. One of the field-workers cursed and complained loudly about the large head on his beer, sending Charlie to the pages of the *Press-Citizen*, and causing the truck driver to leave.

Belinda drank nonstop and talked nonstop, unlike in class where she was completely reserved. Her father was an entrepreneur who bought tainted wholesale food products unfit for humans, and sold them to farmers to feed livestock. She agreed with me that this was not great, but she said he was a good father. She took a twenty-dollar bill from her purse and insisted on buying. She started gesturing with her hands, but the wilder her gestures, the softer her voice, a paradoxical combination. Sometimes she stopped talking, resting her hands in the lap of her dress and staring at the ceiling, so that her eyes rolled up in her head. After four drinks, she told me how unhappy she was and how lonely. She said she usually had affairs with married men, and had just realized this kept her from true emotional investment. She said she had deprived herself of real love in this way, and now she was ready to find an honest guy. I knew right then I was that guy. I knew she picked me because she was ready for someone trustworthy and responsible. I would be faithful and guard her delicate bearing from the crass and shallow world, the workshop world, the world of Donnelly's and beyond. If she stayed with me for the afternoon, her feelings could very well carry over into the night, the next morning, the day after, and the day after that. And through her inspiration, my poetry might grow and possibly rise to match her beauty.

I hardly listened as she went on about her romantic woes, her mistakes and lessons learned. I was preparing for our life together, when she shook me from my reverie by turning and almost shouting, "But why am I telling you all this?" Then she leaned back on her stool as if to get a better, clearer perspective on me, and stared for a few long seconds before saying, "Because you look like a *priest*, that's why!"

At that moment, I felt like a priest, and I might as well have been a priest, as Belinda rose, left our little confessional and walked into the sunshine without another word.

"*Out of Order!*" The professors were still at it, and I was totally drunk, and not from the beer alone. Charlie came over and said, "She's a beauty. And a real lady too." He poured me another, rapping his knuckles on the bar to signal it was on the house.

Donnelly yelled, "Beautiful is as beautiful does!"

"You got that right," Charlie said.

"How about *Dog Bite*?" the bearded professor asked his colleague as they called for two more republicans.

"No, *Fang*! I'll have a *Fang*!"

I staggered out and walked home to Kim and, as I walked, I repeated the first words that came to my mind. They were from Keats:

I have been half in love with easeful death . . .

I was slurring them aloud. I felt I could cry, but crying would be too easy. This was an ache that nothing could erase, except lying down, and not on a bed, but under the earth. I said Keats's line again and again along Clinton Street until I started to mock those words, until I was laughing hysterically, trying to stop when I passed other students, but still smiling, and then I thought of Belinda, remembered our time together, and beamed with the frail hope that a life with her might still be possible.

Kim had made a chocolate cake to celebrate our first month together. I leaned against the doorframe.

"Where were you?" she said. "Are you drunk?"

"I am," I said. "I went to Donnelly's."

"Nobody goes there," Kim said. "It's an old man's bar." She dabbed a knife at the cake, frosting a bald spot.

"I must be getting old then," I said, and went to the bathroom and vomited.

Kim helped me undress and into bed. When I woke in the evening, she was in the chair next to me, reading *Narrative Intellection in the Decameron*. On the stand were the latest copy of *Playboy*, and a cup of chicken soup.

"My mother always got my father the new issue and made him soup when he was sick. Of course, this is from a can," she said.

I finished the soup, guilty about Belinda. I hoisted myself up and said, "How about we get some dinner at the Maid-Rite?"

"Then we can come back and have the cake!" Kim said brightly.

I lifted my black shirt from the chair, and noticed a little white label sewn into the collar. I squinted at the tiny print that spelled out the name of the previous owner, *Father Ignatius*. Kim asked about the shirt and I told her I got it at the thrift shop, but as we went on our way toward the Maid-Rite's loose meat sandwiches, the shirt, the label, and Belinda Schaeffer's remark returned me once more to my anxious and average self.

CHAPTER NINE

KIM JOINS THE FORCE—A CYLINDER WITH A CONE—POWER FAILURE—POEM IN THREE PARTS—A BIG DREAM—APATHY

Kim's only qualification for the position of radio dispatcher for the Iowa City Police Department was a statuesque figure that looked good in uniform. And yet she got the job. We were ecstatic; we needed the money. Our diet was mostly potatoes, and we had become expert at making hash browns, potato pancakes, and baked potatoes with different garnishes. Kim was glad to have something to do outside the university as her classes with Cheyenne Romanelli in the comparative literature department mystified her. Romanelli, a wild-haired Italian who claimed to be part Algonquin, wore shorts through the winter and answered simple questions with cryptic statements like, "The white buffalo, that's what I'm talking about! The white buffalo!" On another occasion, he held a canto of Dante in one palm, and a can of peas in the other, and said, "Weigh them, weigh them!"

In her new job, Kim warned friends of coming drug raids and complaints about loud music. The night before my first workshop with Lawson, she called to say neighbors of The Vine were upset about more than the usual rowdiness. Frosty the bartender was drunk and selling pitchers of whiskey. Kim said she would hold off telling the police. I told Ridge I didn't really want to drink, I wanted to be ready for Lawson's first class the next day, and I was almost relieved to find that when we arrived, the whiskey supply had been depleted. Instead, Frosty poured us half a pitcher of tequila and a pitcher of beer. On this night, the low-life Vine couldn't get any lower. Several patrons were sitting against walls, legs apart and mouths open. Two guys rose from a booth, butted heads and crashed into tables, sending tumblers, whiskey and other patrons flying. An hour later, the glass with my beer chaser exploded in my hand, and I went behind the bar to get another as Frosty had abandoned his post. Soon that too exploded, as did a third. Our table was covered with glass and Ridge cut his hand wiping away the shards. I looked around trying to understand what had been happening. Ridge explained I was slamming the glass full force when I emptied it, and he shattered his in illustration.

The next day I trudged off to my long awaited workshop with Mitchell Lawson feeling as if someone had twisted a garrote around my temples. McPeak sat next to me, already in a feisty mood because Lawson stood for everything he despised—form, decorum, restraint. McPeak's motto was, "Whatever you are criticized for, do it twice as much, it is yourself." He couldn't recall whether it came from Jean Cocteau or Clint Eastwood. Lawson was for full responsibility in life and art. And on that day when he walked into the chatter and laughter of the seminar room, Monique shushed us and we all fell silent, as in a court of law. Lawson took the head of the table and placed a legal pad in front of him. He called the roll, nodding to those he knew, squinting at the rest. Then he lifted a yellow pencil, and held it vertically in front of us, saying nothing. We focused on that simple object for several seconds, all of us fixed on it, expectant, nearly hypnotized. He said, "Ladies and gentlemen, this is a cylinder with a cone attached. A pencil."

The room's taut silence, the almost brittle, glass-like atmosphere was shattered by McPeak, who yelled, "Not so fast! Not so fast!" A few laughed, but most were frozen in the tension. Lawson continued, saying that one end was more important than the other—the end with the eraser. He said it was something he expected us to learn, adding, "Including you, Mr. McPeak."

The first poem was in syllabics and McPeak asked Lawson in a challenging way about the form. Lawson talked passionately about Yvor Winters telling Thom Gunn to write in seven syllable lines. He invited McPeak to stop by and borrow a collection of essays by Winters and a book by Gunn. A few days later, when McPeak went to the office, Lawson had forgotten his offer. He found Gunn but couldn't locate Winters and said, "I guess I have to give you something." He lent him an anthology of imagist poems that McPeak said was lousy, but what annoyed McPeak most was the way Lawson answered his door. "He just said *Come*. Just *Come*. Like I was a dog."

I told him it was probably habit, nothing personal.

"Talk about being stingy with syllables!" McPeak said. "Would it kill him to add *in*?"

Lawson left the Winters book in McPeak's mailbox the next week and to my surprise McPeak loved it, talking constantly about poetic convention and morality. He also never returned it. He began to change toward Lawson, saying, "There's something to be learned from the man." He sat at Lawson's right hand, paying full attention, unlike his other classes where he leafed through *Downbeat*.

One winter afternoon, the power went out in EPB and our classroom was freezing. Lawson seemed particularly cold and his hands shook as he shuffled his papers and expressed his aggravation at the building manager. We sat bundled in coats and hats reading by the sunlit windows. McPeak, who had driven from Illinois, drank coffee from the red lid of a towering plaid thermos. The steam crept toward Lawson's chin and he glanced over at it several times, which McPeak noticed.

"Would you like some hot coffee, Mitch?"

The offer seemed almost maternal—it was the word *hot*, the way a mother would offer specific comfort and also show her importance. Lawson smiled. "That would be very nice," he said, shifting in his icy seat.

McPeak went to the dark lounge and returned with a cup. Lawson leaned away from the table as McPeak unscrewed the cap and poured. A spiral of brown liquid snaked toward the Styrofoam and all eyes watched McPeak as he held the thermos vertically in front of our teacher to coax out the coffee but managing only an inch.

"I thought there was more in it," he said. "I couldn't tell. It's heavy even when it's empty." He whirled it around in a futile spiral.

Lawson seemed angrier at the half ounce of coffee than at the failed power.

"That's the problem with this," McPeak said, continuing to shake the thermos as if motion could refill it.

Lawson looked at McPeak and said what sounded like, "Thank."

Minutes later he canceled class and said he'd be in his office if anyone wanted to meet him, but no one dared. I walked downtown with McPeak who berated himself as he slapped the thermos against his thigh. He blamed Lawson for not having his own coffee. He blamed his wife for possibly having helped herself to his thermos that morning. He blamed the Thermos company for making such a heavy product and then he blamed himself for offering it at all to such a curmudgeon and then he circled back to blaming the curmudgeon.

We went to Epstein's used bookshop and McPeak did what he always did when upset. He bought a book by Henry Miller. He had gone through the novels and was on to the essays. He took *The Cosmological Eye* from the shelf, which I thought would put him in a better mood, but as I walked him to his car, he started in on Lawson again.

"You know, John," he said, "he was mad that he had to depend on someone, the way Ahab was pissed for having to rely on a carpenter for a new leg. I'm the carpenter and he's the pissed-off Ahab who hates human interdependency."

The next week a note appeared on the bulletin board: *Students who have borrowed books from me, please return them—not for myself, but for others like you. ML*

I was standing next to McPeak and we read it together. McPeak whipped out his pen and wrote *NO* under Lawson's initials.

The next day, Lawson replied: *Whoever wrote NO please come and see me. ML* McPeak took out his pen again. *NO.*

A full paragraph by Lawson appeared. It was against the coward who wrote *NO*, the one who refused to accept responsibility and, because of his craven and thieving conduct, his refusal to own up to his own words, would never become a poet. ML.

Barkhausen had gotten into mild trouble because a student named Kristen Ward had been murdered in a dormitory, an unsolved crime that set both the town and university on edge. When Barkhausen gave a major exam to his freshmen, they begged and begged for an extra credit question, and he finally agreed. They sat with pens poised as he said, "Who killed Kristen Ward?" The class gasped and a student complained to the Chair.

Ridge said to me, "It's a shame you never got to teach when a lunatic like Barkhausen runs a class."

"You should have written shorter lines," Pryor advised. "Lawson likes short lines. And syllabics. You should have tried syllabics."

"You guys don't write like that," I said.

"We're different. We came with aid. You had to catch their eye, like Barkhausen did."

McPeak said, "You know Roman Tedington? He sells poems to the *Christian Science Monitor* for a hundred bucks. He told me it's the title that counts, you've got to call them something spiritual like, "Under the Shadow of a Larger Hand.""

Without speaking, we took out pieces of paper and began writing descriptions of nature with titles like "Always Present" and "Thankful Beings," but we did not repeat the success we had with *Rolling Stone*.

Harvey arrived at our Problems in Modern Poetry class in a bad mood because the *New Yorker* had rejected his poems. He had told Ridge he was certain they'd be taken because they mentioned water, and poems in the *New Yorker* always mentioned water. He couldn't find a good line in our work, dispiriting us so much that we began to fight among ourselves. One poem featured a black kid swinging on a park's monkey bars "like an ape." When criticized, the poet denied comparing the child to an ape, saying, "he was just *swinging* like an ape." The workshop's most vociferous feminist wrote a villanelle containing the line, "That's me, the girl with the mouth full of truth." McPeak suggested she edit it to "That's me, the girl with the mouth," and Ridge recommended "The Girl with the Mouth" as the title of her thesis. She stomped out and three women followed. I was next, and very happy with my poem, "The Sadness of Music," in three sections, the longest I'd done. Harvey made fun of part one, tore it from the page, walked around the table and handed it to me. He did the same with the other two, laughing the whole time, as if he and I were sharing a tremendous joke. By the time he had shredded the poem, he was in a good mood. I was not upset, just puzzled. At Fairfield, I had a similar experience. I had taped a cartoon from the *Village Voice* to my dormitory room door—Tomi Ungerer's "Kiss for Peace" which showed the Statue of Liberty bent over and lifting a gown made of the American flag, and a US soldier forcing a scrawny Vietnamese man to kiss the statue's naked butt. When Father Faye, the hall prefect who spouted Latin phrases, saw it, he tore the square into strips and put them into his pocket. I told him he had vandalized my property.

"*Quid nunc?*" he said.

"You had no right to remove that cartoon."

"Yes, I did. This is my hall."

"You didn't have to destroy it."

"I *could* have given it back to you, maybe I should have," he said.

"I'll take it, even if it's torn," I said.

"I do it ex gratia," he said, reaching into his pocket.

"And I believe it cum grano salis."

He looked surprised, as if I could rival him in Latin, which I couldn't. I knew only a few phrases. My stark cartoon had changed from a square of newsprint into a banner, a banner I had overly imbued with meaning, but a banner nevertheless, and a banner I wanted to wave, even in shreds, but I didn't feel the same way about my poem. I was sure it deserved to be destroyed.

When I got home, Kim was still at the library trying to do a writing exercise called "squaring the circle" for Romanelli. Sometimes he made the class read fairy tales starting with the last paragraph and working forward to expose the author's hidden intention. She had left me a note that began, "Dear Snaggle-Tooth." It sent me to the mirror. How could I have never noticed my front teeth did not align? Why hadn't I noticed my poems were deformed as well? I was tired and disgusted because the night before I had worked hard on another poem, and that one, too, in three sections! Harvey was right. I couldn't sustain a narrative. And he had joked that the length of your poems equaled your sexual duration. That poem revealed too much about me. It should have been torn up, along with everything I'd done. Torn up and thrown away.

I lay on the itchy rust-colored couch and had a dream in which Belinda Schaeffer was visiting New York City in the summer and asked me to show her around. She had never been to the Hamptons, so I promised to take her to a special place for dinner. I looked through the *New York Times*, selected a four-star restaurant with great reviews, and made a reservation. To make sure I wouldn't get lost, I drove there early in the week, found the address on Main Street and approached its wooden exterior, thick leaded windows and great brass doorknobs. I shielded my eyes from the sunlight and peered in. The tables and chairs were shrouded in sheets, and a tarpaulin covered the bar. Everything not hidden by cloth was coated with dust. I couldn't understand it, since I had just phoned. It was hot, and I felt dizzy as I stepped into the bright street. I walked to a barbershop where I asked about the restaurant. The barber said, "A beautiful place, but it's been closed for years. For years." When I told him I had made a reservation the week before, he looked at me like I was crazy.

I woke with the bewilderment and fatigue that big dreams bring, feeling not only that I had run a long distance, but had fought through a foreign world. When I replayed the events, I recalled the name of the restaurant. *Moi-Meme.* Untranslated in the dream, I had to use my scarce French to puzzle it out. *Myself! Myself!* How could

I be so unaware of myself? "The unexamined life is not worth living" and "Know thy self" were two staples from my introductory philosophy courses. Once at Fairfield I passed Professor Lou Berrone on the stairs. I was heading to the second floor for philosophy and he was talking to a student about *Ulysses.* He stopped at the landing, and turned to me, saying, "Take John. He likes dark clothes. Blues and browns. He isn't fussy—look at his loose tie. He doesn't polish his shoes and needs a haircut." Students were rushing, edging and squeezing past. The student looked from Lou to me and back to Lou. "Joyce took note of every fiber in a character's appearance—*the ineluctable modality of the visible.*" Minutes later, Father Canavan introduced Aquinas's notion of God as an unmoved mover and, as he spoke, I examined myself more closely than if I stood before a mirror. I wondered about the meaning of my rough shoes, the pilled wool on my sleeves, my miniscule handwriting. Canavan kept proving the existence of God through logic, trumpeting his conclusions with the word *Therefore!* The priest's high-minded syllogisms punctuated my own servile thoughts. I was proving my existence by choosing not to listen. *Therefore!* Proof of God was simple, but I kept thinking, *What made me like this?* Canavan again boomed *Therefore!* A dreamer dreaming an abstract, wan dream of sex because he never had a girlfriend. *Ergo!* the priest resounded. Awakened on a flight of stairs between Joyce and Aquinas, but to what? To the fact that I existed and I did not exist, like the penis on the underside of the mechanical canary.

To make money for an occasional night out, I took a job in the journalism department, working Saturdays, keeping track of supplies in the storage room, and doing odd jobs. On my first day I made pads, sitting in front of four stacks of different colored paper and placing them in a sequence of white, pink, blue and yellow. When the pile reached three feet high, I moved it to a huge vice, locked it down and dipped a brush into a bucket of rubber cement, swabbing the side of the paper into an adhesive binding. I came home that first day smelling of glue. Kim said we should splurge so we went to the Best Steakhouse for cube steaks and Texas toast. The way Kim looked at the several policemen there with their families made me realize she longed for a solvent and stable domestic life.

The next week I found a shoebox filled with tissue on the floor next to the bed. Also a plastic bag with a receipt from a department store's lingerie department. It meant only one thing: Kim had entered another amateur contest at The Dugout. I became angry at her, at the men in The Dugout and at myself. Around midnight, a car dropped her off. We screamed at each other. She thought she would make some money but she didn't win. I said I would get a third job. I was ashamed of myself for asking who from the workshop had seen her. We ended up as we usually did, making love. She got out of bed and threw the lingerie and tiny shoes into the garbage can. We never mentioned it again but the evening stayed between us. I confided the incident to Ridge, saying it didn't bother me. I said I was trying to stay less emotionally invested in the relationship. I used the phrase, "selectively apathetic." Ridge thought for a moment and then asked, "Don't you have a poem called 'Apathy'?"

"Two," I said.

CHAPTER TEN

MARK STRAND—ITCHES AND THIRSTS—
TRY TURNING THE PAGE—BECOMING AN RA—
A DOG NAMED UNCLE—NOBODY BEATS
ARTHUR'S MEAT—GALAHAD—
A POETRY READING AND A SICK CAT

When handsome, softly dressed Mark Strand joined the faculty in spring, every thread of his wardrobe was examined, his every syllable recounted. Pryor saw Strand without a tie at nine in the morning but wearing one at noon, and inquired about it. Strand told him his neck was cold. That Lawson and Strand were good friends we had learned from Lawson's remark in Hamburg Inn No. 3, but no one could imagine it because no one could imagine Lawson having a friend. Lawson was often heard saying in a celebratory way that he was on his way to meet Mark, that Mark was coming to his house, that he and Mark were playing Win, Place & Show, or that he was driving Mark to the Amana colonies. Their relationship made Strand all the more alluring, as if only he could awaken the affection of the teacher McPeak called "our bloodless stalk." I saw Lawson showing Strand his office, and telling him that when he returned from Syracuse, the drawers held some-one else's files. He said, heatedly, "I'll tell you all about it!" That there was more to tell about the occupied drawers was the astounding part.

Strand visited Lawson's workshop and sat across from him and they disagreed at every turn. When Lawson said a poem needed more meat on its bones, Strand said he yearned for even less. Strand complimented a poem that had a nonsense refrain and Lawson thought it weakened the whole. This went on for two hours. I had come to Iowa to learn to write poems, poems of emotional endurance. Now I knew there was no single way, no invisible truth. I felt further liberated by Strand's remark that "no one really knows what poetry is."

The last part of the workshop was devoted to the poems of Rafael Alberti, whose book, *The Owl's Insomnia*, Strand had just translated. Strand read a few surreal poems so different from the usual examples we were given. He ended with:

> It was the day when the last cry of a man
>   bloodied the wind
> when all the angels lost their lives
> except for one, and he was left wounded,
>   unable to fly.

Charlotte said, "Oh Mark! That poem is so beautiful it makes me cry."

"You mean it passes the tearstain test," Lawson said, and all of us turned to him, including Strand. He explained that a poem Byron wrote to his spurned wife was sup-posed to have been stained with tears. "If so," he asked, "would that make it a better poem?"

"Haven't you ever cried over a poem?" someone asked Lawson.

"I think I've been close to tears only twice in my life," Lawson said.

I couldn't resist asking, "What about Pound saying 'only emotion endures?'"

"Technique may last as long as emotion," Lawson answered. "And may be the best way to obtain it."

"Mitch's emotional about craft," Strand joked, and he passed Alberti's book around. It was dedicated to Lawson, with an acknowledgment of Lawson's dry character, and the replenishment of it through the two men's bond:

> If in your country all hope is lost in the long
>   heat of summer,
> The snows in my country will help you to get
>   it back.

The days of playing the horse race board game lasted only six weeks, as Strand received an invitation from another university offering him something we never had heard of—a global travel allowance—and he left midterm.

Ridge's first book, *Itches and Thirsts,* was chosen by Stanley Kunitz for the Yale Series of Younger Poets, so when Strand left, Ridge taught one of Strand's courses. Lawson brought Ridge's book to class and told us that almost all the poems had been workshopped. He flipped through to his favorite, "What Remains," adding that it would have made a better title for the collection. He read it dramatically, appreciatively and, in the Iowa tradition, he read the last line with full-blown, jowl-shaking emotion:

A wild rose on a coffin.

A quiet moment followed, a quiet in which we were all moved—not by the poem, but by our dreams of winning the prize ourselves, having our books published, ascending to faculty rank, and hearing our lines read in an homage to our pedigree and skill. Lawson's reading enveloped us in that fog but a voice snapped us out of it.

"Try turning the page, Mitch," McPeak said.

The poem had begun on the right hand side, and we realized that Lawson had not been familiar with the poem or he would have known it continued. He blushed brightly and read the final stanza. Pryor said that the poem ended better where Lawson stopped.

I had made a fool of myself with Strand. My faux pas came via loudmouth Trotta. He told me that Strand had taken his name from his boyhood on Prince Edward Island, where the fishermen noted the high and low tides by yelling, "Mark Strand!"

"It's a tradition," he said. "Like Mark Twain."

When I was on the elevator with Strand, I asked him what his name was before he called himself Mark Strand. He looked puzzled and said it was his real name. He did not hold that silliness against me. He heard me in the hallway telling Ridge that when I requested Milosz' anthology, *Postwar Polish Poetry,* at Iowa Book & Supply, the clerk thought it was a Polish joke. Strand quickly went to his office and gave me his extra copy.

A week later, Pam Rhodes, the workshop secretary, stopped me in the hall. She said that Lawson's RA had left school due to a family emergency and I could take his place. I told Ridge who said he had heard, but wanted me to get the word officially. We met at The Deadwood to celebrate, and when we walked in, Pryor raised his glass, also in the know. I was thrilled but daunted, and daunted even more because the week before there had been a reading by another workshop graduate who recited a long poem composed entirely in heroic couplets. At the reception afterward, Lawson told the poet that one line was short a syllable. The poet said that was impossible and he and Lawson went off to a corner to consult the text. Lawson proved right, and the reputation of his fine ear grew. Ridge saw it as cantankerous and aggressive, saying Lawson couldn't really have heard the poem, to be so absorbed in syllable counting. On the other hand, I hoped my appointment might get the attention of Belinda Schaeffer who loomed over me, a fantasy like poetry itself. Glimpsing her was like writing a few decent lines that trail away as the muse deserts the page.

I went to see Lawson the next day after visiting the library's periodical section. *Kayak* had sent me a stinging rejection, a drawing of a man strapped to a surgical table and being trepanned. I wanted to check out the new issue and see why I needed my brain drained. When I left, I had to cover my head with a *Daily Iowan* to avoid the rain and the droppings of hundreds of starlings that had nested in the trees at the entrance. My shoulders were splattered when I got to EPB's hall of faculty offices.

"Come."

Lawson sat at his desk in his brown suede jacket and blue knit tie over a tattersall shirt. His horn-rimmed glasses lay on a pile of pages scattered across a calendar. He described the job as making sure the books stayed in alphabetical order, watering the plants, and straightening out the desk at the end of the week. There might be typing. I was disappointed that no research was involved, but then he said Pam was having another key made. I could use his office when it was empty, which meant I could examine his books. We shook hands and he returned to his papers. I felt as if I had troubled him but his dour demeanor did not dampen my delight. Pam gave me a key, and showed me the mailbox, my name above a square wooden grid where Lawson would place any secretarial assignments.

I was on my way back to the library and got on the elevator when Lawson joined me, carrying a beat-up brief-case and an umbrella. He told me he'd be in the office only on Wednesday mornings and for a few minutes before his classes. "So you can spend all the time there you'd like," he said as we got off. He seemed to have softened outside of the fourth floor, and even looked kindly.

"I'm about to walk my neighbor's dog," he said.

I asked the breed.

"All kinds and none," he said, "but mostly pug and bloodhound."

The morning rain had halted, and we walked side by side in sunlight. He was smiling as I had never seen him smile, thinking about the dog. As he turned toward his car, I jumped to avoid something ankle high that swept across my path, almost tripping but straightening my tangled feet at the last minute. Lawson stopped and stared, concerned, and then he put on his sunglasses and headed to the parking lot. There had been nothing for me to leap over; it was only the shadow, the sharp silhouette of Lawson's umbrella, which, in my uneasiness, I had tried to hurdle.

I kept my job as lunchtime supervisor. The kids had gotten to like me. The turning point was my finding them a place to go with their girlfriends. I suggested Black's Gaslight Village and Mr. Black happily supplied his Tarzan room, the bed veiled with mosquito netting below green ropes painted like vines.

The next week I cut through a clump of MFA students reading the bulletin board to get to my mailbox, aware that some were envious of my new post. Many RAs dramatically shouldered past the others on their way to the sanctum sanctorum, usually making their return with bowed heads, seriously reading their supervisors' mail, library requests and other orders. My position was easy to understate, as I carried a white watering can in the shape of a swan. In Lawson's office I stood before the bookcases, almost all poetry. I circled the desk. On the opposite wall was a sign: *Beware the fury of a patient man—John Dryden.* A glass from "The Egg and I" restaurant in Miami held a handful of sharp pencils and a metal ruler. I sat at the manual typewriter next to a ream of that renowned yellow paper. Did I dare open the drawers? No. In a corner of the green blotter was a photograph of a very ugly dog, a dark pushed-in mug, a light tan body with brown spots. The heavy eyelids drooped as if drugged, and uneven bottom teeth jutted from an underslung jaw. The face showed agony tinged with hope, the hope to be rescued from its face. It was the dog Lawson walked. On a shelf next to the desk was a folded length of fabric, with a note pinned to it, addressed *Cher Monsieur Lawson.* The writer told him to enjoy his "smock-frock." It was from Monique—a long shirt, with pockets in front holding pens and pencils. I put it next to a few small cactus plants and a piece of pink coral in a tray of sand. The plants, the coral and the sand made me feel as if I were at the bottom of a fish tank. Even more surprising were the dozen snow globes. I shook one containing a tiny orchestra, but there was no water in it, no water in any of them, and the white flakes sifted and languished along the bottom. On the windowsill, a row of snake plants abutted a pile of miniature dictionaries. I was sifting through a shoebox of tapes of French singers when someone knocked. It was Harvey Clay who immediately sat down. I remained standing. I couldn't bring myself to sit behind the desk. "Working for Mitch?" he asked.

I said I had just started. Ridge passed by and joined us.

"I was in Kansas City for a literary festival," Harvey said. "Arthur Bryant's barbecue sponsors it. His slogan is '*Nobody beats Arthur's meat!*'" He giggled and rubbed the coral against his cheek. "I have the poster in my office. You should see us, all overweight." He curved his hand over his protruding stomach. "Simic, blob! Hugo, blob!" He made the gesture again. "Me, blob! And then in the corner, a little handsome angelic face—Merwin!" He got up "Oh, I'm teaching in a minute!" he said and ran out.

"Did you get that?" Ridge asked.

"Get what?" I said.

"His point. He might not be the most beautiful poet in heaven, but he's in heaven nevertheless."

"That's what he said?"

"Of course," he said. "And we're in limbo." He pointed his finger at himself and then at me.

Pam Rhodes came to the door, freshly made up.

"Are you ready?" she asked Ridge. And they left together.

Harvey and Lawson said the Yale prize would change Ridge's life. And it did. Everyone taunted him. Students touted the fact that Paul Engle had beaten out Theodore Roethke for the award. They cited long forgotten winners and searched for those with the most ludicrous names. When Ridge entered a room, loudmouth Trotta welcomed him with the words, "Thomas Caldecot Chubb!" quoting Chubb's line, "Here's Merlin. A lonely man, his head among the stars." He tacked a list of Yale authors and titles to the bulletin board:

Christiane Jacox Kyle, author of *Bears Dancing in the Northern Air.*

Amos Niven Wilder who wrote, "Those sultry nights we used to pass outdoors."

Darl Macleod Boyle, and her prizewinning *Where Lilith Dances.*

The next day as I was shelving Lawson's books, Ridge brought me a cup of coffee. I showed him the dog. "That is one ugly fuck," he said.

Lawson appeared outside the door, hands on hips, like a suspicious neighbor. He seemed uncertain about entering, so I asked him if he wanted to use his office, and I tried to slide the photo into the blotter without his noticing, but he ran in and grabbed it.

"Isn't he beautiful?" he said, laughing. "That's Uncle."

"There's something about him," Ridge said.

Lawson explained that his neighbor adopted it from the pound for his daughter. "It was abandoned, left behind when a family moved. Can you imagine the irresponsibility of some people," he said.

"Where'd they get the name?" I asked.

"Their little daughter saw it and called it ugly, but they thought she said uncle." He stared at the photo, in his own Uncle universe. "I'm not sure the little girl likes the dog."

"You should bring him in," I said.

"Maybe I will," he said, looking like he wouldn't. "He seems to get cold easily. Maybe when it gets warmer." He put his fingertips to his chin and began to scan the shelves until he found a volume of Guillevic, and turned to me, very pleased. "I've been thinking about one of his elegies," he said, opening the book. He read, "He who harbors fear/Of becoming mist."

"Good line," Ridge said.

"Yes, but the earlier part of the poem mentions the sea, so I don't think 'harbors' is a good verb. Do you?" He was looking at me.

"It's like a pun," I said.

"It's very close to a pun," he said, and replaced the book and left.

"Only Lawson can break into a smile over an elegy," Ridge said.

"He was still high from thinking about the dog. I've never seen him like that."

As Lawson got to know me better, he increased my responsibilities, asking me to type his worksheets on stencils. One assignment called for students to write their obituaries. I ran off copies on the Thermo-Fax machine. I spent my mornings and nights in his office, which I began to call simply, 405. I washed the cups, which he acknowledged with a simple "Thank you ML" on a yellow sheet he left in the typewriter. McPeak finally returned Yvor Winters's *In Defense of Reason* and I read it in a week, sitting at his desk, straining at his marginalia. The book was very worn, thumbed through, read and reread. One day, Lawson left a poem by William Stafford on his desk, typed on the yellow paper.

ASK ME

Some time when the river is ice ask me
mistakes I have made. Ask me whether
what I have done is my life. Others
have come in their slow way into
my thought, and some have tried to help
or to hurt: ask me what difference
their strongest love or hate has made.

I will listen to what you say.
You and I can turn and look
at the silent river and wait. We know
the current is there, hidden: and there
are comings and goings from miles away
that hold the stillness exactly before us.
What the river says, that is what I say.

It was not in my box, not to be typed for class. I wrote a note saying that the most despairing lines I had ever read were, "ask me what difference/their strongest love or hate has made." A few days later, another poem appeared, this time by John Clare.

I AM

I am—yet what I am, none cares or knows;
My friends forsake me like a memory lost:
I am the self-consumer of my woes;
They rise and vanish in oblivion's host,
Like shadows in love's frenzied stifled throes:
And yet I am, and live—like vapours toss't

Into the nothingness of scorn and noise—
Into the living sea of waking dreams,
Where there is neither sense of life or joys,
But the vast shipwreck of my life's esteems;
Even the dearest, that I love the best
Are strange—nay, rather, stranger than the rest.

I long for scenes where man hath never trod
A place where woman never smiled or wept
There to abide with my Creator, God,
And sleep as I in childhood sweetly slept,
Untroubling, and untroubled where I lie,
The grass below—above the vaulted sky.

Beside the underlined words, he wrote, "These, to me, are the saddest lines. ML"

I typed my own poem on his machine, and accidentally left it behind. The next morning, I ran to EPB, hoping to snatch it before Lawson arrived, but in the hall I saw 405's open door.

"Looking for this?" he said, handing me the page.

"I didn't mean to leave it," I said.

"I thought that was your intention." He didn't say any more, so I reached over and took the poem. "Some of your work is witty, some is melodramatic," he said. "It's never really funny or heartbreaking. Your real poems are the ones you haven't yet written."

I wondered when I would begin.

"You know I haven't done a lot," he said. "A reputation as a perfectionist. I wish it were otherwise. I wish that instead of revising and revising a poem, searching for the right word, I had left it alone, or moved on to another. The changes I made which took weeks, well, I think now they made scarce difference."

He looked again at my poem.

"Take more chances, see what happens when you forget all this," he said, referring to the workshop.

I was touched by his candor, especially about his own life, almost a repudiation of his stature as a "craftsman."

I thanked him and moved to the door.

"John," he called, the first time he used my name. "The middle way is the only way that doesn't lead to Rome."

Ridge visited the Fine Arts Work Center in Provincetown at the invitation of Stanley Kunitz, one of its founders. He returned enthused about the staff, which included Alan Dugan, and its mission—giving emerging artists and writers seven-month fellowships. He described the beauty of the town on the water and the charm of the Center, where fellows worked in converted coal bins, lobster-trap sheds and rough-hewn studios. Artists and writers like Mailer, Motherwell and Lowell visited out of goodwill. Ridge was staying in Iowa to finish his doctorate, and urged me to apply. Kunitz edited a supplement for the *American Poetry Review* and included two poems of mine, which Ridge had shown him, so Ridge thought I'd have a good chance. With this report, I saw a path out of the workshop's claustrophobic hierarchy and clawing competition. I imagined the shore, the threshold between land and sea offering a home to struggling unknowns. I rhapsodized about it to Ridge who said, "Don't forget, Provincetown's known as *The Last Resort.*"

Pryor started referring to Barkhausen as Galahad, and the name garnered the interest of many women who flirted with him in the halls. He brought several to 405 where they lolled around the books, shook the dry snow globes and laughed at Uncle's photo. Lawson came in one day and seemed pleased by the little gathering.

"When are we going to meet the pooch?" Barkhausen asked.

"He's in the car," Lawson said.

The girls begged to see him and Lawson said it would take him a while because he had to adjust the new horse blanket coat. "I paid for it," he said. He gave a precise explanation of the buckles and straps.

Half an hour later, Lawson came down the hall pulled by a stubby tan and spotted dog wearing a crimson jacket. A bloodhound and a truck. Loose skin hung from his neck and shoulders so that he seemed more like an old man in a dog suit than a dog. Lawson stopped at the office door while the girls gushed and Uncle looked up with huge red eyes, one long canine rising from his pushed-in muzzle. I bent over the dog, who rested his head on my knee and immediately closed his eyes, as if in relief.

"He's still cold," Lawson said.

"So cute," one of the girls said, squatting next to me. Uncle stayed on my knee, drooling.

"I think he'll grow into that baggy skin," Lawson said, and asked me to put water into a bowl he had brought. We watched in disbelief as Uncle drank for a minute straight.

"He seems to have a hard time getting water through that muzzle," Lawson said.

I rubbed the dog's head and jowls, and Barkhausen joined me, asking, "Why are his eyes so red?"

"I'm not sure," Lawson said.

"I'd have that checked out," Barkhausen said, which annoyed Lawson who said it wasn't anything, and he started to leave on that sour note.

"Good-bye, Ugly," Barkhausen said.

Lawson turned. "It's *Uncle*, Artie, *Uncle*."

"I like *Ugly*," Barkhausen said.

"When you get your own dog, Artie, you can call it *Ugly*," Lawson said.

Lawson ran into Neil Clarke, his friend and teacher of romantic literature. They played a little game. When they met, they spoke *Stevens*. The rule was that their first words had to quote Wallace Stevens and be appropriate in greeting and reply. This involved two things Mitch loved—poetry and competition.

Clarke took a look at Uncle and said, "There are not leaves enough to cover the face it wears . . ."

"The creator too is blind," Lawson replied as Clarke looked warily at the protruding teeth of the gentle pup. I went back into the office.

"That's a funny looking dog," a girl said. "So opposite of Mitch."

"Who's always so neat and refined," the other added.

Uncle left behind a scent like a rainy day in autumn—decay, wet leaves and mud.

Barkhausen went with Pryor and Wendy to lunch. The three of them were often in a booth at The Deadwood and they arrived at readings and parties together. Barkhausen, the odd duck, the isolato of Black's Gaslight Village, was suddenly social. I asked Ridge about Barkhausen's sudden friendship with Pryor and he said, "If I wanted to fuck Pryor's wife, I'd hang around with him too."

Harvey and Lawson gave a reading, introduced by Dan Cook who wore his usual ascot and a tweed coat with patches on the elbows and left breast. Our teachers sat behind him in jackets and ties, which was odd for Harvey who always wore blue work shirts. He had let his goatee grow, and it hung from his chin like the tongue of a shoe. He could have been a high school math teacher who held eccentric theories about alien abduction. Lawson wore a tan corduroy suit with a white oxford and red knit tie, like his neighbor who sold insurance. A chalkboard off to the side emphasized the academy. Lovers of poetry, serious readers, supporters of libraries and arts centers across the state came to see their famous citizen-poets. They circled the stage like people feeding ducks. We were those who watched them feed the ducks. Harvey and Lawson were the ducks.

Harvey went first, and Dan read a list of awards, quoted reviews, and ended with Lawson's blurb, "In his hands, the pedestrian stalks the infinite." Harvey stood at the podium, and gave a little talk about the difference between raw and cooked poetry. He said he was proud to be reading with his former teacher, whose skill was unequaled, and who "edits with a scalpel." He read some funny poems, darting through the pages. He took off his jacket and draped it on his chair. He began one poem with the opening line, "Renoir painted with his dick," then stopped, looked disgusted, tore the page from the book, rolled it into a ball and threw it into the amused audience. He said the room was too warm, and loosened the knot of his tie. At the end of the next poem, he lifted it over his head, placing it on the microphone where it faced us. He thumbed through the book front to back, then back to front, reading poems at random, yet they seemed to have a thread. Sweating, he sipped from the water glass and then unbuttoned his shirt, revealing a red undershirt printed with the words *Kellogg's of Battle Creek*. The poems became more serious, about his dead parents. His long hair fell from behind his ears and he popped on a headband from his back pocket. He ended with a sequence about the Vietnam war, perspiration showing as he now read as seriously as he had recited comically, concluding, flushed and depleted, with a forceful moral outrage. The audience applauded loudly. We had been taken from comedy to tragedy, from formality to humanity. Harvey's spontaneity at the podium somehow arrived at a perfectly shaped performance. When he left the podium, he was an entirely different person from the one who had been introduced, changing from schoolmaster to beatnik stalking the infinite. He left the tie hanging from the microphone.

Dan walked across the stage, clapping, then bowing to Harvey. He leaned toward us, beckoning further applause with his fingertips. When silence returned, he reached for something inside his sport coat. He tried another pocket, his concern becoming panic. He felt the shelf under the podium, as if in the dark, which he was, because he had lost his introduction to Lawson. He touched his chest again, and again scanned the shelf, like an obsessive, compulsive mime. Loudmouth Trotta called for him to begin, which was followed by catcalls and laughter. Dan righted himself, looked directly at us, and said, "This man needs no introduction," which produced an even greater roar of taunts and boos. He abandoned the microphone, headed toward the chalkboard, wrote *Mitchell Lawson!* and left the stage.

Lawson moved like a scarecrow dragged by a farmer to its post in the field. It was tough enough to follow Harvey's transformation and final dramatic subject, but the botched preface challenged Lawson to both obliterate the introduction and rise to it. If before he seemed a man awaiting the firing squad, now he looked as if a few bullets had grazed him at the knees. He winced his way toward the lectern and calmly removed the tie, as if it had caused the commotion. He walked over to Harvey and handed it to him, the way a teacher returns a forbidden object to a student at the end of the day.

When Lawson again faced the audience, he said, "Tonight I'm reading all the poems in my books no one's ever liked." With those words, he had us on his side. He read flatly, his index finger following the list he had compiled for the evening, and his wistful tone permeated the room. Many poems described his own character: the invisible man, empty mirror, skeletal heart. By giving us his negative persona, a three-dimensional human being appeared. He sometimes shifted his shoulder, as if to lean away from a blow or an arrow he had dared someone to aim at him. He was both archer and target, and the only sounds in the hall were his lines across the air. When he finished, the quiet man was met with noisy approval.

Workshop students who never frequented The Deadwood filled booths. Ridge, McPeak, Pryor and I discussed
the reading over a pitcher. We fell into different camps.
Ridge and I loved Lawson's flat delivery. Pryor, who had
gained weight and grown a goatee, praised Harvey's show-
manship, but criticized Lawson for being as stiff as a man-
nequin. McPeak said they couldn't hold a candle to the
best actualists. He quoted a poem by Robert Slater called
"Crazy Lady."

> Look at that
> Crazy lady shopping
>
> In a night shirt.
> *Hey* crazy lady.

A cheer went up near the bar, and Pryor craned around
and announced Harvey's arrival. He went from table to
table, shaking hands, nodding and smiling. He lifted a
chair from a stack, sat at our booth and asked Brandy for
a glass.

"Mitch's a riot, isn't he?" Harvey said, laughing. "That
calm demeanor, but he goes right for the jugular." He lifted
his beard and grabbed his throat.

"But you were spontaneous," Pryor said, shaking his
head in admiration.

"I had a list," Harvey said.

"It looked like you were picking poems at random," I
said.

"That's what it's supposed to look like," Harvey said.
He turned to Ridge. "Was Charlotte there?"

"I think so," Ridge said.

"She liked that poem I threw away," Harvey said. "I did
that to tease her."

"You planned that?" Pryor asked, leaning forward.

Harvey winked.

I was waiting for McPeak to pounce, but his eyes were drifting to a table of workshop girls here for their first time. Even Pryor seemed stunned, maybe by the magician revealing his tricks, maybe from the effort of learning them for himself. Charlotte walked past with Monique, and Harvey reached out and tugged Charlotte's sleeve.

"How'd you like it?" Harvey asked.

"I wish I could have been there," she said. "My cat's sick."

Monique said, "Sheba puked and shit all over the rugs. It's a mess." They took a table in the back.

"I don't believe it," Harvey said to us.

"Come on, Harvey," Pryor said. "She dotes on that cat."

Harvey pushed his beer away as if he didn't deserve it.

"Hey," Pryor said, "Lots a laughs you got tonight."

"Laughs? Thanks, David."

Pryor lowered his head. "I thought it was a good response. They appreciated the humor."

"Please," Harvey said, and got up. He put his chair on the stack against the wall and said good night. Pryor said he would walk him home since they lived near each other.

"Pryor is becoming a little Harvey, don't you think?" McPeak said.

"And you're a little Lawson," Ridge said to me. "In fact, you're looking like him!"

Ridge had a few books with him and one was by Merwin, which I'd lent him.

"Are you finished with that?" I asked.

He handed it to me, saying he liked the way Merwin abandoned punctuation halfway through. I noticed a girl's name and number written on the inside cover. I showed it to him.

"Sorry!" he said.

In the men's room, I saw what Ridge meant. Thinning hair, the beginning of jowls, I was starting to look like the great craftsman, but without the craft.

CHAPTER ELEVEN

CORNEAL EROSION—SAMSARA—HELLO? HELLO?
IT'S ME! IT'S ME!—GROOMING UNCLE—
THE GREAT LOVE OF THE THIN MAN

I met Lawson walking Uncle on South Governor. Students joked about never seeing him on the street, in a store or outside at all, and McPeak referred to him as an air fern. But now he came toward me, a stick figure pulled by a hunk of muscle. I petted Uncle whose red eyes matched his coat and seemed to reach from the depths of hell. Lawson said he thought the dog should be gaining more weight and he worried about his diet. The next day he came to 405 and said the neighbor told him that Uncle wasn't eating because the vitamins they mixed into his dinner tainted the taste. He asked me to type almost twenty pages of material, and I finished it right before his class, when he thanked me distractedly. As I straightened out the desk, I found a revision of his rhymed poem about visiting a dying friend. He had changed a line from:

Blood drained from his face

to:

His father said he lost his place

The rewrite brought another person into the poem. The next time I saw him, I mentioned it and he seemed pleased, saying he had published the original in a quarterly, but was never happy with it.

One day he complained of an error I had made typing a student poem.

"John," he said, calling me by my name, which he did rarely. "Please proof the stencils!"

"I did," I said. "I must have missed something."

He pointed out the line, "I keep my bong in the closet."

"*Bongo!*" he said. "It should be *bongo!*"

I was sitting at his desk as he lurched over my shoulder. I defined *bong*. He put his hands on his hips, but instead of getting into a snit, he laughed, as much with relief that his worksheet was flawless as with the new word.

I was embarrassed when Dan Cook stuck his head into 405 because I was looking in the mirror. My drinker's/reader's eye had worsened into corneal erosion, a condition that tore the thin membrane when I woke up, feeling like someone was scratching my pupil with a pencil point. The doctor at the infirmary had given me a tube of erythromycin, which I hid in my pocket.

"Hello? Hello?" he said. "It's me! It's me!" He grinned from the doorway. "Don't you recognize an actualist poem?" He walked to the pile of new books sent by publishers, discarding them like playing cards. "There's not one here I'd want to read," he said. "I understand you're the lucky man who squires Kim Costigan around."

He inspected the shelves and stopped at the music books.

"Mitch wanted to be a composer, did you know that? He studied with Nadia Boulanger in Paris."

"He writes a lot about musicians," I said.

"What are they saying about me?"

"Who?"

"People have been talking about me, haven't they? About me and Nora."

I said that students talk about faculty all the time.

"I know, but they're critical."

"I don't think so," I said.

"Yes," he said, in a resigned, unhappy way. "They're talking about us." He stood and tried to shake off his mood, saying at the door, "That reminds me of the fortune I got at Fong's last week. It said, 'Good luck in love, and a better position!'"

I mentioned this conversation to Ridge and McPeak in The Deadwood. Like me, neither knew what he meant, but Ridge said Dan had been complaining about *Esquire* rejecting his new stories.

"Why would he talk about something like that?" McPeak said.

"By mentioning *Esquire*, he shows he's a member of a club we might never be admitted to. Even if he was rejected this time, he's still in the club."

"You read too much into things," I said. "Like you did with Harvey and heaven."

"Buddhists call it samsara. He only thinks of getting, and so he's always disappointed. He complains magazines reject his stories. Then they take some. He collects them in a book and complains he doesn't get reviewed. Then he gets reviewed. He says, okay, I get reviewed, but the *Times* doesn't review me. Then the *Times* reviews him. And he says, oh yeah, but it was a bad review."

And so we began talking about Cook talking about people talking about him critically, and then we talked about him critically.

Lawson asked me to help him trim Uncle's claws. He arrived winded from carrying the dog because Uncle zigzagged unexpectedly on the leash and had hurt Lawson's shoulder.

"They're neglecting him," he said, putting Uncle on the desk. "Look at his nails, turning in and curling." I wrapped my arms around him as Lawson plucked a pair of canine scissors from his sport coat with shaking hands. Uncle leapt sideways, as if trying to dismount a rider, veering left and right. Lawson lifted a paw, but his hands continued to shake and then Uncle started to shake, as if an electric current passed between them.

"I used to clip my dog's claws," I said.

We changed positions and I took the hind leg and, as I had been taught, didn't let Uncle see what I was doing. I didn't hurt him, but with each snip, he made a sharp cry, otherworldly, neither animal nor human, but like a fingernail flicking the rim of a glass. I felt I didn't hold a paw, but the palm of a fairy creature and, when I finished, standing in the office of a man who had been such a stranger to me, a man whose poetry I revered, a poet known for his great attention to art, the room shrunk and expanded, as if the walls inhaled and exhaled. Lawson thanked me and lowered Uncle to the floor. He had brought some eye medicine, but put it on a shelf for another day. Uncle looked at both of us and then he turned, facing the door and sitting like a rock, like something timeless and enduring, a boulder in the sea, immobile to everything crashing around it, even over it. Yet he seemed almost thoughtful.

Neil Clarke approached, saying, "At twelve, the disintegration of afternoon began."

"Shrinking from the weight of primary noon," Lawson replied, and continued down the corridor, shrinking from more than the weight of that metaphor, a thin man walking a bocce ball on a leash. He called out to no one, "He'll be fine!" My hands smelled like Uncle, who smelled like burning rubber.

CHAPTER TWELVE

HOT IRIS—THE BLACK ANGEL—
INCREASED DUTIES—THE LEOPARD SPEAKS—
CAFÉ WHA?—COOK DISGUSTS LAWSON—THE
TWIST TIE, THE FLAT BOTTOM BAG AND THE
JOLLY RANCHER—CITY LIMITS

ﾠ

I ris Mendes, a Brazilian student with red hair and pale skin, was having an affair with Dan Cook that went beyond the usual fling. Sexy and daring, playful and saucy, she punched the shoulder of anyone who made a witty remark, throwing her head back in laughter as if catching a rain shower in her mouth. Her straight features were perfect, as were her white teeth, which were often exposed from her habit of dropping her jaw when listening to a conversation, and seeming to pant. She held a part-time secretarial job in the workshop and her desk was always surrounded by men. Ridge spent one night with her and said she was literally hot to the touch. She told him her normal body temperature was 100.6—two degrees above normal. When she smiled, her beautiful face displaced that stuporous, overheated look, although her lipstick looked like it could melt.

Cook usually visited his student lovers in their apartments, dates made in the day and followed up in the dark. They had an understanding; they passed each other in the halls, at parties and in bars with nothing but a nod. He reinforced this conduct in public by constantly mentioning Nora and their two-year-old daughter, so he seemed a perfect family man. With Iris, he was different. He was smitten, besotted, mad. He couldn't keep himself from quoting her translations of Drummond de Andrade in class when they seemed pertinent, and because Iris so dominated his thoughts, everything she did seemed pertinent. Once they met in the back of The Deadwood. The booth in front of them was empty and Dan asked Ridge and me to move there, so other students wouldn't be privy to their words. We heard nothing but whispers, his voice occasionally followed by her long and lovely laugh. He gave Brandy money to keep the jukebox going. In "Hearts," there's a moment when the song seems over and, in a lull before the singer says, "Is everything all right?" we heard Iris ask in her bewitching accent, "Okay, Dan, if you just had three days to live, what would you want to tell me about how you feel about me?"

Ridge said, "Oh boy . . ."

Iris lived with her cousin from Rio, so her dates with Cook took place at the Burlington House, an old hotel next to the cemetery. He had written a story about making love to her near the Black Angel, a florid tombstone, and he showed it to Ridge, who said fucking in a graveyard would only bring bad luck.

Lawson increased my small responsibilities, asking me to write notes refusing invitations to campus events, and to open his mail, throwing out the junk. A square envelope arrived, pale blue, addressed in schoolgirl script, a woman's name in the return address. I placed it unopened with his other letters. It was still there a few days later, the flap torn. The next week, his phone rang and a woman asked for him, saying she had mailed a poem. I mentioned it to him, and he acknowledged it, lifting the envelope as if it weighed a pound. She phoned the following week and I said I would make sure he returned her call, but again he forgot. She called once more, when we were both there, and he answered. He still hadn't read the poem and he fumbled with the envelope, the phone under his chin. Before he had it out, he was saying it was very good.

"Yes," he said. "Quite good." He read the handwritten lines as he spoke. She must have asked for advice because he said, "Well, when you have feelings like this, you might soften the language." He continued, "Violent feelings don't have to be expressed with violent imagery," and he hung up and shook his head.

"I wish I'd read it earlier," he said. "What could I do? At this point I had to say it was good. It's my fault for being rude." He handed it to me and I glanced at the careful script:

> I bite your neck, digging my teeth in
> for a deeper taste.
> I tear the skin from your back with my nails
> and we swim in the blood that flows over both of us
> As you try to escape this devouring mouth . . .

"Good god," I said.

"Wait till I show Harvey," he said.

I was returning the poem when I noticed the title. I pointed to it and he blushed saying, "What did she expect? Why do people send me these things?" He walked out, leaving me with the woman's poem, "The Leopard Speaks."

I enjoyed finding the scraps of paper Lawson copied from his reading and placed on his desk. At night he took them home and entered them into a commonplace book:

"To the French, an amorous relationship is more than friendship, less than love."

"Youth is a disease which time cures."

He kept a folder of newspaper stories: a female high-wire walker called "The Tottering Angel"; strongman Siegmund Breitbart hammering a railroad spike with his bare hands through a five-inch board, and the result of a study concluding that smiling can actually arouse happiness. This piece was underlined and asterisked.

I typed my poems in 405, sometimes using that yellow paper which made my words seem like his. Lawson dropped in occasionally, then made it a habit. He would knock lightly and rush around saying he was going downtown to get new soles on his shoes, or place an order at the butcher. He was both domestic and cerebral, and I watched him in admiration, often asking about a book that intrigued me. His answers were succinct and enlightening. He felt Wallace Stevens was an intimate poet, not at all abstract or distant. He flipped open *Harmonium* and read a few lines aloud:

> The wind shifts like this:
> Like humans approaching proudly,
> Like humans approaching angrily.
> This is how the wind shifts:
> Like a human, heavy and heavy,
> Who does not care.

He looked at the cover, a formal photograph showing Stevens in jacket and tie, and yet a wayward lock of hair rose from the back of his head. Lawson stroked the paper, as if trying to groom it into place. And then he left. I started to feel comfortable calling him by his first name. On occasion, he inquired after other students, curiously, but without gossiping. He knew I was from New York, and asked if I had ever gone to the Café Wha? I told him I had spent many Saturdays there, drinking glasses of limeade, called "Green Tigers," and listening to a group called "Them," whose first album was "The Angry Young Them." He said he was surprised that the Wha? was named after W. H. Auden's initials. When I laughed at what I thought was a joke, he shook his head seriously, putting his chin to his chest, which he did when he was embarrassed by another's ignorance. He said Barkhausen had written a poem about it, that I was mistaken, that Auden lived in the East Village and Barkhausen had the facts. He smiled a forced smile I hadn't seen before, more a grimace than a grin and I realized he was using the information from the article to summon happiness.

Lawson's *The Science of Goodbye* was nominated for the National Book Award. Many of the poems showed the influence of César Vallejo and Rafael Alberti, a big change. At The Deadwood, overly enthused about his book, I bet my friends a night of beer that Lawson would win. I had to pay for my wager by working overtime in the journalism department making pads.

One morning as I entered EPB, Iris ran out in a raincoat though it wasn't raining. She held it closed by the collar, as if protecting herself. When I got off the elevator, I heard Cook and Lawson arguing. Lawson, red-faced, furious, stood close to Cook, who kept asking for a chance to explain. Ridge tried to make peace, but Lawson stamped around the hall.

"Murderer!" he yelled. "You're no better than a murderer!"

Students came to listen and catch a glimpse. Realizing the audience, Lawson went to his office and Ridge escorted Cook from the building.

Ridge told me later that someone had sent a letter to Nora about Iris, and Dan broke up with her in the hotel. The heat of her body reflected the heat of her temper, and Iris walked into the bathroom, removed the lid from the toilet tank and hurled it out the window. The heavy porcelain rectangle fell through a trellis and into the courtyard. The police arrived, Iris left, and Dan settled with the hotel and authorities. When I had seen her earlier, Iris was leaving Dan's office where she had exposed her breasts, which she had cut with a razor. She screamed at him while blood ran down her chest. Lawson walked in and saw her wounds. He tried to calm her, but she ran off. Then he let Dan have it, while Dan pleaded that it was a misunderstanding, as if that word could cover what he had done, not only to Iris, but to dozens before her. Iris, whose wounds turned out to be superficial, left her work-study job, but was hired as a translator by the International Writing Program, through Lawson's influence. Dan canceled classes for the week and left an excerpt of a poem by Theodore Roethke on his door:

> Dark, dark my light, and darker my desire.
> My soul, like some heat-maddened summer fly,
> Keeps buzzing at the sill. Which I is *I*?

McPeak and I parked at the Eagle supermarket where we saw Lawson talking with another teacher. He had let Uncle out and tied his leash to the handle of the car door. As we passed, we heard a terrible squeal coming from Lawson's engine, like a fan belt screeching, about to break. We went to help but, when we arrived, we couldn't detect the source of the sound.

"Is something wrong with your car, Mitch?" McPeak asked.

"No," he said, curtly, and unclipped the leash, hoisting the dog into the back seat.

As we walked away, I said to McPeak, "It was coming from Uncle."

Lawson's concern about his neighbor's pet continued to distract him. He talked frequently about Uncle and said he was considering asking the neighbor if he could adopt the dog. One day on the stairs he looked at Ridge and me as if we were strangers. He paused, confused, and said, "Hello. Both."

A brown bag full of Jolly Rancher sour candy was crammed into Lawson's mailbox with a card that read, "Sweets for the sweet" and was signed "Love, Monique." A few days later, he poured the candy into a crystal ashtray he brought from home, and insisted I try one. He sorted through the bright cubes, choosing two cherries, his favorite. His face was grinning with the irrepressible delight of a man with a crush. We sat across from each other, sucking on the hard squares, but Lawson beamed as if he were swallowing Monique.

"Her father makes these. I mean, he owns the company," he said, his cheek bulging. "But not here, in France. When she was a kid, she lived for a summer in the Versailles palace."

I said I didn't know that.

"Her family was close to de Gaulle. She says that not many people are aware of it, but his wife was an octoroon."

I said, "Mitch, I think Monique makes up a lot of stories. She told me her father invented the twist tie and the flat bottom paper bag."

He looked like I had slapped him. And he looked at me in such a way that I felt immediately guilty, as if I were trying to harm a rival.

"I think you're mistaken," he said, his chin to his chest. "I've never heard that from her. Why would you say such a thing?"

We continued to suck on the sour candies. "It's not called Jolly Rancher in France," he said, sifting through the bowl to look at a label but, not finding it in French, he put it back. "It's '*Rancheur de Joie.*' She's a good kid.

She said she was uncomfortable being so wealthy, that she identified with the servants."

I could feel my face fall at the sight of my mentor collapsing for the fake charms of cheap Monique. But pronouncing the name "*Rancheur de Joie*" must have ignited the tiniest spark of doubt, and he coughed and scratched his neck. He stood, walked past me to the window and looked out, hands on hips. I wondered if he had an "amorous relationship" with Monique.

"She's a nice person," I said, "but she exaggerates at times."

Lawson was reviewing Monique's claims.

"You could be right. You may be right," he said, not facing me. "She has said a few odd things." When he turned, I could see he had been making that forced smile, and an echo of it remained. He left without saying anything else.

I was glad I did not have to mention, "With a name like Smucker's . . ."

Cook came to Ridge's office when we were discussing my new poems. Two lollipop sticks protruded from his lips.

"I've changed," he said, the words garbled. He removed the lollipops. "I want everyone to know. I made a promise to Nora and to myself. Our marriage isn't perfect, but I won't cheat on her in town."

Dan had found a compromise. He would be unfaithful only beyond city limits.

Ridge shook his head.

"What's the matter?" Dan said. "This way I'll keep all private business far away."

We didn't say anything, so he added, "Ah ha! You don't believe I can do it, but I can!" He smiled as if accepting a challenge. He pointed at us. "You'll see!" He put the two lollipops in his mouth, turned, took them out and waved them. "Giving up smoking too!" he said.

CHAPTER THIRTEEN

40 REGULAR—SNOW GLOBES—
BETWEEN COVERS—THE END OF UNCLE—
RIDGE LANDS A JOB—THE ALAMO

A note in my box from Lawson said to come to his office. It was on the usual yellow paper, but signed Mitch, not typed ML. I wondered if it was about Monique, but when I entered 405 he leapt from his chair, showing me a tan sport coat.

"This doesn't fit anymore. You're a 40 regular, right?" He stepped back to gauge my size and helped me try it on. "Looks good," he said. "Now you can get rid of the other one."

I realized I had been wearing a high school jacket without even noticing. Everyone else did. I was more touched by the gift than embarrassed by my need of it and I thanked him. He said it was Mongolian camel hair, and eased me into the hall, insisting I check it out in the men's room. When I saw my reflection—glasses, narrow shoulders, waning hairline and long arms—I looked even more like Lawson. I told him how much I liked it, and he smiled a real smile, not the smile that tricked the brain. Seeing *Iowa City* on the label made me believe it was a poet's coat, or at the very least the coat of a student of poetry, and beyond that, a student of Lawson who resembled Lawson.

I met Ridge on the street.

"What's this?" he asked, tweaking the lapel.

"Lawson gave it to me."

"He gave it to you? It looked familiar. Weird!"

"I know," I said. "I feel strange wearing it."

"You can't win. To wear it means ridicule and to wear your old one means ridicule."

Lawson ordered expensive books from France, and didn't want his wife to know. As he spoke about this secret vice, he rubbed his hands together, gleeful, expectant. It was nearly comic to see a man who prized integrity relishing these covert purchases. Boxes arrived from Paris, pasted with colorful stamps and crushed at the corners. A note told me to come during office hours. He handed me his long brass letter opener and said to be careful. The books were packed in pages from *Le Monde*. I removed ten or so thin books from each carton. The pages had to be torn, and Lawson said he would do that himself with a special blade. I knew some of the authors before I came to Iowa: Apollinaire, Valéry, Claudel, but most were new. I found his favorite, Eugène Guillevic, which he grasped with both hands. He piled them on the desk and I knew to leave him alone. It was the only thing I had seen him romantic about, and a kind of cheating on his wife as well. He said he would have to get rid of some books to make space. I said things could be arranged without that and he nodded. As I was leaving, I saw him holding Guillevic to his nose and inhaling.

The next time I went to 405, I shifted magazines to the lowest shelf and moved the dozen snow globes. I shook one containing an owl, forgetting they held no water. I turned it over and saw a little plug. The tip of the swan watering can would fit perfectly. Half an hour later, I had snow in the air.

Ridge had gone out with many of the students in Kim Merker's class, The Hand Printed Book, and three of them printed his poems on broadsides. His latest girlfriend didn't want to be part of that group so, for her final project, she printed a leaflet of my poems, *The Sadness of Music*, on beautiful, thick paper, letterpress, a jacket with folders around it. Now I had a "book," something to give friends. Without telling anyone, I placed a copy in Belinda Schaeffer's mailbox, and signed it

> *To Belinda,*
> *Love, John.*

With this exquisite, minute publication, I vaulted into another dimension. I joined those with poems "between covers," a phrase used often in the workshop. "I can't wait to have those poems *between covers*," we would say to each other. It was as if our poems had been wandering the streets, insomniac, and had finally been put out of their restless, wide-eyed misery by lying down, tucked into a bed from which they would rise and shake the world.

Pryor published his own book, *Tightrope Walking in the Rain*, fifty poems bound expensively "between boards," meaning in hardcover. The lush and delicate paper looked like silk strands ran through it, so it seemed a defilement to turn the pages. Pryor pointed out the colophon, which named the typeface and paper stock, a poem in itself. He numbered and dated each book, with a line drawn through his name on the first page and signed again. Instead of Iowa City, it said Poet City. I was shocked to see the book was not dedicated to Wendy, but to Barkhausen. When

I mentioned this to Ridge, he said, "If I was trying to keep Artie from fucking my wife, I'd dedicate my book to him too."

One night when I opened the door to 405, I jumped when I found Lawson there in the near dark. It looked like he'd been crying. Cabaret music played from the small cassette recorder.

"They gave him to a cousin in Council Bluffs," he said.

It took me a second to realize he referred to Uncle. I went behind the desk and put my hand on his bony shoulder.

"They said the cousin has a farm, but I think they euthanized him," he said. "This voice," he said, referring to the music. There was something about the vocal just like Uncle, a quavering, otherworldly keening. "It's like him talking from beyond the grave," he said, as if daring me to disagree. I went to get him a glass of water and when I came back, the music was louder.

"Thanks," he said. "Please leave us alone."

I closed the door and heard him wail, an Uncle-like sound, a cry for only the third time in his life, floating through that hall of callow pangs, those rows of cubbyholes holding our poems etched in blue Thermo-Faxed ink.

My mailbox held a large manila envelope with Belinda Schaeffer's name on the return address. I couldn't bear to open it in the elevator or on the street. I rushed to my apartment and put my books away, sat at the kitchen table, and cleared off a wide space. I opened the clip, sliding out a book. I hoped to find a letter. I shook the envelope, but it was empty. The front page had an inscription:

> *For John,*
> *With thanks for The Sadness.*
> *Warmest personal regards,*
> *Belinda*

Warmest Personal Regards. Warmest Personal Regards!
Not *Love*, and nothing "personal" about it. In my rush to
see if there was a letter, I hadn't noticed the book's title—
it was used, from Epstein's, Galway Kinnell's *The Book of
Nightmares*. I already owned a copy.

I called Ridge and told him about the dog. When I hung
up, I felt closer to Lawson. He loved so little that I hated
to see him lose the one thing that seemed to fill his trim,
well-metered world with a cockeyed delight. I realized how
many of his poems were about loss:

> The missed train, the platform empty
> except for petals from a dropped bouquet.
>
> ∽
>
> The mirror displays a lost reflection,
> the no-man, the no-body,
> the nothing
> that means everything.
>
> ∽
>
> The child has lost his ball,
> the grandfather his memory.
> The years have lost their months.
> The months, their weeks . . .

English departments solicited Ridge because of his
Yale prize, and he accepted a job as assistant professor
at McGuire University in Dallas. This irritated Pryor who
was rejected from everything and was flying at his own
expense to an interview at a community college in the
same state, right near the Alamo. I took him to the airport
and wished him luck, but he was bitter about fate casting
him toward the landmark of annihilation. The next morning
Kim and I drove out of town early to apply for jobs grading

high school seniors' exams at the American College Testing program. Afterward, we stopped at a remote diner for breakfast and saw Barkhausen sitting with Wendy on the same side of a booth, both with wet hair. Wendy waved. Barkhausen came over. He was revved up, from coffee or from romance, and he talked nonstop, madly, recommending the diner's freshly *squozen* orange juice. He said he was in love with Wendy and that Pryor should see the "right thing on the wall." He called our waitress by her first name, so we guessed he and Wendy had been coming there for a while.

In the parking lot, I said to Kim, "I wonder if Pryor knows."

"Where is he?" Kim asked.

"I put him on a plane last night. To the Alamo."

CHAPTER FOURTEEN

STANLEY KUNITZ ON TWELFTH STREET—
A FIGHT WITH KIM—THE FIFTH SEASON—
KANE IS ABLE—ANTHROPOMORPHIC
DOORKNOBS—THE HABIT OF ANALYSIS—
LEFT IN THE DARK

I flew with Ridge to New York where he was giving a reading at the Poetry Society of America while I was going
to Queens to celebrate my mother's birthday. He stayed
at our apartment, but when my parents and I came back
from dinner, he called to say he had met a girl, and wondered if my mother would be upset if he didn't return
that night. She didn't care, but my father said he must
be a real operator. The next day I met him outside Stanley Kunitz's Twelfth Street brownstone. Stanley's wife, the
painter Elise Asher, short, lithe, and wrapped in a silk robe
with prints of red and green parrots, opened the door. A
fat cat twisted around her ankles, and she pushed it away
with her sandals. She saw us gawking at the hefty pet and
said, "Twenty-eight pounds. Celia won the fat cat contest
in Provincetown last year."

Elise had a way of welcoming and appraising. The taut
skin on her face seemed freshened in the light that broke

through the back of the apartment, traveling from the garden, which burst with green even in midwinter. Stanley ran down the stairs, a youthful seventy-four, wearing a flannel shirt and an ancient sport coat with wide lapels. Ridge introduced me and he took my hands in his, his lively eyes peering out from above two sacks like tea bags.

"Helloooo! Helloooo! Let me get you some coffee!" He sang his greeting. Elise went to her studio. Stanley darted to the kitchen, as if we were the distinguished poets and he the one paying homage. When we settled in armchairs, Stanley pumped us with questions about our work, our loves, our plans. At the first syllable of each reply, he hummed a little, as if he already knew the answer. Ridge had separated from a girl he had raved about in a letter to Stanley, and he hoped Stanley had forgotten his earlier, effusive account. I hadn't admitted to myself that Kim and I might be about to part ways, but Stanley brought out the truth in me. It was like being in confession, except I felt a real unburdening. Stanley was surprised by little, seemed to understand everything, and yet lived for surprise. His responses were optimistic and heartening, as if nothing was really wrong, everything *could* change, and in fact, *would* change for the better.

When we talked about our work, I told Stanley that I had been revising my poems overly, and that when I finished a poem, it was so far from the first draft that I felt I had wasted a lot of time.

"Try making two poems," Stanley said.

"Suppose one of them's lousy?" Ridge asked.

"Better average than most," Stanley said.

He was translating Anna Akhmatova and not using exact rhymes. He said prosody came from the way we breathe and speak. And as he spoke, his speech seemed both colloquial and incantatory. An hour later, he saw us to the door. In the vestibule, he asked Ridge about the girl.

Ridge said the affair was over and Stanley asked if he was sure, as his letter waxed so romantically about her.

Ridge said, "I'm certain."

Stanley said, "When we are uncertain, that's when we are most alive."

Kim had two more years of course work before her dissertation. I didn't want to join the Iowa City hangers-on so we agreed I'd find a job in New York, visit often, and be together when she received her degree, an understanding that immediately led to warring accusations. When she came home from the police department wearing an officer's windbreaker, I charged her with having an affair. Her doctor, known as "the workshop doctor" because he freely dispensed painkillers, phoned one night to check on her sore throat. I had never heard of a doctor calling a patient for something so trivial, and another fight began. To smooth things over, we drove to Celebration, an out-of-town restaurant. We crossed Old River Road and New River Road, Beverly Park and Beverly Gardens, getting lost and confused. We turned back after a dispute about whether she had said "parallel" or "perpendicular" when she read the map. That summarized our relationship at its disintegrating point, but a particular episode defined it further. Kim said she would pick me up at Epstein's after work. I ran into McPeak and we went for a drink. Just before five, I realized she'd be on her way, so I left and walked in the street, along the row of parked cars facing the traffic so I could flag her down. In front of Epstein's, a taxi arrived and a woman who was waiting on the sidewalk got in. As she did, she dropped her newspaper. I tapped her window. She smiled and I opened the door, handing it over. Just as I turned, there was Kim, in front of the bookstore, arms crossed, saying, "Who was that woman? And why were you riding in that cab with her?" My laughter enraged her further. What were the chances I'd be closing the door to a taxi, a taxi with a woman in the back seat who just dropped a newspaper on the street? When things are going bad, the chances are good.

Every thesis had to be signed by Chair and Reader, either Lawson and Harvey or Harvey and Lawson, then submitted to the Office of Graduate Studies. McPeak worried how they would react to his actualist influences. He fretted over poems like:

> Okay, will do.
> Yeah, me too.
> Good-bye.

and:

> I don't want no ptomaine pussy.
> I don't want no po' man's pussy.
> Who do?

McPeak's fears were needless. I had brought mine to Harvey's office early, and he signed his name without turning a page, and the same would go for McPeak's. I met Jen Thacker in the hall on the day they were due. She showed me the vertical black stripes on the left and right margins. "I hope they'll accept it," she said. "I used a new ribbon, and it smeared on the rollers and the rollers smeared the pages."

Grad studies was ticklish about format. Numbers in the upper right corner had to line up exactly on each piece of twenty-pound bond. A crinkly librarian held the pages to the light. Jen's thesis was sure to be refused. I asked her the title.

"Death's Dark Kiss and Kaboodle."

I was absorbing this nutty bleakness when McPeak trotted toward us with his book in a box and Jen asked him his title. Instead of answering, McPeak pushed it at her.

He couldn't bear to say it since Barkhausen told him *The Fifth Season* was the name of the bar in the Cedar Rapids airport, and Ridge said it referred to Indian summer.

She paged through it. "Is this a joke?" she said.

"I know, I know," he said. "It's the name of the airport bar."

"No," she said. "I mean . . ." She pointed to a poem.

McPeak looked at lines that were pale, unreadable. He flipped through page after page, each one blank with the faintest lettering. I found out later that he had broken up with Stavrula the week before and, in a furious fight at dinner, he threw her collection of slides into the sink, poured lighter fluid over them and struck a match. When he went to apologize the next day, he found his belongings on the steps, including the boxed thesis he had been proudly reading to her by candlelight before the flames hit the slides. It was only at the moment with Jen that he learned Stavrula had wiped each poem with a bleach-soaked sponge. *The Fifth Season* had become one huge snowstorm, a whiteout, but it was signed by Harvey, just as he had signed mine, without a glance.

Lawson had diligently reviewed my manuscript, but I needed his signature. When I handed him the approval page, he said, "Harvey's out of town. How did you get his name?" I explained that I had gotten it weeks ago, disappointed he would think me a forger. He seemed unsettled that he had reverted to his usual suspicions, and he forced that smile to banish displeasure. He picked out his favorite poem, and said, "I'm glad you cut all the adjectives and adverbs—they were like sexy cheerleaders distracting from the game." Then he did something extraordinary—he invited me to dinner the next night at Marino's, his favorite restaurant in Cedar Rapids. At that moment, Monique appeared arm in arm with Falcon Namiki, and followed by Tim Kane, a hippie student running for sheriff. The three of them were posting placards around campus for Tim's campaign. Since the student body numbered forty thousand, Kane hoped to overwhelm the resident populace. The signs showed him in shoulder-length hair, with the slogan: KANE IS ABLE. Monique returned books I had loaned her. After she left, I thumbed through the Paul Carroll anthology, looking for Strand's poem, "The Marriage." I wanted Lawson's opinion, as it was the poem's minimal emotional display that helped me break away from the New York School. A photo of each poet prefaced his poems, but Monique had sliced out Strand's photograph, which made Lawson chuckle as he snapped his case shut and went home.

My left eye burned. The corneal erosion came and went, but made me very sensitive to light. I had run out of the sample erythromycin. I sat at Lawson's desk, turned off the overhead, and covered my eye with my hand, which gave some relief. I noticed a tube on a bookshelf, Uncle's eye medicine. A dab of the GenTeal Gel stopped the tears from running down my cheek.

Pavese's statement, "Give company to a lonely man, and he'll talk more than anyone," proved true the night Lawson took me to Marino's. We met at 405, where we packed two boxes of books he wanted to bring home after dinner. He opened one of the desk drawers, which I had never looked into, and showed me his collection of antique doorknobs. He lifted a knob with a lion's face, and another made of crystal. He pointed to his favorite, called "broken leaf knob," the carving of an urn on brass. He weighed another in his palm, a hand holding a scepter. Turning the scepter opened the door.

"Do you like this?" he said. "If you do, you can have it. I'm getting rid of my anthropomorphic knobs." He held it out. I jiggled its heft, imagining turning the handle. "Thank you," I said, "but I'm moving. And I don't know where I'll be. So I don't, I don't really have a door." I gave it back.

Lawson blushed as he was greeted as "Il Professore" by Gianni Marino who served us what he called the best bottle of wine in Iowa. Lawson looked like a different man against the restaurant's maroon wallpaper and deep wood—as if he had always been there, a comfortable expatriate of the academy slouching in the round booth, his arm over the soft leather, twirling his wine glass. He thanked me for my work with him.

"Especially for your help with Uncle," he said, and looked away.

"He'll be happy on that farm," I said.

"John Stuart Mill could read Greek when he was three," he said. "After a nervous breakdown, he wrote that the habit of analysis has a tendency to wear away the feelings." He paused. "I felt that was happening to me, but Uncle somehow got me past analysis. He was so bumptious, so wrong, he just couldn't be dissected."

"That's what people like about dogs," I said.

"Something changed in me when I saw him. He was not of this world because he didn't enjoy the world. I recognized something of myself in him." He ordered for both of us. And he ordered enormously. Appetizers of calamari, scungilli, and octopus, followed by steak pizzaiola, side dishes of linguine, salads, a second bottle of wine and rum baba for dessert. He ate just a bit of everything while I ate everything. When he got the bill, he made that grimace-smile to cheer the brain.

It was raining, and we dashed to my car. Lawson talked all the way home, an elliptical monologue expressing his hatred of Dan Cook, his disappointment in the Iowa administration, and even the football coach. He had spoken rarely about his poems, but he said he felt good about *The Science of Goodbye*. I pulled into his driveway and he was about to get out when I reminded him of the books. We grabbed the boxes and headed toward his front door in the downpour, covering the contents with our arms, crossing a lawn of deep puddles and divots.

"Thank god the outside light is on," he yelled.

In the hall, I put my box on top of his. We were both soaked and laughing. He held out his hand and said to stay in touch. He closed the door behind me and I stood on the porch planning my route around the deep troughs. I took my first step when the porch light went off, leaving me in the dark as I slipped and twisted in the ditches, almost falling. Once inside the car, I leaned on the steering wheel and laughed, my shoes and socks saturated, covered in mud.

CHAPTER FIFTEEN

A FURIOUS MAN—COOK'S BIG PLANS—
ADVENTURES OF THE LETTER I

I had lunch with Ridge at the Hamburg Inn No. 3 the day before I left Iowa City. We sat beneath a poster advertising the actualists' evening of Double Croakers:

"This meat is hard to chew," Tom beefed jerkily.

and:

"I hate reading Victor Hugo," said Les miserably.

Ridge told me that Lawson was on the warpath against Uncle's owners. He was certain the dog was dead, but wanted the name of the cousin with the farm and the neighbor wouldn't give it to him. Ridge passed Lawson's office just as Mitch slammed down the phone. Embarrassed, Lawson smiled and quoted the Dryden line he had posted on his office wall, *Beware the fury of a patient man,* but Ridge said he misquoted it, saying, *Beware the patience of a furious man.*

He told me about his dinner with Dan Cook at Lum's in Coralville. At the end of the meal, Ridge said Cook got very serious, stared into his cup of coffee and told him that NYU was about to offer him a full professorship and a named chair. That's what Dan's novelist friend in New York had told him, that he was at the top of the short list. When Ridge congratulated him, Cook said if took the job, he would have to leave Nora. As his former student, she wouldn't be happy in the New York literary world, she'd be over her head. Ridge told him that being young meant she could grow, that she was charming and attractive and that he should think twice, but Cook's mind was made up. He planned to build an addition onto their house and had already ordered the river stone. He was making an apartment, a bedroom, a bath and kitchen. Ridge couldn't get the point, but Cook said it would be a source of income for Nora when he was gone. "Who knows?" he said. "She might fall in love with the tenant, someone her own age, and be better off." He talked about the New York novelists he hoped to meet, like Vonnegut, as well as editors, and all the career opportunities this position would bring.

Ridge said to me, "It's weird to think of Iowa without Cook chasing women."

"You should know," I said.

"You could have done better," he said.

Ridge said, "I have something to tell you. I've been nominated for the National Book Award."

I congratulated him and we clinked glasses.

"I got a postcard from Porter Reed, who runs Provincetown's writing program," he said. "He wrote, 'I hope you win the fucker.' That's what they're like out there—writing *fucker* on an open-face postcard!"

Ridge had his mail with him. He'd heard from other poets and received invitations to read. An airmail envelope with a return address in Ethiopia turned out to be from Abe Gubegna, saying the novel they worked on together was being published in England. It also contained his new poem:

> Every day in Africa a gazelle wakes up.
> It knows it must run faster than the fastest lion
>   or it will be killed.
> Every morning a lion wakes up. It knows that it
>   must outrun
> the slowest gazelle or it will starve to death.
> It doesn't matter whether you're a lion or a
>   gazelle.
> When the sun comes up, you better be running.

Ridge recalled how Barkhausen encouraged Gubegna to mobilize an insurrection against Halie Selassie and fight with street weapons, such as "Mazel tov cocktails."

"And he said to him, 'One day tyranny will seize and desist!'" I said.

After lunch, we passed the university band marching along Jefferson Street and then dispersing. The musicians went their own ways, instruments under their arms. Each wore a black windbreaker emblazoned with a large gold *I* on the back. We turned to each other and said, at the same time, "Which I is *I*?"

CHAPTER SIXTEEN

SKELETON JANGLE—THE ALHAMBRA—
P'TOWN—THE BULL RING WHARF—
ANCIENT AGE—MOCHAHAGTDI!—BLACKOUT—
A NOBODY

I visited McPeak on my way to Queens. Despite his house's wide porches and airy rooms, he spent the summer in the dim finished basement, listening to jazz, reading biographies of musicians and drinking Scotch. His wife sat across from him smoking marijuana. Every so often, he rattled the ice in his tumbler, saying, "Nancy," who sighed, got up and tilted Johnny Walker into his glass from a bottle with a metal spout. No time wasted unscrewing a cap. After a day in his cellar, I mentioned the music had a common thread. Bill Evans, Chet Baker, Dave Brubeck: all white. He said most of his collection came from his racist father who used to watch the Chicago Bulls on TV, but didn't root for them. Instead, he tracked the scoring of white players versus black, telling McPeak at the end of the game, "how we did."

Having gotten his degree, McPeak lost his excuse to carouse in Iowa City, so he flirted with his high school students, waited until they graduated, and tried to seduce them at their colleges. He told me this new strategy on our way to lunch at Auntie's Road House outside of Moline, where we were meeting Didi, his new love. We reminisced about the workshop and I told him I missed Kim and he said he missed Stavrula in spite of their battles. He had hoped to reconcile, but she refused. He had gone to her house with a fresh copy of his thesis, which he now dedicated to her. She accepted it, and asked for the bleached version as well—she said she wanted a record of their vanishing. He mailed her the whited-out copy and never saw her again.

McPeak led me through Auntie's bar, out the back door and into a barren yard with one picnic table and two weary sunflowers. We were soon joined by Didi, a blonde and childlike college freshman. A waitress brought beers and hamburgers and Didi excitedly told me that this was their secret rendezvous, that the table we sat at was special, as it belonged to Auntie, who allowed them to sit there, hidden from the view of the bar as the bar was hidden from town. When Didi smiled, her tiny rows of white teeth looked like kernels of baby corn, and that's what she was, a baby. I felt McPeak and Didi had misunderstood their relationship with Auntie, a wrinkled woman in a wrinkled apron who came out several times, frowned, and banged the door closed as she returned to the bar. Didi was talking excitedly about an upcoming ABBA concert when Auntie tossed a pile of tablecloths onto the patio and shook them, sending ash and crumbs in our direction.

On my last night, McPeak drunkenly made much of the fact that Bix Beiderbecke, of nearby Davenport, died a few blocks from my birthplace in Queens. He tapped his fingers on his knees to repeated playings of "Skeleton Jangle," and gave me his lucky white-on-white shirt, with its pattern of cornets and trumpets. I left McPeak's with my pallor whitened further by his basement and its steady stream of jazz, along with a head full of facts such as Cab Calloway firing Dizzy Gillespie for hitting him with a spitball when it was really Jonah Jones.

The neighborhood surrounding our Queens apartment building, The Alhambra, had become plagued by drug deals and muggings. The barren lobby once held highboys, couches and overstuffed chairs, but the landlord hadn't replaced them when they were stolen a second time. A milk machine stood alone in a corner of the marble floor. I thought of the summer Ridge had visited me. When we walked from the Roosevelt Avenue subway, he remarked, not unkindly, "It's funny that you come from here, and I come from a nice area." That being Morristown, New Jersey. He said that after a rat crossed our path.

I walked to the elevator where ten-year-old Tony waited with two friends. He pointed at me with his thumb, saying, "This is John. He had his picture on the cover of *Rolling Stone!*" The kids gasped, but I couldn't begin to correct them. I was too stunned that my poem on the farthest back page had been transformed into my portrait on the front. The word *Spick* was scratched into the new paint. It seemed strange, since most of the building was now Latino, or maybe this was why it was done. I hesitated before the door to 5D. I had a key, but debated between using it and ringing the bell.

When my mother answered, I heard my father's cocktail shaker. She gave me a hug and I brought my bag into my unchanged room: single bed, dresser next to a triangular desk facing the corner, two bookcases, a wastebasket stuffed with bayonets, including a spear held by John Wayne in the movie, *Hatari!*, and Jim Morrison staring out of a milk crate of records. I looked in the mirror at my shaggy hair, frayed collar, and green army jacket with an ink stain on the pocket. I hadn't noticed any of this in Iowa. In my childhood mirror, I saw myself through my mother's eyes. I took a shower in the jury-rigged bathtub—a hose jammed onto the faucet and looped over the curtain rod.

I tried for a job in publishing, sending résumés to Scribner's, Random House and Morrow. I toured my old neighborhood. Jahn's ice cream fountain continued to serve the giant sundae, The Kitchen Sink, for six dollars; a glass of seltzer was still two cents. I had hung out on that corner where every night a motorcycle cop went in for coffee, every night someone spat on his seat, and every night he left the shop with a wad of napkins to wipe it off. I passed Elmhurst Lanes, where my friend who had never seen a urinal, mistook the pink round deodorizing cake for soap, and rubbed it between his palms. I went into Weiss's Stationery and bought a pad of graph paper, perfect for my handwriting which was getting smaller and smaller. When I returned home, my mother was on the phone, but she cupped her hand over the receiver and asked what was in the bag. I showed her. She said to her caller, "John just came home, thrilled with a notebook. You'd think it was a Lincoln Continental." Like the mirror, her words showed me myself.

My writing in miniscules in eighth-of-an-inch squares reflected my diminishing world, expanded only when letters from Ridge arrived. He was getting ready to leave Iowa and wrote that, as he was packing his office, Harvey told him that Barkhausen and Wendy had run off together. Barkhausen bought a motorcycle and they zoomed out of town for Fort Madison where they were living in a motel. Pryor was facing the community college near the Alamo alone. Ridge drove to McGuire University, which he jokingly called the Harvard of the southwest.

Porter Reed called from Provincetown and told me I had been awarded a seven-month fellowship to the Work Center starting in October. He said Stanley Kunitz and Alan

Dugan had liked my work. I felt as if a tunnel had been dug for me that reached from the Midwest to the Atlantic. I returned to my summer job at the Associated Press, filling in for vacationing typists, copy boys and messengers. Kim wrote that she had fallen in love with a policeman. We knew something like this would happen to either of us, and I sent a letter of good wishes written on graph paper with an extrafine point.

In late September I jammed the nozzle onto the bathtub faucet for the last time and took my suitcase and typewriter to Port Authority. The bus driver yelled, "P-town," and I got on a line where everyone knew each other. A black man in a safari outfit was greeted as Prince Kelly by his friend whose gray hair was swirled high on his head in a bun. He wore a shirt with the logo *Top Knot* and a caricature of his profile. A musician carried a guitar case and a harpoon, which he told me was a sculpture from his upcoming show. The bus driver, Ronnie, announced he had been born in Provincetown and had driven the route for ten years. He described the Portuguese community as a home to artists and writers, calling it "A little drinking village with a fishing problem." We went down Forty-Second and along Twelfth Avenue, passing Italian delis where I had gone with my father to buy prosciutto, mortadella and capocollo for Christmas dinner. The harpoon maker asked Ronnie if he could sing, and Ronnie said just one:

> Traveling down the highway
> In my brand new Adidas
> Traveling down the highway
> Nothing but Hojo's to feed us.

We passed through Providence and New Bedford where we stopped in front of the Moby Dick Travel Agency. We crossed the Sagamore Bridge to the Cape, the canal below like the waters of Lethe, forgetting the past and heading into the unreality of seven months in a seaside town. Tall privet hedges allowed only quick flashes of the screened porches of antique homes on 6A.

Ronnie parked near John's Foot Long Hot Dog Company at Provincetown's MacMillan Wharf. Fishing boats with peeling paint on their hulls docked there, winches holding tons of seaweed-entwined rope. Gulls fluttered to the pier where they walked among packs of dogs, the whole town presided over by the Provincetown Monument, an almost 300-foot granite tower. Many of the people lurching by were drunk.

Porter met the bus, and picked me out of the crowd. "Do you want to eat or drink?" were his first words. His blue eyes swept across the street like the beam from a lighthouse and he showed the way. Although it was night, the bright streets were swarming. Same sex couples walked hand in hand. The fragrance of garlic drifted from Ciro & Sal's, and a similar wave came from Plain and Fancy. Everywhere cats and dogs. There was no leash law—both beasts and men were on the loose, and the first song I heard blasting from The Surf Club was "Unchained Melody." Commercial Street ran parallel to the bay, and the glimpses of the blue water between buildings gave a feeling of transience to the town. When I told McPeak where I was going, he showed me a passage from Henry Miller—"In their dream of love or lack of it, the lost are ever wandering to the water's edge."

We drank bourbon on varnished benches in the window of The Fo'c'sle. The table, deeply carved with names and dates, unsteadied our tumblers. Heavy beams loomed over red and white buoys and orange life preservers on the dark walls, but the effect was not touristy—nothing could shake the shadows from this den-like room. Everyone greeted Porter by name. When I went to the bar to buy a round, the bartender poured the whiskey right to the top. I thanked him, and he placed his palm over his chest, saying, "I understand." In the Provincetown bars, it was always midnight, and on the streets, it was always noon.

A patron wearing a green silk windbreaker leaned over the jukebox, which blasted the refrain, "Mi-a-mi Dolphins! Mi-a-mi Dolphins," a child's tune. As I lifted the drinks, he returned to his seat, the team logo in script above his heart. He told the bartender about seeing Don Shula in an airport and said he knew he should be a Patriot but he'll always be a Dolphin.

Porter introduced me to Vince Leslie, a grizzled man with a goatee, author of fourteen books. Not even at Iowa had I met anyone so prolific. He planned to go to Mexico to interview Pancho Villa's widow for a biography of the revolutionary. A photo of the car where Villa was shot would serve as the cover. Elliot Darmody, wearing a duster coat that reached the floor, joined us. He was a poet who told me he had just legally changed his name to *Post-Elliot*. He smiled as he said this, his beautiful white teeth contrasting with his worn, smudged face. Vince talked about preparing mackerel with mayonnaise and Post-Elliot told me the fishermen would give you a free fish if you went to the pier at the end of the day.

"It's usually a trash fish like hake, and it helps if you take a pretty girl along," he said. "By the way, Porter, is Hester back?"

"Any day," Porter said. They talked about Hester, a poet, second-year fellow from New Orleans, and a great chef. She had gone to Louisiana for the summer to care for her sick mother.

"You'll love her!" Post-Elliot said to me. "Her squid stew is better than the restaurants'."

Porter and I left for The Bull Ring Wharf, the motel on the water where I'd be living, as there wasn't enough space for all twenty fellows at the Center. On the way out, I accidentally bumped into a man entering and I apologized, but he ignored me and headed straight for the bar.

"He can't talk," Porter said. "He lost his voice last year when his wife left him."

Porter said that neither Vince nor Post-Elliot had jobs. They spent most of the day in the bar and, if they could, wrote late at night. He asked me to guess their ages. I said midfifties but they were both forty. Porter said you'd think that schedule would have given them a longer youth, but they worked so hard wasting time that it took a toll.

My place, ten by ten with a kitchenette and bath, had a picture window that angled onto the bay. The couch served as a bed, and chairs of aluminum tubing and cross-hatched vinyl surrounded a glass-topped table. A fireplace, at odds with the beach furniture, gave the room a paradoxical coziness, as if winter and summer had come to terms. It reflected the state of the fellows: none could afford to be summer residents, but we clung to the town in winter. Porter said he'd come back in the morning and take me to breakfast and an introductory meeting at the Work Center. I piled my clothes in the dresser and tossed my bag into the bottom of the closet. My minimal possessions gave the room a feeling of spaciousness. I lined books along the mantel, and was reading a welcome card from the Bull Ring owner when the lights went out. The illuminated bay turned black. The manager's office across the parking lot was also dark. I walked Commercial Street to the sound of fog horns until I found The Fo'c'sle, Vince and Post-Elliot's faces flickering with light cast by candles in tin ashtrays.

"Welcome to P'town," Vince roared. "This happens all the time." I walked to the bar for a drink, happy to be in literary company. The bartender didn't recognize me in the dark and handed me a flashlight, saying, "Top shelf, a dollar twenty-five. Second shelf, ninety cents. Bottom, seventy-five." I drank Ancient Age from the bottom, as we'd been doing, though I briefly considered moving up to Ancient Ancient Age. I joined my new friends as the bartender brought a cup of coffee to a skull-faced man in a black suit, who sat alone facing the street. He held the mug shakily. Vince said, "Sad story. A Harvard professor struck by lightning."

Vince and Post-Elliot began a friendly argument. Provincetown-Boston Airlines was holding a contest, inviting suggestions for a marketing slogan. Vince had sketched his idea on a brown paper towel from the men's room and Post-Elliot was shaking his head. Vince pushed the paper toward me. A stubby pencil had written, *MOCHAHAGTDI!*

I sipped my drink.

"Well," Post-Elliot said, smiling. "Think it'll go over?"

"Don't push him," Vince said. "Let him digest it." He left to get another round.

"Is this Portuguese?" I asked Post-Elliot. He started to laugh, harder and harder, until he wiped the tears from his eyes with the slogan. I was laughing too when Vince arrived, holding three drinks in his big hands and frowning. Post-Elliot repeated my question.

"Portuguese?" Vince yelled. "It's an acronym! I thought you were a writer!"

He sat down and pointed his thick forefinger at each of the capital letters, "Make Our Customers Happy And Have A Good Time Doing It!" He took a swallow of Ancient Age. I was embarrassed by missing Vince's acronym, and relieved when another customer approached our table. The man swaying at my side was a housepainter, his overalls and balding head flecked with white.

"Hey," he said, poking my arm. "Weren't you in here earlier with Porter?"

I said I was.

"Porter. What a great writer. I love his stories." He was slurring, but his admiration seemed real.

"What's your name?" He leaned on my shoulder to steady himself.

I told him and he blinked. "Who?" he asked again, and again I told him.

He dropped his arms to his sides. "I come all the way across the room to meet one of Porter's famous writers, and who do you turn out to be—a nobody!" He faltered back to the bar.

Tired, a bit drunk, I felt like a spectacular nobody as I sat between the prolific author and a poet. I hoped that I was not as diminished in their eyes as I was in my own. Vince seemed affected by the painter's verdict on my name, and my verdict on his slogan. He took another sip and talked about the novel he'd begun that day with a great first sentence. In a stentorian tone, he said, "He was a tall dark Armenian whose mind was a clear pool of doubt," and then he yelled, "Got ya! Got ya!" lurching for our throats in a choking gesture.

The bartender told us that the sixteen-year-old boyfriend of the owner of The Rooster Bar crashed his new Cadillac into a telephone pole, downing the power lines.

Vince said, "That's batting a hundred."

Post-Elliot corrected him. "Vince, you mean a *thousand*, right? A *thousand*! That's the expression."

"I've had it with you two," Vince said, finishing his drink and walking out.

Post-Elliot and I sat in silence and considered our wavering reflections in the window.

"You know, John," he said. "There's a reason why so many of us end up here in P'town."

And the lights came on.

CHAPTER SEVENTEEN

THAT'S P'TOWN—THE MEAT RACK—FAWC— EVERYONE BUT HESTER—A FREE FALL INTO RELATIVITY—THE VICTIM WAS ALONE— THE DROP-IN CENTER—CORSO ARRIVES

There are two main streets in Provincetown: Commercial Street, along the water, and Bradford, parallel to it, once simply called Front and Back Streets. Porter and I walked past Town Hall's little rectangle of benches known as "The Meat Rack," an after-hours cruising place. He told me that when the bars close in summer, it filled with hundreds of men. Although it was October, tourists still paraded the streets, mixing with gay couples and fishermen in rubber boots on their way to the wharf. We passed the library where the housepainter, still wobbly, shook his tarp over the grass next to the building and wandered through his truck looking for brushes. A library official stood on the steps, arms folded. "No ladders today!" he said, "today, no ladders!"

It was then that Porter spoke the slogan, the short anthem of the area that I heard for the first time—"That's P'town."

At Tip for Tops'n, we had a breakfast of coffee and flippers—fried dough sprinkled with powdered sugar. The menu explained the restaurant's name—The Tip of the Cape for The Tops in Food. I thought Vince's acronym might win after all.

A sign on Pearl Street read *A Winter Community of Artists and Writers.* The Fine Arts Work Center, FAWC for short, was a converted lumberyard, and the rickety, worn façade looked more like a set for a western than a forge of artistic activity. It consisted of a long two-story wooden building, unheated coal bins, a shed once housing lobster traps, and a barn. Raised windows showed the studios of the visual artists who worked and slept in the same space. We ducked under a white oar painted with the word *Office* nailed to a doorframe tangled in wisteria.

Bonnie, the secretary, handed me my stipend check of a hundred fifty dollars across her IBM Selectric, and said to Porter, "Would you talk to Case about keeping the shower curtain *inside* the stall! This is the third time." She pointed to a full bucket.

"Sorry!" A voice came through the ceiling. Exposed wires and pipes crisscrossed the rafters, dangling with tags written in shaky cursive.

"Thank you, Case," Bonnie yelled, and we could hear his footfalls creak. She answered the phone and, when she got off, she said it was the new pastor of the Universalist Church who wanted the name of a carpenter. "He said all the windows stick and he has trouble opening them."

"He better get used to it," Porter said. "There's not a right angle in town."

Porter took me down a narrow hall crowded with books, paintings, and cartons leading to two wooden crates that served as steps to the sunken common room. A pay phone hung between a row of wooden mailboxes and a tilted metal bookcase. Jeanne East, a second-year writing fellow, entered through a sliding glass door facing the parking lot. A short broad-shouldered brunette, she carried herself with authority. In New York, I had received a copy of *Shankpainter*, FAWC's literary magazine, and remembered her lines:

> When you come, leave your bones
> in the hallway. I like you soft.

She introduced her husband, Wayne, as a carpenter and "bedfellow." A visual artist named Les carried a huge cone of twine, his heavily callused fingers rubbing the fiber as he asked Porter in a worried way about the 250 bikers he heard were coming to town.

"That's the Entre Nous Motorcycle Club," Porter said. "Two hundred and fifty members, and not a bike among them."

"They just like to dress up," Jeanne explained.

Les joined the artists who were meeting in the trap shed. I recognized Jack Tworkov, a well-known abstract expressionist, walking in the parking lot, a small, compact man, his bald head like a fist. Porter said that Les was a fiber artist who made huge towers of rope on display in the gallery next to the office.

Two second-year poets took seats. Stephen Greene huddled in a dark raincoat. Barry Mengas wore black jeans, black T-shirt and a black zippered jacket. I recognized them, they were familiar to me from the way Hemingway described such figures: poets marked by death. Others entered, including first-year fellow Ted Page from Tucson, blond and handsome, with Gail, his blonde wife. A ring of keys dangled from Ted's belt, and Porter warned him that keys on your right side meant you were gay, and submissive. Ted grimaced and Gail jangled the ring to unfasten it.

Alan Dugan and Stanley Kunitz arrived. They were united in their generosity toward young writers, but opposites in every other way. Dugan lived a solitary life in nearby Truro. His drinking binges had given him a poor reputation and invitations to teach or to read were few. He wrote, smoked and drank in his house overlooking Cape Cod Bay. His first book, *Poems*, which he published at thirty-nine, won the Yale Series of Younger Poets Prize, the Pulitzer, the Prix de Rome and the National Book Award. Each book that followed was dedicated to his wife, Judy, and each book was titled the same, *Poems 2*, *Poems 3* and *Poems 4*. In Provincetown's west end, Stanley's house was renowned for its exquisite garden and many visitors. He was active in New York poetry circles, judged contests, served on the boards of foundations and taught at Columbia. Everyone referred to him as Stanley and to Alan Dugan as Dugan, just as we had done with Lawson and Harvey, but there the similarities ended. Dugan and Kunitz, both Pulitzer winners, had eclipsed the Iowa hierarchy, but you wouldn't have known it. They had formed a peerless community in Provincetown.

Dugan pulled two thick envelopes from the breast pocket of his jacket and handed them to the poets marked by death. They thanked him and he sat down and began writing in a legal pad. Although in his early fifties, Dugan's face was cracked and lined, his fingers brown from chain-smoking Pall Malls. The poets marked by death opened Dugan's envelopes and removed pages filled with Dugan's looping scrawl. He had also line-edited their poems in pencil. They thanked him again and he said, "You're welcome," in a deep Brooklyn accent that banged the walls. He went through his mail, which included a cookbook of poets' recipes to which he had contributed. The collection of rhapsodies by sensitive males involved bib lettuce, sautéed endive and pea tendrils, but Dugan's entry began, "Take two hot dogs and throw them into a frying pan until they turn black . . ."

Stanley sang his sentences, bounding from fellow to fellow, introducing himself. He knew something about each of us. He grasped my forearm and asked after Ridge. When Page said he missed the desert, Stanley waved toward the water and said, "You'll love the ocean even more!" He took a chair next to Dugan and they discussed a former fellow who had just died. Stanley said, "It was a relief, he was so sick." Kurt Becker, a poet and secretary of the committee, explained that the fellow had become paranoid and believed The Red Inn, a restaurant near Stanley's house, was run by communists. I hadn't noticed Kurt. He had blended into the shoddy armchair with his thrift-shop clothes and glasses held together by brown pipe cleaners.

"How'd he die?" someone asked.

"A car crash in Boston," Porter said.

Dugan stabbed the air with his finger, accusing Detroit and Madison Avenue at once, saying, "The ads say the car goes from zero to sixty in five seconds. They don't tell you it goes from sixty to zero in twenty seconds."

"And that's when the pole gets in the way," Stanley said.

Dugan took a drag on his cigarette, flicked ash into a hubcap of cigarette butts and said, "That makes what, three fellows who went nuts now? What happened to that guy from Alaska, the one who left wearing spoons on his head?"

Stanley clapped his hands, trying to brighten the meeting. "Welcome, everyone, welcome! I think everyone's here but Hester." He told us we had no responsibilities except to do our own work and that members of the committee would look at manuscripts any time. He asked for suggestions for visiting writers and we decided on John Updike, Robert Bly, Mark Strand and Bernard Malamud.

Jay Hankard, another new poetry fellow, swished his ponytail and jutted his square jaw forward. "Why only writers?" he asked. "How about radical lawyers or religious leaders?" His buck teeth helped push his words across the room. Everyone was silent. He continued, "Farmers? Gurus? People who break the mold!"

Stanley said, "Some of these names have distinguished themselves in ways you mention. Let's see how this first round goes." When Stanley spoke, a gentle smile peeked from his lips, and he often ended his sentence by making a little hum of finality. While Stanley was talking, Hankard caught Gail staring at his hand, and he brought his ring close to her eyes and said, "Bone of Tibetan Monk!"

Page said he was satisfied with the list, and Hankard threw his arms over his head, saying, "I'm just trying to save us from a freefall into relativity!"

Kurt would write the invitations on a manual typewriter in the office, on a Formica table which served as his desk. The letters I had received from him were pounded hard into the paper because of a worn ribbon, and the frayed words had to be puzzled out.

Hankard said, "The fishes live in water but they do not see the water."

Porter announced that Robert Creeley was arriving in a week and that Hester would be hosting a brunch in his honor.

"You won't want to miss that," Stanley said. "She's quite a cook."

"Stanley! Stanley!" Dugan said so urgently the whole room turned. "Is Hester making beignets?" Dugan's cracked brow, combined with his deep monotone, made even this trivial question seem grave.

"I guarantee it," Stanley said.

Porter said the date would be posted above our mailboxes.

I imagined Hester again, the sultry New Orleans poet with a domestic touch. Part cat on a hot tin roof and part plantation hostess. I had read her poems in *Shankpainter* about municipal statuary in the French Quarter, which added another dimension to her portrait.

Porter took us to the gallery to see the work of the visual fellows. The walls hung with paintings similar to de Kooning and others to Kline. Les's coils of heavy hemp dominated the space. On the way out, I stopped at a stand displaying a manuscript. The typeface was faded; it was impossible to read but interesting to try, and I could see the outline of poems, the shapes of stanzas. I deciphered a few titles and then a few more. I couldn't believe it, but there it was in front of me—McPeak's bleached thesis. I found the artist's name: Stavrula Pallas. Her fellowship had come, in part, for obliterating *The Fifth Season*.

Although it was only eleven o'clock, Dugan suggested the Fo'c'sle and we followed Stanley, who trotted at the head of the pack, the sun angling off the shiny brim of his fisherman's cap. The late morning light hit the street, flaring the asphalt, but the Fo'c'sle remained a shroud. We shielded our eyes as we navigated through the benches to the bar where everyone ordered Narragansett, the only thing on tap. Hankard asked for Perrier but the bartender's stare transformed his order, like alchemy, into beer.

Post-Elliot was at the bar. "I wasn't entirely truthful with you last night," he said while I waited for my drink. "I haven't written whole poems for a while. I'm into titles."

"He has notebooks of them," the bartender said. "Yesterday he wrote the title of his autobiography." He raised his eyebrows in appreciation.

"*The Victim Was Alone*. It's one of my mystery titles," Post-Elliot said. He asked if I was going to sit with Stanley Kunitz. I said I was, and I noticed a dog at Post-Elliot's feet, a tiny brown dog with three legs and one bulging eye.

"That's Major," he said. "He was buried alive for two days, but dug his way out." The bartender handed Post-Elliot a brass ship's clock and a long screwdriver, and Post-Elliot left the bar for a bench under a lantern where he started dismantling the face.

I joined the table where Stanley held the bar's orange cat in his lap. One of the patrons came in and he and Dugan saluted each other. I asked who it was, and Dugan said it was an old army buddy. He smoked and stared out the window. Stanley served in World War II as well, but as a conscientious objector, refusing to bear arms. Jeanne said she had a cat, and could tell Stanley was a cat person. Stanley said he'd never been without one. Jeanne asked Dugan if he liked cats. Dugan turned from the window and said, "I like animals in the wild where they belong."

Stanley said, "When I was in high school, I found a cat near our house in Worcester. My mother loved him and he kept growing and growing. Then I went to Harvard, and I missed him."

"Oh, that's so sad," Jeanne said. Her eyes also said she was not used to drinking beer in the morning and she had finished the tall glass as if it were orange juice. "What was his name?"

"Dart," Stanley said. "For D'Artagnan, one of the three musketeers." He continued to stroke the purring cat. "But one day my mother phoned and said, 'You must come home, Stanley! Right away! It's Dart!' She wouldn't tell me what was wrong and I imagined the worst. I took the next bus and when it pulled into downtown, there was a big commotion, sirens, horns, policemen everywhere. The city in knots! In the middle of the intersection was Dart, larger than I ever thought possible, surrounded by drawn guns! I begged the driver to let me off, and he said he could only make regulation stops, but I told him about my cat, and it turned out he was a cat lover too and he opened the door. I ran to Dart, right through the police, and he rolled on his back—he had grown immense because he was, and we didn't know it, he was a mountain lion!"

"Oh my god!" Jeanne said as Stanley's eyes blazed. "What happened?"

We had finished our beers in the rush of the story and Porter brought another round.

"Well," Stanley continued. "He followed me home." He giggled and said, "I built a pen and he stayed with us for years."

"Then what?" Jeanne asked.

"When he reached adolescence, he leaped over the fence and went back to the wild." He made a farewell gesture. "Where he belonged, really."

Dugan looked over but said nothing.

A loud moan came from Post-Elliot. He had nodded off with the clock in his lap and the screwdriver upright in his hand, so his face plunged onto the point, catching the side of his eye. The bartender gave him a wet rag, which Post-Elliot held to the wound as he left for the Drop-In Center, the town's free clinic.

The cat sprung from Stanley's lap and Stanley sprung up at the same time. "Good-bye, my darlings," he said, and Porter and Kurt followed. Dugan trudged off with the others but I stayed behind with Gail and Ted. The whole time, Gail held Ted's keys in her fist. Their two tanned faces and blond hair, fresh from Arizona, almost lightened the dim bar. Ted said, "I'd like to take a walk on the beach, okay, babe?" And they, too, left the Fo'c'sle.

I moved to Dugan's place by the window. A thin parade continued—fishermen, tourists whose children held balloons, and then someone I recognized but not someone I knew. He dragged a knapsack, his shirt unbuttoned, a pair of glasses hanging from a rope around his neck. I couldn't place him, a poet, a beatnik, a hippie or a yippie? Then I got it—Gregory Corso. He was shorter than I thought and his face was like a gnarled root. I had read everything of his, and everything Kerouac wrote about him and Ginsberg. They were mythical to me, and I never thought of any of them doing something as simple as walking down a street, especially a street in a town where I lived. Post-Elliot returned with a gauze strip over his eye and sat next to me. The bartender brought beers. "You can fix the clock another time," he said. I told Post-Elliot about Corso, and he quoted, "'Should I get married, should I be good?'" We agreed what a great poet he was and I said I hoped to meet him.

"Not me. I'm not wild about meeting poets," Post-Elliot said. "They have a bad effect on me. Stanley Kunitz, for instance," he said. "Do you know that whenever he's around, something bad happens?"

"Really?"

"I could feel it the minute I spotted him at your table." He pointed to his eye. "Two summers ago, I saw him looking in the window of the bookstore, and just then a madman on roller skates jabbed my neck with a knife!" He showed the scar.

"Why?"

"Don't know. Just zipped through the crowd and kept going. I walked to the Drop-In Center with blood running to my shoulder. I'm not crazy about being around poets, like I said." Then he looked at me.

"Well-known ones, I mean."

CHAPTER EIGHTEEN

OLD MR. BOSTON AND HAFFENREFFER
PRIVATE STOCK—PARALYZED—IRON MAN—
EDDIE BONETTI AND JACKIE O—
DEAN MARTIN—AN UNMAILED LETTER

K urt had invited the fellows to stop by anytime, so the next morning I walked west to his place on Cottage Street. The entrance was through the garden, and I stepped over enormous zucchinis, tripping on the tangled vines. His wife Penny, a former visual arts fellow, sculpted in papier-mâché. I had to squeeze between a six-foot crucifix holding a dying German shepherd, the words above it saying, *The Last Dog to Shit on My Lawn*, and an equally tall lady lobster, claws raised like castanets, nipples adorned with clamshell pasties. They had just returned from the liquor store. Penny held a bottle of burgundy and Kurt a six-pack of Haffenreffer Private Stock, a malt liquor. That, and a pint of Old Mr. Boston gin would float him into the evening. Penny's friend, Carole, knocked at the door, and she, too, carried wine. The women began drinking at the kitchen table among shredded newspapers and a gallon of wallpaper paste. A gray cockatiel whistled in a cage, and Penny poured birdseed from a huge bag into a small feed dish and it splashed across the floor. She opened the cage and dropped the bird to the linoleum, trusting he would devour the mess.

Bookcases surrounded Kurt's desk, a door propped on saw horses. I joined him in a glass of Private Stock, which he served in a mug smudged with fingerprints. He wore a heavy sweater with moth-eaten holes on the sleeves, and wide-wale corduroy pants thin at the knees. An old phonograph played scratchy Mozart. A big dog snoozed on the rug, its square head on Kurt's boot. When it rolled over, I saw a stomach of scabs and scales. Kurt called it autumn eczema, and scratched the dog's belly, causing his glasses to fall from his nose. He grabbed them from the rug and adjusted the pipe cleaners. In the next room, Penny and Carole loudly affirmed that each should drink from her own bottle of wine and not try to share, a pact made from experience.

I looked at a copy of Pound's *Personae*, a former library copy stamped *Discard*. Every book in Kurt's library was damaged and every book a classic. He had the best of everything in the worst condition. When I remarked on some arcane volumes, he said, "Many books are unjustly forgotten, but no book is unjustly remembered." He was working on a first collection of poems, some of which he had published in the *New Yorker, Harper's* and *Poetry*. He wrote every day, rising early, but expected little attention. He felt poetry had no place in shaping the world, and yet he made a world of it. When I asked him how his work was going, he said, with the happy cynicism of the creative mind, that he was already ahead of last year.

After an hour, Kurt walked me to the door and told me not to miss the upcoming brunch at Hester's, which overlooked the bay. He complained to Penny, "That mineral oil you put in the dog's ear got onto John's pants." I hadn't noticed the stains on my knees and said it didn't matter as I edged past a five-foot swordfish standing on its tail. Back at the Bull Ring, my ankles began to itch, and black dots on my cuff bounded toward the rope rug. The result of my first visit to a house in P'town were oil stains from a dog's ear and a family of fleas.

I spent the next week watching the tides come and go, and leaves fall from the slender oaks outside my door. I walked through town, browsed the shops and crossed the breakwater at land's end. The beauty of the town hypnotized me into paralysis, but there was something else. I felt I had to write significant work to justify my time there. I finally placed my typewriter on the glass table. With each clanging keystroke the machine inched away from me. I moved to the bed and filled a few pages of graph paper with gobbledygook, which made me feel I had done something. I heated a can of Campbell's clam chowder. The label said you could use water or milk. I had to make the stipend last, so I chose water.

I tried typing a letter to Ridge, but the metallic thudding on the glass felt like banging out a bad drum solo. I wrote again by hand, describing the coast, the people, and my plans for a long poem. Each section would focus on a part of P'town: the bay, the wharf, the boats, the fishermen, the dunes, the beech forest and more. I would pattern it after Galway Kinnell's *Book of Nightmares*, as he had followed the *Duino Elegies*. Happy with the accomplishment of defining the architecture of my poetic sequence, I left to mail the letter.

Post-Elliot urgently waved me in from the Fo'c'sle window. I approached his table, but he rose and walked to the bar, ordering me a beer. The bartender yelled, "Wait till you hear!" Post-Elliot couldn't stop grinning as the bottle was opened.

"You know that poet you like?" the bartender asked. "The one from the beat generation? He was knocked stiff at the Governor Bradford. The bouncer tossed him out the door, and he stayed there all night, curled on the sidewalk, wearing a jester's cap."

"He's clever," Post-Elliot said. "He's already moved in with Connie who owns the New World Deli." I had gone there once for a sandwich, the sticky hardwood floor grabbing the soles of my shoes as I approached the register. Connie rose lethargically from a booth where she sat with friends, and said, "I can't believe you want to order something . . ."

Post-Elliot continued talking in a dreamy way, "He's all set, got plenty to eat, a place to stay."

"John," he said, as we moved to a table, "Corso is the only poet who makes me want to take up the whole poem again." Before I could reply, he continued, "He caused a big ruckus at the Bradford, insulting women. Howlin' Jack coldcocked him. Either him or Crobar." I had seen Crobar and Howlin' Jack, huge bearded fishermen, through the Bradford's window, holding forth at its circular bar amid loud music and bustling pool tables.

"Uh oh," Post-Elliot said. "Here comes Iron Man. What's he carrying?"

Porter had pointed out Iron Man, banned from every bar in town, a swarthy mesomorph walking a bicycle whose handlebars sported a row of American flags. He got his name from the time he found an abandoned boat engine on the wharf and asked his longtime friends to help him load it onto his truck. When no one volunteered, he lifted the huge hunk of metal himself and threw it into the payload. His family said he was so hurt by the incident that he went to the liquor store that afternoon and kept drinking for thirty years.

The bartender was washing glasses and didn't notice Iron Man enter holding a large wooden top painted with a map of the world. He sat down grasping the toy by a cord in his left hand and spinning it with his right. Post-Elliot told the bartender he had a customer.

"Okay, Iron Man, you'll have to leave," the bartender said, lifting mugs from the sink. "And take your world with you."

On his way out, Iron Man dangled the top between our faces and said, "It's not funny. I can send you to the cemetery." He spun the top. "I have nothing to lose, you know."

Post-Elliot and I watched him mount his bike. "He's harmless," Post-Elliot said. "Unless he drinks, that is."

Vince Leslie and Eddie Bonetti walked in. Eddie, a short dark man with a broken nose and bowlegs, shook my hand heartily. He was a writer friend of Norman Mailer's. He went to the bar and came back with four tumblers of Jack Daniel's. He downed half his drink, said he had just finished a story about killing a lesbian on the beach with a shovel, and left. When I asked where he went, Vince said, "He keeps drinks in each bar. He's got one at the Bradford and one at the Old Colony."

"And fights too. Last month he got in a fight at each place, " Post-Elliot added.

"You know that big brick house in the east end? That's Mailer's. There's a boxing ring in the basement," Vince said. "Eddie was a pro. He once fought Willie Pep. Now he spars with Norman."

A pretty woman walked past the picture window wearing a white rabbit fur jacket, tight white pants, and a red wool hat. Her skin seemed whiter than her pale clothes.

"There goes Lint," Post-Elliot said, as I leaned forward to get a better look.

"Who's Lint?" I asked.

Vince said, "I crowned her with that nickname last year when she came to town. You must have met her by now. Hester."

I said I hadn't.

"She stopped in a few times with Porter," Post-Elliot said. "She didn't take to the place."

"I went to her reading last year," Vince said. "And I never go to readings, but she's a good looking woman, so I thought what the hell, but how can I listen to any poet after hearing Alexander Scourby read Whitman!"

"She's a good writer," I said.

"She didn't care for Vince's moniker," Post-Elliot said.

"She's not lint," Vince yelled. "She's more like virgin wool."

"She outran the shepherd!" Post-Elliot said.

Bonetti passed the window and, as he did, he dropped lower and lower, as if walking into a hole in the street until we could see just his head and shoulders. Everyone laughed as he entered.

"Descending imaginary stairs!" Post-Elliot explained. Eddie swallowed his drink, walked to the bar, again lowering himself with each step, and returned with another round.

"Whoa, Eddie," Vince said as he stared happily at the full glasses, their fragrance lifting toward us.

I hadn't eaten anything. I had been reading the soup can labels and I learned that each had three grams of protein if you made it with water, and nine grams if you made it with milk. I decided to just drink a glass of milk.

"I'm feeling great!" Eddie said. He had returned from New York, where he met Jackie Onassis who was editing his book of stories, *The Wine Cellar*. He described her gardenia-filled office at Viking Press and how she praised his prose, telling him that a lot of writers write with their wrists, but he wrote with his whole body.

"She whispers," Eddie said. "She never raises her voice so it's rude to disagree. If she shouted, well, then we could have gone at it!" He made two fists and ducked a shoulder forward.

"A pug like you with a lady like that," Vince wondered. "I heard the compound in Hyannis Port has heated towel racks."

"And her favorite dish is unborn calf," Post-Elliot said.

"I was on my best behavior," Eddie said. "Though a big guy at the reception desk gave me some guff when I asked for Mrs. O. But I knew I could take him." He stood up, pointing at his thick thighs. "The guy had spindly legs. You should have seen his face when we left for La Grenouille. By the way, Mrs. O never says hello, just smiles." Eddie's deeply turned-down mouth tried to imitate Jackie's greeting, a twitch that lifted his lips slightly upward from their usual frown.

"Did you fuck her?" Vince asked.

Eddie didn't answer. He was registering the question.

"*Eddie*, did you fuck her?" Vince asked again.

Eddie continued thinking and I wondered if he'd get violent but instead he turned indignant, then gallant, raising his chin in the posture of someone who had escorted the wife of a president.

"Of course *not*. She's a *nice woman*, Vince. A *nice* woman."

Hester walked past in the other direction and I was the only one who noticed. She carried a brown paper bag, a loaf of French bread sticking out of it along with the *New York Times*.

Vince bought a round, then Post-Elliot and then it was my turn. At the bar I crammed a bag of pretzels into my mouth. Porter walked out of the library across the street and joined us. It was getting dark and I was drunk. The jukebox played "Best Thing That Ever Happened To Me," and a man at the bar began singing along, "If anyone should ever write my life story . . ." He was smiling, but his eyes were watery and my eyes got watery watching his. Vince said that if his life were made into a movie, Anthony Quinn would be a good choice. The sad singer at the bar continued with a keening mew, "For whatever reason there might be . . ."

Post-Elliot chose Steve McQueen. Bonetti said his life couldn't be portrayed by an actor, but only by someone who had endured real pain. Like Rocky Graziano, the middleweight champion.

Porter was not interested in the game, so Vince said, "Ichabod Crane would play your life." He paused. "If you had a life!"

Porter just smiled. He enjoyed the atmosphere, the company, even the insults. He was memorizing their words to record verbatim in a book of monologues called *On the Cod.*

Vince turned to me. My forehead felt numb, and my body paralyzed, encased in a block of ice, ice that was beginning to melt onto the ragged floorboards. When I announced the man who would play my life, I meant it with all my heart and with all my soul.

"Dean Martin."

Vince, Eddie, and Post-Elliot all repeated the name at once. Everyone in the bar turned around and shut up. There was one second of silence before a thunderclap of laughter stormed around me and over the puddle I had become. I was smiling a dumb smile, the smile I hated in myself when I did something stupid, or found someone doing something stupid and was afraid to call it stupid. But no one was afraid to call me stupid, and amidst the horselaughs, which reached me as if I were underwater, Porter helped me from the bench.

"Let's get something to eat," he said.

I kept smiling, but I knew I'd made a fool of myself before the author of fourteen books and Mailer's cohort edited by Jackie O.

Over fishwiches at The Post Office Café, I remembered the letter in my back pocket. It was wrinkled and smudged and looked like it had been mailed, received, and remailed.

I put it by my plate and told Porter about my plans for the long poem. He said he was writing a short story about Isaac Babel, in the way Babel had written about Maupassant. Porter's literary talk and the sandwich almost snapped me to my senses. He paid. He always did. And I stumbled to the Bull Ring, past the Fo'c'sle's continuous roar, holding the letter outlining my plans.

CHAPTER NINETEEN

HESTER'S BRUNCH—STATUES AND STATUETTES—
COCKS AND COCKERELS—ONE POTATO—
A MOUSE-LIKE DOG—DON'T BE A RAT—
A NEW START FOR STAVRULA

A stairway on the side of the Flagship restaurant led to Hester's second-floor apartment overlooking the bay. Robert Creeley sat at the kitchen table surrounded by the writing fellows. Dugan's wife, Judy, cracked eggs into a bowl and beat them with a whisk. Hester came toward me wearing an apron. A tumult of hair sprung from her head, hidden the day before by her hat. Her breasts, tightly checked, rode high on her body. She wore no makeup, eyeliner or lipstick. Her pale skin made the streak of flour on her cheek seem gray.

"I'm Hester," she drawled, offering her hand. I was so struck by her that it took me a moment to notice the Chihuahua under her arm. "Would you like a Bloody Mary or a bullshot? Heretofore, I served only beer, but Porter brought vodka. This is Pepe." Pepe's eyes bulged as if overinflated.

It was eleven A.M., the appointed time, but everyone was drunk except Judy and Stanley. I learned that Creeley had arrived the night before and asked to meet the fellows right away. Porter herded them to the Fo'c'sle and then to his place after the bar closed. Many left, but this group had not yet gone to bed. Hester said that she and I missed it because we didn't live at the complex. Dugan downed a glass of vodka. Porter had told me that Dugan drank in the morning and through the day until, as he put it, "the curtain dropped," around eight o'clock, and all communication ended.

Hester poured a Bloody Mary for me from a silver pitcher. I couldn't come up with anything to say to her, my pulse had raced all the way there and was still pounding. Kurt waved from a white wicker armchair where he wrote on a paper plate, printing along its circumference. Hester brought me to the table, which was cluttered with glasses and lit candles. "We're having a conversation of interest to some. We're naming our five favorite sea foods." She raised her eyebrows to show it was not of interest to her.

I said hello to Ted and Gail, Jeanne and Wayne. Creeley was not wearing an eye patch. His black hair fell over his forehead like a wing. Creeley said to me, "In reverse order! You have to name your favorite sea foods *in reverse order!*" He stared at the table as he spoke, and tapped it with the heel of his fist, as if he had made a significant point.

Gail counted on her fingers, saying, "Scallops, squid, shrimp . . ." Dugan tallied her choices on his legal pad.

Judy interrupted from the kitchen. "Squid? Before shrimp? Are you crazy?"

"Well, I like squid . . ." Gail said shyly. "I never had it until last week."

"Ridiculous!" Judy said, leaving the stove. "I'll serve you some rubber bands!"

Stanley said, "At Ciro's they do it right. Sautéed lightly, they turn it out on your plate."

Gail looked at him thankfully. "We should try Ciro's," she said to Ted who closed his eyes, nodding off.

Stanley made the motion of a spoon above a dish, and said again, and with such feeling, you could see the squid being served. "They turn it out on your plate . . ."

Dugan drank from the vodka bottle at his right hand. "I'll go for smelts, cod, oysters, clams and lobster." He said it again as he wrote.

"Smelts first?" Ted said.

"No," Dugan said very deliberately. "Number one: lobster! Number two: clams!"

"Dugan," Judy yelled, "You said smelts first!"

"Okaaay," he said, pressing down on the pen, saying, "Number one: smelts!"

Creeley asked him, "How many had lobster first?"

As Dugan flipped the page, he flipped his glass over as well and everyone tried to lean out of the way, but no one moved. A puddle formed on the pad, which Dugan bent into a crease, pouring the alcohol into his glass. He took a swig of the now blue vodka and smoothed the blotted pages. Kurt stumbled over and showed him the poems on paper plates. They had written circle poems that could start anywhere in the sentence. Porter showed me Dugan's:

You do what you can do and I'll do what I can do

Dugan turned Kurt's plate in front of his eyes like a steering wheel and read:

I was giving blood to soldiers who were giving blood

"Nice work, Kurt," he said and lit a cigarette. "Hester, do you have any buttermilk?"

"No, Dugan, she doesn't," Judy answered.

Hester spun the dial on a large radio, bending close to read the numbers and soon the room filled with Souza's marching music.

"I know the DJ," she said. "He's very well-spoken." She took my hand and pressed my palm to the polished mahogany. "It was my father's," she said. "A Jackson Bell from the thirties."

"It has a warm sound," I said.

There was a break in the music, and the disc jockey read copy, inviting listeners to a benefit for the Drop-In Center. He said, "Come on, come all!"

"Shouldn't that be 'come *one*?'" I said. Hester might not have heard me, because she raced over to the pan where linguica fried.

Creeley asked Wayne what he did, and Wayne said he was a carpenter.

"You sure picked a poor place to stack sticks," Creeley said.

Jeanne tried to change the subject, and found a baseball on the floor and rolled it at Pepe, but she threw it hard and the dog yelped. She said to Kurt, "I'd like a big dog like yours."

"Why do you want a dog?" Dugan asked.

"Oh, I don't know," Jeanne said. "For protection, and a big furry thing's nice to hug on cold nights . . ." She smiled crookedly and wrapped her arms around herself.

"Isn't that why you got married?" Creeley asked, and then he began a story about his friend Bill Glover who lived in Clarksville, and his friend, Jack Clark, who lived in Gloversville.

I stood near the kitchen with Judy and Hester. Ted rose from his chair with difficulty. He cupped his hand to my ear and said, "I saw Creeley's missing eye. I saw under his eyelid when he turned toward the bay. There's a tiny black dot in there." He raised his forefinger to his thumb. "A dark marble!"

Hester was saying to Judy, "It is not the oath that makes us believe the man, but the man the oath," as she sprinkled powdered sugar over a tray of beignets.

Dugan called to Judy, "Is there any buttermilk?"

"No, Dugan. There is no buttermilk. Shut up!"

Page said to Stanley, "Have you read *What's O'Clock?*"

Stanley said, "Okay, just one more," and held out his glass.

Creeley tilted a candle, pouring hot wax into his palm. "Statues and statuettes," he said as the wax solidified and we watched the gathering tallow. Jeanne leaned toward his hand, closer and closer to the flame until it snaked up and caught her hair, spurred on by hairspray and perfume. Kurt leapt from his chair, paper plates flying, and slapped his palm against the side of Jeanne's head as she laughed drunkenly, hysterically and, when the fire was out, she was bald at the temple but not burned.

Stanley said, "You're lucky. You're very, very lucky," and his words were echoed by Kurt, Gail and Ted, who all chimed in about her good fortune.

From the kitchen, Hester said, "True love is friendship caught afire."

Creeley spoke about how much Provincetown meant to him, that he had lived here with his first wife. He motioned toward Pearl Street and said the first poem in *For Love* is dedicated to Slater Brown, a friend of Hart Crane. He said he sat in Brown's studio, now part of the Work Center, and listened to his stories about poets. Then Creeley grimaced about his marriage, working the wax and getting tearful. He sipped his Bloody Mary and composed himself.

"Did something happen to your wife, Bob?" Stanley asked. We sat in wonder, guessing illness or death.

Creeley squinted. "It was terrible," he said. "Munchies, pasta, chocolate, day and night. She gained fifty pounds."

Hester set the tray of her specialty on the table. "My mother used to say, eat what you like and let the food fight it out inside."

"Easy for a skinny malink like you," Creeley said, looking Hester over and at the same moment each of us stared, admiring her shape under the apron.

She pointed at me and said, "I need help in the kitchen."

"Look!" Creeley said. On his palm stood a horse he had sculpted out of wax. He combed its neck with a toothpick, making a mane. "Funny how it looks more real without eyes or mouth," he said, and placed it on the table.

Judy served eggs and everyone praised the beignets. Hester did not seem interested in the food. I was hungry but hungrier to be alone with the strange hostess who spoke strangely. She opened a slider onto the bay, and we stood on a small deck looking at the lighthouse on Long Point.

Judy was scolding Dugan for drinking so much.

"Why, Dugan? Why?" she said.

"Hester, is there any buttermilk?" Dugan called to the deck.

"Dugan, there is no buttermilk. Shut up!" Judy yelled.

Dugan poised a fork before his lips. The trembling mound of scrambled eggs on the silver tines seemed strangely more alive than the man holding it.

Wayne looked at Jeanne, pointed to his bullshot and said, "What is this I've been drinking?"

Creeley praised the eggs and explained that he left Cape Cod in 1946 and raised chickens in New Hampshire. He became very animated describing their mating rituals saying, "The cockerels are tempted . . ."

"You mean the cocks, Bob? Don't you mean the *cocks*?" Dugan asked.

"The *cockerel*, Alan, is what a young rooster is called, an immature bird."

~ 179 ~

Stanley had also raised chickens, and talked about losing his entire brood of leghorns to disease. "They had to be given cyanide by a county agent to make sure it didn't spread," he said. "I've written about it." He spoke as if long finished with both the chickens and the poem.

"'Not one of them was spared the cyanide,'" Porter said, quoting him.

Hester said to me, "This talk makes me sick on my stomach."

"I like your poems," I said.

"Thank you," she said. "I'm only here because of Stanley. He was my teacher at Columbia and fought for me." She tossed her wild hair to get it out of her eyes but it also had a touch of glamorous self-righteousness and I was hit full in the face with a tsunami of patchouli.

"That's nice that he supports your work," I said. A second wave of fragrance arrived as I spoke.

"Yes, it is, because unlike everyone here, I eschew the autobiographical."

"Like the others, I embrace the autobiographical," I said.

"To do so, you must first know who you are," she said.

Ted was telling Creeley about his zebra finches. "If I had a permanent address, I'd have a large cage," he said.

Gail thought for a moment and then burst into tears at the remark.

Creeley was back to Glover from Clarksville and Clark from Gloversville. He lamented a trip that Glover took to see friends in Gloversville where he got very drunk. His hosts did not look out for him and he spent the night in jail. Creeley said it was Gloversville's responsibility to take care of Glover.

Hester answered the phone, describing the brunch to a friend. "It is a spectacle to be witnessed," she said.

Stanley clapped his hands and everyone rose as best he could.

"The beignets were superb as always," Stanley said, embracing her. Stanley's balding head disappeared in her cyclone of hair.

"See you at your reading tomorrow, Bob," Stanley said.

I was about to ask Hester if I could help clean up, when Creeley began to stack the plates. She smiled at him with feeling.

We trailed out, and I overheard Hester say, "I retire early."

Dugan walked behind me on the stairs. He said, "Skoyles, what do you think about that cockerel/cock distinction Creeley made?"

Porter answered, again quoting Stanley, "They indulge their taste for chicken from behind."

Kurt slipped and had to grab the railing with both hands, sending his morning's work, several paper plates, careening down the stairs, and rolling to the beach where they blew away.

That night I listened to the *Sports Huddle* on the radio and drank a glass of milk with a piece of Portuguese bread. I nursed my pang for Hester and wrote all the words I could think of describing white. When I finished, I felt very dark. My fixation with Hester kept me from eating anything at the brunch, and I opened the bag of potatoes I'd bought at the food co-op, which was housed in the Center's coal bin. I dropped one into a pot of boiling water and was standing over it when there was a tap on my door. I lifted the long shade and saw Hester with a picnic basket, her hair like cotton candy from the fog. She noticed the steam and pushed past me, right to the stove. "What are you doing?" she asked, peering into the pot. "Boiling a potato?"

"Yes," I said.

"Why?" She seemed incredulous, and poked the water with a fork. Her white finger looked like a lily petal next to the misshapen globe.

I usually went into contortions to avoid an embarrassing truth, but there was nothing else to say when faced with the boiling potato. "Because I was hungry," I said.

"Beignets were left over, and linguica." She put the basket on the counter and looked around. "Cozy," she said, sitting and wrapping her coat around her. I turned up the thermostat.

"That was fun today," I said.

"I'm glad you enjoyed it." She sighed. "It took me a while to get rid of Creeley."

"*For Love* is one of the few books I brought," I said, nodding to the shelf above the fireplace.

"He passed out on my couch whereupon he almost crushed Pepe. When he awakened, I served coffee, but that drove him to more statues. He made a very accurate hurricane lamp."

"Are you glad to be here?" I asked. "I mean, away from New Orleans?"

"I like the north, but I'd prefer it if it were in the south," she said, going into the kitchen.

"Your potato is ready," she said.

Why those words gave me the impulse to put my arms around her I don't know. Maybe two hungers merging, maybe the pot of cloudy water stirred by her genteel hand. I kissed her by the stove, holding the back of her neck to make sure I reached the chalk face camouflaged by hair. It was like leaving a forest and entering a field, a field covered in snow.

"Let's go to my place," she said and moved toward the door.

"Why not stay here?" I said. "The heat's starting to come on." I touched the baseboard.

"Short the way," she said, "but pitiless the need to walk it." I spun around. She had spoken in Stanley's quavering lilt.

I put on my jacket and we left to the ticking pipes.

Hester's apartment smelled like pastry and hairspray. She handed Pepe to me. He was eagerly licking my hands when she poured two glasses of wine from a bottle with the label, *Laughing Bride/Weeping Wife,* and set them next to a plate of beignets. With the lights off, we could see the moon brightening the moored boats in the harbor.

"I forgot to feed him," she said, and poured kibble into a bowl. We sat on the couch and kissed again, then refilled our glasses. A few minutes later she got up and called me to her bedroom. A picture window faced the ignited harbor and Hester looked ghostly, even whiter in a black slip. I undressed and got in bed.

"I have to tell you something," she said, leaning on her elbow. "I'm demanding."

"That's okay," I said, moving closer. "Don't worry."

"You have to be gentle."

"There's nothing stronger than gentleness," I said.

"Repeat?"

"Don't worry about me," I said.

"You have to follow my instructions," she said.

I lay on my back and breathed upward as if exhaling smoke.

"Did you have sex education in school?" she asked.

"No, it was a Catholic school."

"I did, and the teacher, Miss Louise, said on the last day we should bring in our questions about sex on index cards. She read them and answered them."

"Did you bring one?"

"Yes, but I was afraid she'd recognize my handwriting, so I went to the typing room and typed it out." Hester was laughing, laughing hard, which got me laughing.

"I typed, *What is considered unnatural between a man and a woman?*"

"Uh oh. What did Miss Louise say?"

"She skipped it! She shuffled through all of them and she didn't read mine!"

"There's a finite number of combinations."

"Stanley says that man gets his greatest gain by going against what comes naturally to him."

"What are you talking about?" I said, and turned to get my arms around her.

She put her lips together in a child's imitation of a kiss. She was even prettier like that, her snub nose, her crazy hair on the pillow.

"Things that take place without effort are rarely remembered with pleasure." She sang the line in Stanley's knowing, mischievous voice as my face leaned over hers. It was creepy enough so that I asked, "Is this your idea of foreplay?"

"Be patient, doctor."

The combination of coquettish sayings and non sequiturs in Stanley's voice was keeping me off balance, and this last remark confused me entirely. She had a strange locution, but I could make even less sense out of the *patient* and *doctor* wordplay.

"I'm not a doctor," I said, imagining all the guys in Columbia's doctoral program who had gone to bed with her.

"Yes, you are," she said, yanking the sheet off and saying, "I like to lie very still." She was rigid, arms at her sides and legs closed. Her taut slim body seemed made of plaster, or clay into which god had not yet breathed life. She ordered me to massage her, to pinch her, to mouth her, all the time calling me *doctor*.

"Put your whole hand in, doctor," she said, writhing and sighing. *Doctor, doctor, doctor* . . .

When we finished, she brought a bottle of brandy into bed, and two crystal liqueur glasses.

"That was okay, wasn't it? Not too weird?" she asked.

"It was great," I said. Weird did not describe making love to Hester.

"If I'm screwy, blame my breeding," she said. "When I was a girl, my mother sent me to our doctor to teach me the facts of life. He described fucking through hand gestures like charades, he kept pushing a pencil into his closed fist very violently. It was like he molested me via finger puppetry."

"Everyone learns those things in odd ways."

"Do you think so? What about you?"

"By watching dogs mount a bitch in turn."

"Don't quote Yesenin's worst line," she said in Stanley's tremor. "Tell me the truth."

"My father used to kneel by my bed and read from a book called, *Listen, Son*, which he kept in his sock drawer."

She turned very earnest and said, "Our doctor told me that many men would want to have anal sex, but I should never do it. He was insistent. Of course, that made me wonder." We had another brandy and she put the bottle in the hutch. She went to the bathroom and came out with a jar of Pond's cold cream flat on her palm.

"I'm all set," she said. "You just have to do yourself."

She lay face down on the bed and I pushed into her. She turned her head, and said, "You're in my asshole, doctor," and closed her eyes.

Afterward we took a shower together. "I think sex is a sad thought danced, don't you?" she said, soaping herself.

"I don't know," I said. "I never thought about it that way."

"Stanley thinks like that. That's why he's so great. A really great poet."

"Yes, he is," I said.

She got into bed and leaned against the headboard.

"If only he weren't so old, but even so, he's with Elise," she said.

"He's over seventy," I said.

"You know what he told me once," she said. "After a few? He said, 'Just because the head of the leek is white doesn't mean the tail isn't green.'"

"He is a great poet," I said.

"I retire early," she said. "You can stay if you like, but I've got to get some sleep. It's my turn to work the food co-op tomorrow." She lifted a brush from the nightstand and dragged it through her hair, which filled the room with a boisterous fragrance.

She slid under the covers and in a few minutes breathed deeply. I looked out the window and at the odd woman next to me. As I was daydreaming, Hester got up and drew the heavy opaque drapes, so the room went black.

"The moonlight was erasing my dreams," she said, collapsing into bed and falling asleep.

My stomach rumbled. I went to the table and ate a beignet. Powder drifted along the front of my chest and glittered in the moonlight. Hester called from the bedroom. I said I wanted to look out the window for a moment and stuffed an entire donut in my mouth and drank some Laughing Bride before returning. When Hester drifted off once more, I raided the plate again, this time bringing two beignets to bed. The two I chose were hard and I tore them into pieces. Hester rolled over, facing me, eyes shut. I leaned off the side of the bed and felt Pepe at my fingers trying for one of the beignets. I broke off an inch. He took it and raced, nails clicking, to his round cushion. The sound of his little crunching teeth made me laugh, and I wanted to hear it again. I flung a crust. The room, silent except for the foghorns, came to life with the sounds of Pepe's scrambling claws, sniffing in the dark, and then the happy victory of his minute mouthfuls. I tossed another piece, and another. The sniffing followed by the chewing turned me into a chuckling fool. I was happy, thrilled to be in a bed by the bay with a pretty woman, a strange one, yes, but a fellow poet and protégé of a famous poet, casting pieces of Louisiana pastry into the air, and sharing them with a mouse-like dog.

Hester was gone when I woke up. A note on the kitchen table said she was at the food co-op and asked that I take Pepe for a walk. A PS read, "Please keep our little tryst to yourself. Don't be a *rat*!" Her script was wild and thick and signed, "Your precious pup." She had made French toast, wrapped a few slices in plastic and left them next to a bowl of berries and carafe of chicory coffee. Sun illuminated the weirs, fishing traps made of long poles. Gulls flew past the second-floor window, giving the apartment a celestial feel, as if we were living among clouds in an afterlife. The phone rang and I answered, sure it was Hester, but getting a surprised Porter. I told him she was at the food co-op, but I felt guilty about exposing our affair. I didn't want to be a rat. In the shower, I faced the spray and looked at a bottle hanging from the wire rack. The label said RAT! I lifted it and saw I was reading it through the transparent back and it was a TAR shampoo. I dried off in front of the picture window visible only to seabirds.

I carried Pepe to the lawn of the Flagship. We had bonded over beignets, and a few minutes later we shared French toast. Hester's place was filled with poetry, many books signed with the date and the place, New York, from her Columbia days. A framed photograph of Paul Prud-homme with other hefty Louisiana chefs leaned next to her high school yearbook, *Absinthe,* which I opened. She looked the same, but under her portrait, partially cov-ered by her swaggering hair, the editors had captioned: "Her heart is buried in the Swiss glaciers . . ." They had the color right, glacial white, but her heart did not seem buried to me. I hoped that her odd way of speaking, espe-cially in Stanley's rhythm, was the effect of his powerful presence, something unrelated to emotion.

When I got to the co-op, Hester was instructing Stavrula how to choose the best mushrooms. "They should look like they can bounce!" she said. It was the first time I had encountered Stavrula. She had avoided me, wanting to forget our Iowa past. Hester continued packing mushrooms into bags, quickly weighing and marking them as Stavrula stared in admiration. They conspired and giggled, laughed and whispered. They were like a couple from a foreign country who did not expect to be understood by others.

Hester said, "Are you here to replace your potato?"

"I still have it," I said.

"Want to help?"

I scooped coconut granola from an aluminum garbage can into one-pound bags. At three, when the co-op closed, I stood around waiting and not waiting for Hester, but when she saw my indecision, she walked over and said, "Last night was nice, but I'm having dinner with Zoe." She nodded toward Stavrula who counted the money.

"Her name's Stavrula," I said.

"No longer," Hester said. "She's starting anew."

"This is a local neurosis," I said. She said she would call me. When I walked away I remembered I didn't have a phone.

Chapter Twenty

POST-ELLIOT TAKES PHOTOS—
BLACK MIRRORS—A STOPPED WATCH—
AN ANAL HISTORY OF PROVINCETOWN—
MONT BLANC—CRAZY COWBELL—
CREELEY GOES TO JAIL—MY GIRL

I knocked on Hester's door before Creeley's reading. I could hear music and talking and I wished I hadn't come, but it was too late to turn around—I'd be caught on the stairs. The door opened slowly, just barely, and Hester peeked through the crack. All I could see was white, her white face above a white dress, but more, white shoes. A nurse's uniform.

"I have company," she said.

"Another time," I said and ran down without touching the railing.

Kurt barely managed his short introduction, listing left and right, squinting at his index card. After a day of Haffenreffer Private Stock and Old Mister Boston, he was not often seen at night. Creeley graciously thanked his host and told stories and reminisced. He exaggerated the sounds of some poems, reading the ending line:

Oh love, where are you leading me now?

and then reading it again:

Oh love, where are you leading me-now, men-ow,
meow!

Hester never showed up.

Jeanne had taken the job of manager of the Bull Ring because it came with a large apartment, and she threw the party for Creeley. Porter had hired Post-Elliot to take pictures for next year's brochure, and he blinded everyone with flashbulbs. Wayne invited us to his room to see his artwork: Jockey shorts dabbed with flaking dayglow orange paint hung from the tips of fishing rods. A joint dangling from his mouth, Wayne waved one of the poles very somberly, saying, "We do not surrender, but want peace." Jeanne stood in the doorway next to Creeley and shook her head. Hankard said, "I find that people who talk with cigarettes in their mouths are seldom modest." Hankard's cheeks remained dark no matter how often he shaved, and he shaved often, making a study of it. We all knew he used straight razors, preferred badger brushes to boar and loved bay rum. He poked his chin in Jeanne's direction, beckoning her to touch his cheek, and when she pronounced it smooth, he grinned and stroked it himself.

Creeley circled a bottle of tequila on the dining room table like a wrestler trying to get a good angle on his opponent. Then he swooped, grabbed it, took a big slug, and backed away again as if it might retaliate. He did this several times before wiping the sweat from his forehead with a red bandana. I wondered what happened to Hester and I turned to the door at any sound from that direction. And I wondered why she had been dressed as a nurse. I tried to talk with Kurt who sipped from a bottle of gin he kept in his overcoat. I asked him about the piece Creeley read on the sculptor Marisol, but his body had drifted into a mushy plane, and he did not slur his words as much as words slurred his tongue. His eyes rolled toward the ceiling and he gently chopped the air with the side of his hand, swallowing and stuttering until he gave up trying to talk, shook his head, put his arm around my shoulder and smiled.

Page laid a broomstick on the table so that its bristles hung over the edge. Then he raised his boot high, trying to flip it and catch it in the air, but he kept missing and the broomstick crashed to the floor again and again. The poets marked by death, Stephen and Barry, brought a case of their home brew. Jeanne and I sipped the vinegary beer, but when we put the bottles down, foam rose in continuous volcano-like spurts, flowing onto the table and floor. Stephen and Barry said in unison, "Too much yeast!" and clanged their bottles together in a toast to their failure. Post-Elliot caught the moment.

Jeanne invited seventy-year-old Spooner, a Southern woman who lived in the Bull Ring. No matter the weather, she walked the beach in a bathing suit. She had beautiful legs, which had caught my attention one day as I sat at my table with the blind half drawn over my picture window. I saw the legs go by and raised the shade to find my gray-haired neighbor. This evening she showed off those legs in a short skirt.

"Creeley, Creeley," she called, and the poet came politely toward her.

"What's your favorite spa?" she drawled, sipping a cup of tea.

Creeley scowled at the floor and then grinned, "I haven't been to many, but I did go to Baden-Baden years ago."

"I mean baseball, football, golf?"

"Oh, *sport!*" Creeley said.

"How did Baden-Baden get its name?" Porter asked.

Kurt seemed to know the Baden-Baden answer but fell forward trying to cough it out.

"Kurt, Kurt," Jeanne said softly, steadying him.

"Is his name Kurt-Kurt?" Spooner asked, as if uncovering a key to the conversation.

Post-Elliot bragged about capturing Kurt in his nonverbal state, and Porter reminded him to take photos without drinks, dope or drunken behavior. Stephen and Barry were in Wayne's room painting nautical images on the frames of mirrors they planned to sell to summer tourists. Hankard, the only sober one, walked with his hands folded behind his back, saying nothing.

Page yelled, "Did you see that?" He had caught the broomstick.

Everyone missed it, but Post-Elliot got it perfectly.

Jeanne and I talked about the books on her shelf: Kenneth Patchen, William Carlos Williams and Louis Zukofsky. She had come to P'town straight from managing a restaurant in New Jersey, and her tastes were not academic. She asked me if I would like to have dinner sometime, that she would make spaghetti carbonara. Jeanne was level and steady, unlike Hester. And plain, unlike Hester. She wore denim jackets and white blouses with multi-colored hand-stitched beads across the chest. She was usually in a cotton dress with a paisley pattern. At our first meeting, Hankard had asked her where she got the chicken-chasing skirt. She ran every aspect of the Bull Ring, taking reservations, doing the laundry and she was still able to write poems. I couldn't link her to Wayne, who seemed totally disoriented. We sat on the bed, looking at a catalogue of drawings by Patchen, when we heard a ruckus in the bathroom. Kurt had passed out on the toilet, thwarting Page's desperate need to relieve himself of home brew. Porter and I maneuvered Kurt against the sink and pulled up his pants.

"There's no beer left and the liquor stores are closed," Jeanne said. I escorted Kurt to the couch as Porter dialed the local cab company.

"Have one of your drivers drop off a case of beer at the Bull Ring," he said, adding, "and a couple of pizzas." He explained that the cab company kept a supply of booze and pizzas for after hours.

Jeanne put on disco music and Creeley danced with Spooner to "Love Train." Spooner was now saying everyone's name twice and leaping on the grass rug. Jeanne stood at the edge of Wayne's room where the poets marked by death had a new idea for the mirrors. She motioned me over. Wayne's dope-sick stare beamed at their plan to make the mirrors unique. They would paint the glass black. Barry had been reading Fernando Pessoa who said that god gave us the gift of not being able to see our faces. He looked up from the mirror in his lap, which he tortured with a brush, and said, "The inventor of the mirror poisoned the human heart," and his friends nodded at this truth.

"I don't have enough black," Wayne lamented, checking his tubes.

"You can paint them any color, can't you?" Jeanne said. "As long as it's opaque."

Wayne leaned forward in his squeaky chair and said, "I love you." His earnest eyes extended to everything and everything he saw shook with significance. The poets marked by death got hungry and left for the kitchen. I inspected the smudged mirrors and Wayne said, "Not being able to see yourself. Think about it. It's a gift." He asked if I wanted to get in on it, but I joined the crowd, leaving Wayne holding a painted mirror, looking deeply into his nonreflection.

When the boom box blasted "Bennie and the Jets," Wayne hopped from his room, playing the guitar and accompanying himself with percussive sounds made by jumping on boards he had strapped to his feet. Springs nailed to these platforms lofted him into the air. The boing-boing of his bouncing almost kept time with his strumming. When the song ended, Creeley asked Porter to take him into town, and he left to wait in the parking lot. Porter was worried about Kurt, whose face had widened, thickened and fallen. He couldn't move his mouth, much less his legs. Porter and I thanked Jeanne and walked Kurt down the stairs. Creeley held out his hand to Kurt, introducing himself to the man who had introduced him but who now was unrecognizable.

"This is Kurt?" Creeley said, astonished.

"Yes, it is. We'll get you home, my friend," Porter said. Post-Elliot's flashbulb ignited the asphalt.

When the cab arrived, the poets marked by death retrieved the pizzas and beer. Porter paid the driver and asked him to take Kurt to Cottage Street. We pushed him into the backseat, where he smiled straight ahead, and I wondered how he would make it up the path to his house, over those giant zucchinis and vines hard to navigate even in sober light. I stared at Kurt through the cab window. He did not look like a man, but like something I'd seen before, something strange I'd seen recently, right here in Provincetown. And then I got it. He had become one of his wife's papier-mâché sculptures, the last dog to shit on her lawn.

The three of us started downtown, but Post-Elliot called me from the deck and I asked Porter and Creeley to wait. When I got to the top of the stairs, Post-Elliot had a crazed face.

"See my watch?" he said, holding out his wrist.

I examined the dial.

"What time does it say?"

"Nine twenty," I said.

"That's right," he said. "And what time is it now?

"Twelve thirty."

"See what I mean? My watch stopped when Creeley walked in!"

"Come on," I said.

"The exact second!"

"I have to go," I said.

"It started again when he left."

"It's a coincidence," I said.

"It could get worse!" he called after me. "It could get worse! Next time it could be my heart!"

At the window table in the Fo'c'sle, Creeley talked non-stop. When he went to the bar, I told Porter that he must have taken speed. He returned with six bourbons, two of which he downed immediately. He began to clap his hands together as hard as he could. They sounded like gunshots, but in the Fo'c'sle, no one noticed.

"I have to start some action," he said. "I was in Toronto a few months ago, they took me to a really dull place, no one talking, no one dancing. I wouldn't stop clapping. I had blood blisters on my hands." His one eye was wild and happy at the thought and he held out his palms.

Vince rumbled over. Porter made the introductions and Vince said, "You know what I'm working on now? *An Anal History of Provincetown*. About all the assholes I've met!" His big laugh showed his brown and gold teeth. "Corso is the opening chapter."

"Is Gregory in town?" Creeley asked

"Getting fucked fore and aft!" Vince said.

"I'd like to see him!" Creeley seemed almost sober at the prospect.

The rich scent of coconut announced the arrival of Jay Hankard. The emollient he had run through his hair gleamed even in shadow, the result of brushing his fragrant mane for hours while sitting on a sawhorse in the Center's parking lot. Standing by our table, he seemed both totally out of place and perfectly at ease. Porter invited him to sit and Creeley placed one of his drinks before him, nodding. Vince lit a pipe and chocolate-flavored tobacco merged with Hankard's perfume.

"Corso's made a nest for himself at the Old Colony," Vince said. "Right now he's at a table wrapped in a blanket."

"Let's finish these drinks and go!" Creeley said. "Go!"

Hankard slid Creeley's offering back to him and left to get a beer. He jumped when the football-loving barfly sang at the top of his lungs, "Miami Dolphins! Miami Dolphins!" as the jingle came on the jukebox. He was trying to drown out a loud fisherman who was yelling at the captain of a dragger that he served lousy food to his crew.

The men at the bar were at war and at peace at the same time, just as we were living in a summer place in winter. Conflicts, internal and external, abounded. When Hankard returned to the table, he took out a black pen with gold trim the size of a cucumber. All eyes turned to it. "It's a Mont Blanc," he said. He didn't pronounce the two syllables as much as snort them in French so they sounded like two honks from a goose. He started to write in a moleskin notebook with ink he called "Ebony Green." The whole production annoyed Creeley who said Joseph Cornell made great art out of bric-a-brac from thrift shops and Ginsberg wrote poems at his kitchen table.

Hankard handed me the pen and notebook. I wrote my name in the most beautiful letters that ever flowed from my fingertips.

"Some writers care about their writing utensils," Hankard said. "What do you care about, Creeley?"

"I care about the freedom to be absolutely who I am at any given moment. I thank the sun for that every morning when I open my eye."

We stood, leaving Hankard with Vince, but Vince left him with the words, "Did you just say *cosmologically speaking*?" and moved to the bar. Porter told Creeley that the Old Colony was a short walk, and part of a bad restaurant called The Sea Pool, nicknamed The Cesspool.

The OC's rafters hung with the name of local businesses, many of them defunct, and many unreadable from years of smoke, dust and grease. Duarte Motors. The *Provincetown Advocate*. Days Propane. At a corner table, Corso sat wrapped to the nose in a brown blanket, looking more like a tepee than a man. A young blonde talked to him earnestly.

"Gregory!" Creeley called, a thunderclap booming from his hands.

Corso tossed his blanket and embraced his friend. We sat at the table and Porter went for drinks. Corso introduced us to the blonde, saying, "I just gave her an Indian name, *Angel with Jet Lag*."

"What's your Indian name?" I asked.

"*Crazy Cowbell*."

Creeley and Corso had a lot to catch up on, so Porter and I went to the Back Room, a dance floor with a swimming pool on the bay. It was two-for-one night, the whole place reeling. Loud music made conversation impossible, but keeping to yourself amid the rollicking atmosphere was a certain pleasure. An hour later, Corso entered in a gold lamé gown. Creeley wore the blanket and headed straight for the bar where he pretended not to speak English, and made gestures until the bartender served tequila. When Creeley approached our table, Porter advised not matching him drink for drink. Corso joined us, and despite Porter's wisdom, we continued amid the voices of Barry White and Gloria Gaynor. Creeley suddenly pounced onto the floor, his dancing a kind of running in place. Corso snatched a bag of chips from the adjoining table that held a dozen empties. The two women didn't seem to mind, which Corso took as a sign to slide his chair over and sip their bottles of Bud. Despite the deafening music, which blared through the air without a halt, I could hear Corso screaming at them, "There are more things in heaven and earth than are dreamt of in your philosophy!" The women remained calm but after a few more pronouncements from Gregory, the larger of the women stood, and with one great motion, gathered all the bottles into the crook of her arm and swiped them into Corso's lap. Creeley's dancing had devolved into jumping jacks, which he stopped only to pilfer drinks from surrounding tables. When the bouncer grabbed him by the collar, he pretended not to speak English again and we left followed by Corso who couldn't stop laughing. We were heading for Porter's when Creeley threw himself across the hood of a patrol car, pounding it with both hands. He was cuffed and taken away. Corso vanished. Porter and I sat on the benches in front of town hall with cups of coffee until I left him at two A.M. The streets thickened with a fog so dense that pedestrians banged into each other. As I neared the Bull Ring, I heard music. On the corner I recognized the song, and in the parking lot I recognized the singer. Wayne perched on the top deck, strumming his guitar and hitting a bass drum with a foot pedal. He sang into a microphone, which had a kazoo taped to it. *Here comes the sun, Toot-Ta-Toot-Toot. Here comes the sun. Toot-Ta-Toot-Toot. It's all right. . . . .* I waved and he nodded as best he could. I fell onto my couch, drifting asleep to Wayne's one-man band, and I promised myself to start writing the next day.

The next day I was too dehydrated to do anything but walk to the A&P for a can of soup. I met Kurt in the juice aisle where he had regained his human shape. He held a piece of tailpipe in one hand and a can of V8 in the other, hoping to find the right circumference to patch his exhaust system. I called Hester from the pay phone in the vegetable section.

"You missed a good time last night," I said.

"How was the reading?" she asked. "I was erstwhile occupied."

"Great," I said. "And so was the party."

"What can I do for you, John?"

I said I just wanted to tell her about the reading and we said good-bye. Over the next weeks, I saw Hester walking into Dave's Clockhead, a gay bar with a wall of cuckoo clocks; knocking on Zoe's door at the Work Center; strolling with Synchro, the owner of Café Blase, and sometimes with his business partner, Arnie, and sometimes arm in arm with both. A car passed me, and a man with a condom over his head poked it out the passenger side window. Hester was driving. I saw her with the transvestite Musty Chiffon and the puppeteer Wayland Flowers.

She was not going to be my girl.

Stanley was leaving for New York in mid-November, and Porter advised me to make an appointment with him. He had told me Stanley's life story, his father killing himself when his mother was pregnant with him, that he graduated summa cum laude from Harvard but was denied the teaching post automatically granted to those with that honor because he was Jewish. I sorted through my best poems from a year ago and in doing so realized that Stanley's presence, his faith in all of us, had intimidated me into editing myself before I even began to write. As Post-Elliot had become an author of titles alone, I was a one-line wonder. I saw myself years later, next to him on a bar stool, our collected works amounting to a few inches of text.

CHAPTER TWENTY-ONE

NOT MANY BUT MUCH—PO-BIZ IN
THE GARDEN—THE ART SPIRIT—
PIPE STEMS—NEW FRIENDS

I'd been circumnavigating The Fo'c'sle's beckoning beer
mugs and rocks glasses by cutting over to Bradford
Street until I was beyond it, then walking back to Commercial, making a circuitous box of a path. I went that
way to see Stanley, who lived near land's end. I opened
the metal gate to tiers of flowers and herbs that curled
over the timber edging their beds. Oriental cherry trees
and weeping birches added privacy. Bluestone squares led
to a porch where, to my surprise, Stanley sat with a large
man in suspenders and a straw fedora. Chet Cunningham
directed the Poetry Society of America and, when I shook
his hand, he nodded to the rolled-up poems I carried and
asked if I had come to see the oracle. Stanley explained I
was a fellow. I took a seat next to them, our three chairs
facing the garden. Stanley looked at me over those enormous bags under his eyes and said, "We're talking po-biz,"
and chuckled.

"Make all the connections you can while you're here," Cunningham said.

Stanley seemed embarrassed. "I don't know about that," he said.

"Sure!" Cunningham said. "Visiting poets tell editors who they met. Stanley, I wouldn't mind giving a reading and spending a few days in P'town."

"I think Porter already has the list," Stanley said, "but we'll see."

"If someone cancels, I'm here!" he said, poking his palm with his index finger. "Tell Porter. He's in charge, right?"

"That's right," Stanley said in his singsong way.

"Where have you published?" Cunningham asked.

"Not many places," I said. "A few quarterlies."

"Keep sending your stuff out," he said. "Reputations are made by quantity."

"The Italians have a saying, *Not many but much.* I think that's a better way," Stanley said.

"Why not both?" Cunningham said. "Swing for the fences! By the way, Stanley, did you see that the governor asked Rod McKuen to that group he invited to Albany? There are a hundred better poets. *I* would have gone!"

Stanley's wince was not enough to stop Cunningham.

"Don't you think I'm right Stanley, it's a disgrace?"

"He's no worse than many who were invited," Stanley said.

"I know you don't mean that, Stanley," Cunningham said. "You just can't mean that."

"Let me show you the garden," Stanley said.

"Love it," Cunningham said.

We followed Stanley as he passed each specimen, concerned over some, joyful at others, like the Montauk daisies. We reached a stretch of herbs. Cunningham took me aside and asked me to tell Porter he'd like to be a visiting poet, as he felt Stanley might forget. Stanley bent down, tore off a few green curly leaves, and brought the cluster close to Cunningham's face. "What's this?" Stanley asked.

"I don't know," Cunningham said.

"Catmint," Stanley said. We took a few more steps, and Stanley pinched another clump. "And this?" He pushed it under the big man's nose.

"Not sure, Stanley."

"Thyme."

"I don't know herbs, Stanley," Cunningham said.

"Um hmm," Stanley said, bending again and repeating the same gesture.

Cunningham didn't answer.

"Calendula," Stanley said. He did the same with comfrey and wormwood. Cunningham put his hands in his pockets and said, "I should be going." Stanley poked another sprig at him. This time, he didn't wait for an answer. He looked Cunningham in the eye and said, "Chive."

Stanley turned, and Cunningham touched his shoulder to get his attention, saying loudly that he was leaving, but Stanley kept walking and raised the back of his hand in farewell.

"Good to meet you," he said to me, and left.

Stanley pointed out a darkened basement window next to a rank pile of compost. I looked into his study—a desk and chair, two bookcases. The room was smaller than mine at the Bull Ring. We entered the house from the back, walking through the kitchen to a round coffee table near the porch.

"Isn't he awful?" Stanley said, shrugging and laughing. "He's making a mess of the poetry society, everyone's quitting. He wanted my advice."

I told Stanley how much I liked his last book, particularly, "An Old Cracked Tune." He said that when he was a boy, he was taunted in his neighborhood with the anti-Semitic jingle, "My name is Solomon Levi! My name is Solomon Levi!" He made a poem of the ridicule:

AN OLD CRACKED TUNE

My name is Solomon Levi,
the desert is my home,
my mother's breast was thorny,
and father I had none.

The sands whispered, *Be separate,*
the stones taught me, *Be hard.*
I dance, for the joy of surviving,
on the edge of the road.

Stanley put on his glasses and read my poems while
I browsed through stacks of new books. The mailman
placed packages in the basket on the door, but Stanley
did not break his concentration. When he finished reading,
he spread them across the table, saying I should work on
texture, and to pay attention to my endings, which he said
"came thudding to a close." I agreed with the texture. Flat
language was a weakness. But the endings! I worked so
hard on my endings! Stanley said the poems were just getting interesting when they circled back to the first lines.
Worst of all, I was not realizing my whole self and soul.

"In these poems, you're only halfway down the well,"
he said. "You must rake the bottom slime." I couldn't resist
quoting the edict that drove my lines across the page like
battalions on a forced march. "What about Yeats saying
that a poem should close with a click like the lid on a box?"

"The ending should be a door and a window," he said.
"It should close, but you should be able to look through it."

I followed him into the kitchen where he made martinis. We took our glasses to the porch. Stanley's neighbor, Jack Tworkov, entered the garden. He sat with us and
praised the flowers, asking Stanley how he found the time.
Stanley said he did a lot of his work there, it was medita-
tive, and he didn't like to be interrupted. He said Rothko

never forgave him for not inviting him in when he passed by, but Stanley considered the garden his real study.

Jack said he had just wiped away most of a big painting he had worked on for weeks. He crushed his bald head with the palms of his hands, but his gesture of angst had more than a bit of hope in it. He was eager to get back to the studio. Stanley said I had just shown him some poems. Jack said he gave a crit to a fellow but it went badly. He wondered if he had been too harsh.

"When you point out someone's flaws," Stanley said, "they sometimes resent you for it. But when a mirror reflects our ugliness, we call it a good mirror." He peeked over at me, chuckling.

"How's your fellowship going?" Jack asked.

I went into a long monologue mentioning my sliding typewriter, the Bull Ring's noise, the temptations of the bars and female fellows, my doubting my ability, my writing only first lines—in general, the answer of an idiot.

Jack said, "You can draw a dream with a number two pencil if you're open to the dream." Stanley walked him to the gate then hopped to his study, returning with an old paperback of Robert Henri's *The Art Spirit* that he said I could keep.

"You'll see why," he said.

In my motel room, I opened Henri's book to the sentence, "A man must be master of himself and master of his word to achieve the full realization of himself as an artist." Stanley had written about perishing into work and, at our first meeting, Dugan pointed out that we were at the Fine Arts *Work* Center. He lent me Rilke's book on Rodin, whose first sentence read, "Rodin was solitary before he became famous, and he was more solitary after he became famous, for what is fame, but the accumulation of misunderstandings that surrounds a name." I had brought Pavese's *Lavorare Stanca*, or *Hard Labor* with me, but Pavese meant the labor of everyday life. Here I was free of that, and yet everywhere I turned I saw work I wasn't doing. The *New Yorker* took a poem by Ted Page and we were all thrilled. At Iowa, the news would have sent students and teachers running with their heads in their hands. Stanley said, "Live in the layers/not on the litter," and poetry business, gossip and envy were all consigned to the litter. That there were larger issues than craft had escaped me, issues that could be addressed in a dank study near a compost heap, or with a humble nub of lead.

Jeanne invited me to dinner, for the promised carbonara. I walked across the parking lot with a bottle of wine and we talked about life in the Bull Ring. Spooner had been taken to the hospital for breaking one of her beautiful ankles at a polka lesson. Jeanne asked if the noisy weekend visitors bothered me and I said no, but the truth was that on Saturdays and Sundays I heard the sounds of hetero sex on one side, gay sex on the other, and most mornings, the artist Jackson Lambert above me purging the previous night's binge. I saw the table set for two and asked about Wayne. They had separated. She thought he had crossed from eccentricity into madness. She went in the other room and returned with a cigar box containing hundreds of tiny white twigs.

"They're clay-pipe stems. Wayne's obsession. He finds them on the beach. From early Dutch settlers."

"That seems harmless enough," I said.

"He has about twenty boxes like this," she said, and sighed. "He combs the flats at every low tide."

Jeanne's managerial duties took a lot of time, particularly on weekends when she checked in guests. I helped her by painting rooms and sanding and staining railings. She wrote from six until nine every morning, and whenever I spent the night there, I left at dawn after a cup of coffee. In the evenings we compared what we had done.

Jeanne's job put her in touch with the town. One night in her study I asked about the tall Infant of Prague statue wearing his many slips and ornate gown. She said it was a gift from the owner of the Glorified Grocer who told her that if she kept a penny under it, she'd never go broke. I admired the friends and acquaintances she'd made in such a short time. I told her about my first weeks, spent unwisely but with an accomplished writer like Vince.

"Have you read Vince's books?" she asked.

"No, I've been meaning to."

She went to her shelf. "He's a friend of Wayne," she said, handing me *The Complete Guide to Wood Finishes; How to Turn an Orange Crate into an End Table* and *Tips from a Flea Market Maven.*

"That's not what I expected," I said.

She walked over to the infant, lifted his dress, and said, "I just realized maybe I'll never go broke because I'll always have the penny."

I read Stanley's suggestions—Hopkins, Pasternak, Akhmatova, and unknowns like Hyam Plutzik. From Dugan, I got Oppen and Cavafy. I sent my new poems to Ridge and he said I had forgotten the importance of craft. His being a finalist for the National Book Award made his criticism sting even more. I applied for a second year, wondering what outside judges would think.

The painter Janet Fish gave a slide show of her elaborately colored water glasses set on mirrors, work that had made her reputation. Then she showed paintings of packaged apples, tomatoes and oranges, complete with green corrugation and plastic wrap. She said her gallery disapproved of this new take on the still life, formerly favorable critics panned her, and she even lost friends. But she said she found another gallery, different critics, new friends.

CHAPTER TWENTY-TWO

NEAR THE HOPPER HOUSE—STALIN'S SPERM—
PAJAMAS—THE WORK—ASK ME IF I'M
A DOCTOR—THREE IDS—
TIME TO LEAVE

✑

In March, Porter asked me to accompany him to pick up Stanley at the airport. The writing committee was convening to choose the fellows for the coming year. We had dinner at the Mayflower. Stanley mentioned a favorite applicant from Columbia, a former student like Hester, who was about to have a great breakthrough. He said he found one manuscript that had a passion like a "burning wheel." When we asked what he meant, he said, "They're angry poems, and angry poets are best."

"What's his name?" I asked.

"Let's see," Stanley said, taking out a notebook. "Number seventy-three. Barkhausen." Stanley's blessing of Barkhausen made me wonder if I had him wrong. I wished I had kept copies of *La Huerta*. Barkhausen wasn't on Porter's list. I was pulling for Artie, always interesting to be around, to get another look at his work.

Page and I were chosen for the second year. Hankard did not want to return and sneered whenever we were in the same room. I spent most nights with Jeanne and we rued the coming of May, when my stay ended. I would have no choice but to return to Queens. We weren't ready to move in together, so I was happy to get a call on the Bull Ring's pay phone from a local writer I had seen at openings and readings. I didn't recognize the name, but when Jeanne handed me the receiver, I recognized the voice of Phyllis Sherwood by her heavy lisp. She was a sixty-year-old writer who needed an assistant for the summer to help her with a new project. She had a spare room in her Truro house for the right person, and invited me to dinner to discuss it. Phyllis had recently discovered she was part Iroquois and had given a talk about it at the Wellfleet library. Posters showed her in full Native American dress, a white leather blouse and skirt, beads and a headband. Her gray hair was done in a pageboy, popular in the fifties, and revived in the sixties by English rock groups, putting Phyllis twice behind the times.

I took the bus and she met me at the grocery store and post office that comprised downtown Truro, eight miles from P'town. Her place was near Edward Hopper's and overlooked the bay. She told me the other guests would be Arturo Vivante, the Italian fiction writer who was a member of the writing committee; his wife, Nancy, and J. D. Harrell, the translator of Lorca whose work she knew I admired. I also admired Arturo, a big, gentle man with a large soul who seemed to walk through life as through a dream, wistfully gazing at the beauty around him, especially when that beauty took the form of women. He had published nearly a hundred stories in the *New Yorker* and was well outside the Wellfleet circle of psychiatrists and remittance men who on weekends traded their expensive suits for frayed shirts and drawstring pants. Stanley called them cases of arrested development. Porter called them upper crustaceans. Dugan called them the white wine swillers.

I had to duck under the doorframe to enter the antique house, which opened into a kitchen with a cast-iron gas stove surrounded by heavy oak hutches. Phyllis showed me the view of rolling hills of bayberry and bearberry and her path to the beach. I stared at the landscape and at the house where Hopper had painted, but my reverie was broken by Phyllis, who spun through the kitchen and started toward a flight of stairs, unbuttoning her blouse and saying over her shoulder, "I'm getting changed. If they arrive, fix them a drink!" As I looked at the bottles of gin, Scotch, and vodka, I felt transformed into an intimate or a houseboy, I couldn't tell which. I called for a jigger. She yelled from the landing that I would have to estimate. I had failed my first test for the summer position, and walked around the dining room's wall-to-wall bookshelves. I found her novels and her recent book of nonfiction, *The Heirs of Stalin*, which contained clippings of rave reviews from the *New York Times* and the *New York Review of Books*. She had tracked the lives of the dictator's children. I could hear water running upstairs and her stepping across the floorboards. A few minutes later, she descended the stairs exuding Shalimar, my mother's scent. She removed a large pot from the oven, stirred it and asked me to take the pie off the stove. I stood above the burners, facing a deep dish of berries, and said, "What pie?"

"The pie!" she said, pointing.

"That's a pie?" I said.

Arturo and his wife arrived. Nancy wore a pageboy like Phyllis's. Arturo's hair flew in many directions.

"You need a haircut, Arturo," Phyllis said, kissing him.

"I told him to get a haircut or get a cello," Nancy said, looking over the booze.

Harrell, thin as a string of bones, shook my hand but focused on the rug. I made martinis and poured wine while

Phyllis sat with her guests and criticized Princess Nina Georgievna's house in Wellfleet. She asked me for the bowl of peanuts on the counter. I joined them with a Scotch, and tried to draw Harrell into a conversation about Lorca, but he put me off. After drinks, Phyllis served kale soup with bread and salad. Harrell hardly touched his food and I hardly spoke, having nothing to add to the discussion of pond algae and the architecture of the new police station. I followed Phyllis's orders and asked everyone to go back to the living room while I cleared the table and she brought pie and coffee to the guests who seemed accustomed to frugal dinners.

Harrell left, and Arturo told me in his soft voice that Harrell and Phyllis had just ended an affair, and he was jealous of me. Arturo, looking for an excuse to get to Provincetown, asked if I would like a ride. I didn't want to impose on him so I said I didn't need a ride. His eyes widened. He thought I was spending the night with Phyllis, and I wondered if he was right.

When we were alone, Phyllis escorted me to an armchair by the fire. My houseboy role had ended and I again became a guest. She tossed the newspaper and *The Heirs of Stalin* on a brocade-covered footstool and went to do the few dishes.

I leafed through her book again. "The title's from Yevtushenko," she said, arriving with two glasses of brandy.

"I know," I said. "The translation I have says, *Stalin's Sperm.*"

"Well, I couldn't call it that, could I?" she said, and shifted in her chair. She placed her feet on the stool, and her dress ran up her legs.

"You read a lot of poetry?" she asked.

"That's almost all I read," I said.

"Do you know Leger Leger?"

I said I didn't.

"Oh, that's right, only his friends call him that. You probably know him as Saint John Perse. He used to visit here. He wrote wonderful poems, but some awful lines. I recall 'the vulva smell of low waters,' about Blackfish Creek." She closed her eyes while she spoke, opening them at the end of each monologue. It was like watching a canoe that had capsized, and I wondered if it would ever right itself again.

She poured more brandy, and nodded to the door behind me. "That would be your room," she said. "Take a look." I opened the door onto a single bed, dresser and rolltop desk. The white wooden floor had been stippled with red and orange paint.

"My new book's a memoir about my first marriage to a satyr," she said. "But it involves all the people we knew in the sixties who have now became famous. I need fact-checking, that kind of thing." The shutting and opening of her eyes added tension to our conversation.

"I'm sure I could do that," I said.

"Too bad we didn't have any time today to see if you liked the work."

"I think I understand. Editorial and research."

"That's right, but more. Like helping with dinner and driving me around." A breeze kept opening and nudging shut the bedroom door.

"I wish you had brought your pajamas," she said. "Then tomorrow you could see if you liked the work."

"I didn't expect to stay," I said.

"But you can. And tomorrow you can get an idea of what I do."

"But even if I liked the work, I'm not sure this would be the right thing for me."

"I think you might like it," she said.

"Maybe another time," I said.

"Well, down the hatch," she said, tossing off the brandy.

Phyllis chattered nervously in the car, pointing out the houses of writers and painters I would meet. All the while, I hoped her eyes weren't continuing to close. She dropped me at the Bull Ring, and we said good-bye like those who leave a failed date. Jeanne didn't answer her door, so I walked downtown. I sat at the bar of the Governor Bradford, wondering about "the work," and unhappy to be returning to my parents' apartment, when I heard a voice from a table behind me.

"Ask me if he's a doctor!"

I turned to see Hester, very drunk, with three women, one of them Zoe. I also recognized beautiful blonde Claire Fontaine, slayer of men and women. They were laughing. I smiled and turned back to the bar, my receding hairline in the mirror above the bottles.

"Go ahead," Hester continued. "Ask me if he's a doctor!"

"Is he a doctor?" someone said.

"No!" Hester said, and burst with laughter, the table joining in. A momentary silence occurred as they sipped their drinks, and Hester said again, "No, really, ask me if he's a doctor."

"Cut it out, Hester," Zoe said.

"Please," she said. "Ask me."

"Is he a doctor?" Claire Fontaine said.

"No!" Hester yelled, and the table roared.

I faced them once more, and Hester said, "This time, I'm serious. I'll tell you the truth. Ask me, go ahead. Ask me if he's a doctor."

"No way," Claire Fontaine said, and the others muttered they were through with the game. Hester pleaded, and finally someone whispered, "Is he a doctor?"

"No!" Hester shouted. Against their wills but pushed forward by alcohol, they laughed all over again. I finished my bourbon and turned to leave, when Hester rose from the table and came toward me. Too drunk to walk, she tried to steady herself by leaning against a wooden column. She put her hands against it to move forward, but slid very gently, almost gracefully, to the floor where she came to rest on her beautiful rear end, twisting off one pink shoe.

Before I took the bus to New York, Jeanne thought it would be fun to go to the Back Room, where Creeley's calisthenics had cleared the dance floor. As we approached, we saw the women who drank there all winter standing at the threshold while a bouncer examined their identification cards. One of the women looked at Jeanne and said, "They want three IDs." The bouncer waved me in. I didn't want to go to a place that didn't want women now that the season was arriving, and neither did she.

"Maybe it's time to leave after all," I said.

CHAPTER TWENTY-THREE

THE KIBBUTZ—PRIVATE LIVES— UNDER A SPELL—BARKHAUSEN COMES TO P'TOWN—ELMER DUGAN— DICK'S DICK

I looked forward to Jeanne's letters when I returned to my parents' apartment after a day at the AP. She wrote me every week, reporting follies that took place in town, like the Fourth of July fireworks ignited despite heavy fog, unseen by twenty-five thousand tourists. Jeanne closed each letter, "That's P'town."

In September, Ronnie the bus driver dropped me at Jeanne's, where Wayne answered. He didn't care that we'd been seeing each other. Jeanne came out and walked me to the middle of the parking lot and said they had gotten together again. I had had a twinge that something might be wrong because she had always answered my letters by return mail but our correspondence lagged in the last weeks. I carried my suitcase and typewriter down Commercial Street to the Kibbutz, a two-story complex on the water where Kurt, who had taken Porter's place as chair, had found me a one-bedroom apartment. The editor of *Mad* magazine owned the place and the nameplate on the doorbell said *Alfred E. Neuman.* It had leather furniture, a phone and a sweeping view of the bay. Moonlight jarred the water, the deck and the room. The next day I saw Porter at the Work Center. He gave me a copy of his new story, the one about Isaac Babel. He had also xeroxed Babel's piece on Maupassant. I went to the food co-op coal bin with the perverse feeling of seeing Hester. She was weighing radishes, and blithely looked over the scale, saying, "I made use of your absence to remember you," casting me again under the spell of her strange locution and her white languorousness, which seemed to have progressed even further, to a translucence.

"It was only a couple of months," I said.

"Pepe asked about you the other day. You're the only man he liked, you should say hello."

"I will," I said. "I'll call. I have a phone."

"Let's go now," she said. "Zoe can finish up." She tossed her hair, sending a waft of fragrance across the coal bin. Porter had speculated that her presence could deodorize an airplane hangar, and now the air in that room with a twenty-foot-high ceiling swirled with her dizzying aroma. She grabbed her shopping bag and took my arm.

Pepe remembered me, jumping onto my knees as Hester made grilled cheese sandwiches.

"What happened to Jeanne?" she said.

"She's back with Wayne."

"Really? He must have a big one." She said she had been working as Stanley's helper, driving him and Elise to the store, typing and cooking. As soon as she mentioned Stanley, she used her Stanley voice, and said, "He says you have 'a detective's perception and a surrealist's imagination,' but you still haven't become yourself." Then Hester got a raving look in her eye as she sliced tomatoes. "He never said that about me. He just finds me interesting as a woman is all."

"If he didn't like your work you wouldn't be here."

"You're always so moral. Like Christ with a hard-on."

"Funny you'd say that," I said. "That's the title of my book."

"You think I'm strange," she said. She moved to the refrigerator. "What did you read this summer? Have you seen the book Stanley chose for the Yale prize? It's terrible. He should have picked me."

"Did you submit?"

"Can't you find a better word than *submit*? And besides, what difference does it make? He could have *asked* me!" She put a pan on the stove.

"My mother had a book of Noel Coward's plays and I read *Private Lives*. One line said, 'I think very few people are completely normal, really, deep down in their private lives . . .'"

Her eyes moistened. "You and your memory," she said. "Say it again."

I repeated the sentence. She kissed me very hard, banging her teeth against mine. "I love you," she said. "No matter what you think of me." She slapped the spatula against her thigh. I repeated something Stanley said—"The impossible is sometimes easier to achieve than the difficult." And it came out of my mouth in his voice.

She said, "Want to try again? So I can forget all others?"

"Even Claire Fontaine?" I said.

"A bagatelle, ill bestowed upon me."

When we woke toward evening, Hester said, "I don't want to play house with you. You have to know who I am."

"I think I know," I said.

"But who are *you*? Did you fuck Phyllis Sherwood? Everyone says you did."

"Hester, she's sixty."

"You might go for that."

"Please," I said.

"That's the difference between us. I use my imagination off the page." She went to the bottom drawer of her dresser, took out a shoebox marked *Herman Survivors* and brought it to the bed. I sat up next to her. She placed it on her lap, lifted a long curved purple dildo, and shook it at me. Another was ribbed. A long feather. Leather fly swatter. Restraints. A monster hand from a costume store. Then she dumped out the whole contents. "Mostly from Toys of Eros, and some from The Pink Pussycat," she said. "Don't you love the word *eros*? It's so muscular and sleek." She lifted a harness and said, "I'll fuck you sometime. You'll like it. I know just how. And you can use the double-headed one on me." She rocked it through the air like a scythe.

"Let's go downtown," I said.

We passed the Bull Ring and I saw Jeanne's light on. Hester noticed me looking and pulled my elbow in the other direction. She was right, I missed Jeanne, the steady one, not the one with the box of tricks. As we passed the Fo'c'sle window, I caught Vince's eye and he made the sign of the cross. One spring night, I had drunkenly expressed my disenchantment with Hester to my drunken friends, and here I was with her to start the fall. She chose a table in the Bradford where passersby could see us from the street. It was a display Hester heightened by holding my hand as if we were about to arm wrestle.

Barkhausen knocked on my door before the opening committee meeting. I was exhausted by my night with Hester and still asleep.

"Rise and shine!" he said. "I got your address from Porter. What a view!"

I made coffee while he rattled on about the beauty of the sea and bay. He shook a paper cup of sand. "I just had to look at it closely," he said.

"Where are you living?"

"Right on the premises. Number 11."

"Oh yeah," I said. "That's a good one, with the fireplace."

"It's perfect. Two little bedrooms and a counter, like a bar." He trembled in his seat and pulled scallop shells from his pocket, laying them on the table. "Do you know they sell dried sea cucumbers at Marine Specialties? I bought one, and a batfish." He was picking up speed, his words running together and jumping off his sentences in different directions. He quoted a poem:

> Cold are the crabs that crawl on yonder hills,
> Colder the cucumbers that grow beneath . . .

but in his unstoppable haste, in his urgency to name the author, no period could halt his sentence and an additional noun ran right through the stop sign. He had called the poet "Edward Lear Jet." We talked about Kim, and he said she had married the policeman and they lived in Fort Dodge. I mentioned Wendy.

"Wendy! Wendy! Oh, man, to a grad school kid she looked like a woman, married and all, but guess what? She asked me, 'Don't you ever get tired of reading?' She thought poets made money, that I'd sell a book and buy a new car. She belongs with a breadwinner like Pryor. She joined him in Texas."

"There aren't too many women in this town," I said.

"Porter said you have two."

"One. I'm going out with Hester, a fellow for the past two years."

"I've seen her, she's beautiful, but there's something weird."

"I know, but I like even what's weird. She's erotic."

"Always Eros," he said. "Backward, it's Sore!"

As before, Stanley embraced the fellows and Dugan smoked. There was confusion about one new fellow, Millie

Harari, who had changed her name to Allison Stone. She said, "I divorced my husband in Seattle, and sold our farm. I wanted to get rid of everything." Someone suggested her new name was too stylized, and others agreed, but Dugan calmed the room, saying he changed his name too. "I didn't know that, Alan. Tell us your real name," Stanley sang. "Elmer," Dugan said, and everyone laughed. "And my nickname was Bud. Everyone in my family had a sexual nickname." Kurt tried to call the meeting to order but Dugan continued, "I had an Uncle Dick and an Aunt Tittie." When Dugan said this, the cracks and crevices on his face disappeared, and he smiled, reversing gravity. I had seen this happen on other occasions—when a group of children ran through the common room, and the time he found a piece of quartz on the dunes and said it would fracture nicely.

We made our visitors' list: John Ashbery, Grace Paley and Tomas Tranströmer. When business was over, everyone left for the Fo'c'sle, but at Pearl Street I continued to my room because of a problem. A tiny fern protruded from the opening of my penis, like a small and irritating pine tree. I didn't want to go to the Drop-In Center, because I knew the doctor. He wrote poetry, and I had given him and his nurse a tour of the Work Center. I made an appointment with a urologist in Brewster.

Hester didn't answer her phone. I kept dialing. To distract myself, I read Babel's story on Maupassant. On page two, I found an almost perfect description of Hester, "The high-breasted maid moved smoothly and majestically. She had an excellent figure, was nearsighted and rather haughty. In her open gray eyes one saw a petrified lewdness." Lewdness! Yes, lewdness, hers and mine, which is what had given me this fern! Maupassant went mad from syphilis, enduring headaches, blindness and fits of hypochondria, dying in an insane asylum eating his own shit. My hands twitched as I put down the pages. Maybe the tiny fern came from hypochondria: maybe I had, like Hester, carried my imagination off the page and onto my penis. Checking again proved it was not imagination but reality that stuck out like the last Christmas tree on the lot. Or was it the first! Suppose there were more! I kept looking and dialing.

Barkhausen came over in the evening after drinking all day with the writing committee, but he seemed sober. What McPeak said about him was true: he seemed drunk when sober and sober when drunk. "The Fo'c'sle's a weird place, full of hangers-on and artists manqué," he said.

"Was Vince there, and Post-Elliot?"

"Oh yeah," he said.

"Vince is a writer," I said.

"Yeah, books on varnish and yard sales. And the other guy doesn't write at all."

"You figured that out quicker than me," I said.

Barkhausen was on his way to the breakwater to meet a few fellows to get periwinkles for dinner. He invited me, but I declined, hoping to reach Hester.

"Cook them in garlic and white wine, then pluck the snail out with a bent pin!" he said, trying to tempt me. He left, but lingered on the deck, looking at the beam from Long Point's lighthouse. Abby Swan, who owned the windsurfing shop, came out of her apartment next door. Barkhausen struck up a conversation. I never had the nerve. Her name alone froze my heart. She was muscular and blonde and tan all winter. I met her in the building's laundry room but she flung her underwear out of the dryer with such abandon that I decided to come back later, which she didn't notice.

Hester was at her desk when I entered, her phone off the hook. I told her my problem and she asked to see it.

"It's like an arrowhead," she said. "Are you sure you didn't fuck that Indian squaw Phyllis Sherwood?"

"It's not funny," I said.

"Does it hurt?"

"It feels strange."

"You know what I like about you, your dick has a dick!"

"I made an appointment with a urologist in Brewster."

"Why not the Drop-In Center?"

"I'm embarrassed. I know the doctor."

"I wonder if I have anything like that," she said. We went into the bedroom and she got a flashlight. "Do you see anything unusual?" she said to the ceiling.

"Everything looks unusual," I said.

She sighed and got a mirror. "I don't see anything like what you have," she said, but feel this. She put out her hand and smeared my fingers. "After all, you are a doctor," she said. "A bad doctor, but a doctor," and she pulled me on top of her and I fucked her with my dick and my dick's dick.

CHAPTER TWENTY-FOUR

A STRANGE COURAGE—DUGAN STRANGLES A
WRITING FELLOW AND TRIPS ON A SEAGULL—
I'M NOBODY, WHO ARE YOU?—
SECRET STORIES—SELF-SWINDLER—
GAL-ALLELUIA

Porter asked to use my place for a fund-raising, friend-raising event. He was inviting a couple of local writers who did not usually come to the Center and a few wealthy people from town. Dugan would read beforehand as an added attraction. I once asked Dugan what poet meant the most to him and he said William Carlos Williams. He recited "El Hombre":

> It's a strange courage
> you give me, ancient star:
>
> Shine alone in the sunrise
> toward which you lend no part.

A fitting poem for a man who shunned celebrity, but, on this night, he was in the spotlight, giving a reading in the art gallery under life-sized bandaged figures swinging from the ceiling on wire trapezes. Dugan sat at a table, hunched over his manuscript, a pack of Pall Malls, an ashtray and three cans of Bud. I took a seat next to Barkhausen, who was introducing him, and pointed out Marge Piercy and Robert Boles. The chair of the Work Center's board escorted a wealthy couple, Bernard and Elizabeth Gildroy, and several of their friends. Hester came in with Claire Fontaine. There were no seats, so they leaned against the wall. I tried to get Hester's attention, but she wouldn't look my way.

Barkhausen's tide of critical superlatives washed over Dugan. He read a page and was on the next when Dugan interrupted, saying, "Okay, thank you!" in a voice that seemed to rise from the bottom of a well. A few sentences later, Dugan said, "Enough!" Everyone laughed. Was there the start of a smile across Dugan's Mt. Rushmore face? No. He ignited his cigarette lighter, aiming the flame at Barkhausen's introduction. The room laughed harder because it seemed a rehearsed routine, and Barkhausen continued.

Mindless of trend . . .

At these words, Dugan jumped up and his chair fell backward. He lurched toward Barkhausen whose last words tripped from his lips even as Dugan seized his throat with both hands and drove him across the room. Dugan was not only serious, he was enraged. His red face grew redder from the effort of pinning the younger man to the wall, where Barkhausen dropped his papers, trying to pry Dugan's bony fingers from his windpipe. Dugan let go and returned to the table while Barkhausen left the gallery.

"Graduate student-ese," Dugan said.

Major, the one-eyed, three-legged dog who had been buried alive, wandered in and flopped at Dugan's feet. Dugan began to read, but whenever someone caught the dog's eye, he wagged his tail heartily, slapping the floor.

Claire Fontaine snapped her fingers for Major's attention, enjoying the back-from-the-dead dog looking at her and thumping. Hester moved Claire's hair from her ear and whispered something that made her hysterical. A moment later, they opened the side door to Pearl Street and left. When the reading was over, the chair of the trustees apologized to Dugan for the noisy dog and Dugan said, "I've been places where the academics are worse than dogs."

I raced to my apartment wondering about Hester. Why was she with Claire Fontaine? Would she bring her to the party? I decided to be done with Hester for good as I put out the beer, chips and clam dip Porter brought earlier. There would be no photos. Post-Elliot complained that at the last party he couldn't get a clear shot without booze. The new brochure showed us starry-eyed, every hand cropped at the wrist.

Stanley arrived with Elise, which was unusual; she skipped social events, but on this night they hoped to win friends for the Center. Jeanne came with Wayne and we glanced at each other but didn't speak except when she asked for a knife to cut bread. Hester walked in alone and helped Jeanne, whom she caught looking at her earring— two dangling pink babies, a male and female. The female had holes in three places and the male a stiff penis. Hester told Jeanne she fit them together according to her mood. Barkhausen introduced himself to Marge Piercy, saying, "It's nice to meet you, Margin." The trustee chair arrived with the Gildroys. Their friends had fled after Dugan's pugnacious display.

Dugan and Barkhausen patched things up and were in deep discussion over a bottle of Heaven Hill, trading shot for shot. Barkhausen said, "I want to write a poem that is there and not there." Dugan didn't understand. Barkhausen clarified, "A poem conceived in a dim light." A poet from town with a crush on Hester followed her around.

She had shown me a poem he wrote about her called, "Ice Sculpture in a Snowdrift."

Mr. Gildroy said in a loud voice to Stanley and Elise, "Last week, two college presidents came by. They want my art collection! The question is, where do they house it?" Stanley spoke softly and then Mr. Gildroy burst forth again so their conversation was like the sound of a crashing wave followed by the receding tide.

One of the fellows sneezed and someone asked if he had a head cold. He said it was a face cold. Wayne strummed and sang, "The Night They Brought Old Dixie Down," but Dugan stopped him, saying the chorus went "No No No" and not "Na Na Na," insisting it was a refusal to capitulate. Considering what happened at the reading, Wayne revised the refrain. I told Mrs. Gildroy I was a writing fellow. She poured herself more wine and asked what I liked to read. I told her poetry. She clapped her hands, an ounce of burgundy flying to the rug. It was her love too, especially Emily Dickinson. She grasped the stem of her glass with both hands, and recited:

> I'm nobody! Who are you?
> Are you nobody, too?

Mr. Gildroy surged toward Stanley. "I gave them a hundred shares of IBM and got a thank you for a golf cart! That's the last they'll hear from me!"

A female fellow said the guys at the fish market were cute, and a fellow who liked her tried to discourage her by saying they can never get that smell off their hands. An artist had given me a painting of a mackerel on a dish, the oil still wet, and Kurt shouldered into it, smearing it to abstraction. Porter passed around a plate of oysters. Stanley said they were an aphrodisiac because they were shaped like testicles. Dugan said his testicles were not shaped like oysters and the Gildroys left along with Marge Piercy.

At midnight Judy and Dugan said good-bye but Judy ran back, poked her head in, and said Dugan had fallen on the lower deck. Porter and I grabbed flashlights, but by the time we arrived, Dugan was on his feet staring at the dead seagull he had tripped over. Jeanne joined us.

"It must have crashed into one of the windows," Porter said, nudging it with his foot.

With Dugan gone, everyone surrounded Stanley and Elise. Stanley talked of his love of birds, even seagulls, and described the time he brought singing finches to New York from the Canary Islands. Customs officials confiscated his cages, but the chief inspector, who also loved birds, admired Stanley's exotic collection, and allowed him to enter. Stanley said as a boy he had read that an owl couldn't be tamed, so he made it a point to go into the forest every day after school. "One of the greatest moments of my life was walking out of those Worcester woods with six owls. Three on each arm," he said, flinging those arms open and knocking over his martini.

Jeanne was commiserating with Kurt, having seen him under his car at the Center taping his dangling muffler with a roll of Tiger Patch. Stanley said his car, loaded with rare books, once died in the Mojave Desert. Each time someone offered a ride, he refused. "I couldn't leave my books!" he said, shaking a fist. "Three days passed," he continued. A Fuller Brush salesman, who also loved books, stopped and Stanley showed him the first editions and signed copies. The man threw away his sample cases to make room for Stanley's library. Stanley's stories had a similar mythical pattern. He always seemed to meet a man who loved what he loved and that person saved him. And in a way, he was a man who saved us.

Elise stood up to leave, but not before saying, "Now he's in the desert for *three* nights. Used to be two." Porter drove her home.

Hester suggested we reveal something we regretted, something we were ashamed of having done. Barkhausen went first. He thought a cat and a mouse were playing together in the common room, but then the cat killed the mouse. Jeanne had heard a rumor that the Holiday Inn was interested in buying the Bull Ring and, when a letter from the chain arrived for the owner, she threw it out. Hester didn't stop for a boy hitchhiker in Louisiana who was later kidnapped. Porter returned and said one of the fellows had a crow named Charlie that pounced onto the head of anyone riding a bicycle. Porter tempted him into a car and drove him off Cape. Hester looked at me and asked directly, incriminatingly, "You've gone to confession your whole life. You've legion sins to share."

"I told a woman I loved her," I said.

I was sorry to see Jeanne flinch. I meant to hurt Hester, another thing I immediately regretted. Hester straightened her shoulders and said, "After the final no there comes a yes, and on that yes the future world depends."

Stanley said he had an experience that combined ours. He loved a woman who was also a poet, and they lived together. One day, alone in their apartment, he read a letter she had received from a mutual female friend, and learned she was having an affair with that woman.

"Jean Garrigue," Hester whispered and Stanley nodded.

At dawn, the party ended. Barkhausen was hugging me and hugging everyone. Porter said to him, "Tell me, Artie, did I hear you right tonight? Did you call Marge Piercy *Margin?*"

"Yes, Porter," he said. "I didn't think I knew her well enough to call her Marge."

Porter was telling Stanley that he should write about Jean Garrigue. Stanley said, "I don't want poems that tell secrets, I want poems that are full of them." Porter followed Stanley out, along with the others, except for Hester, Jeanne and Wayne.

Wayne had fallen asleep in the bedroom and Jeanne helped me straighten up. Hester pitched in and we dumped the ashtrays, poured dregs down the drain, and stacked the empties on the deck. In the clean room, which the sun had brightened, Hester said, "The three of us have a lot in common."

"I don't think so," Jeanne said.

Hester moved to the couch and Jeanne and I leaned against the kitchen counter.

"The more varnish you apply, the more the grain shows," Hester said in her Stanley rhythm.

Jeanne said, "You don't know what you're saying, Hester. I'm making my marriage work."

"Face it, Jeanne, Wayne's a loser."

"I'm leaving," Jeanne said, and walked to the bedroom to get her husband.

"So am I," Hester said. I watched her put on her sunglasses before she descended the stairs. She stopped, looked over and said, "Self-swindler!"

"And other poems!" It was Barkhausen, rushing right past her with two cups of coffee and the Boston Globe. Jeanne and Wayne came out a few seconds later. Artie handed me a coffee, went in, fiddled the radio to the news station and started paging through the paper.

When they reached the first floor, Jeanne yelled, "John, that gull's not dead!" I ran down to find Wayne vomiting over the railing. Jeanne and I stood by the broken bird. It lay on its side, blinking.

"In the dark, it must have looked dead," I said.

"You stink," Jeanne said to Wayne who had joined us. She pointed to the front of his shirt.

I knelt by the bird, and saw no wound, no sign of injury. I touched its wing and it didn't move.

"I think it's dead now," I said, and went upstairs.

"On my way here I saw a dog holding two balls in its mouth," Barkhausen said. "What happened to your Gal-Alleluia?"

"Over," I said.

"I told you she was weird," he said. "I liked Dugan's new poems, I don't care that he strangled me. Are those stories of Stanley's true?"

"I think so," I said. "Though he does say poets must turn their lives into legend."

"You know what I like about this place?" he said. "You arrive needing a flashlight and you leave wearing sunglasses."

CHAPTER TWENTY-FIVE

VD—GOING FOR THE JOCULAR—A DONALD
DUCK, STRAIGHT UP—THE SICK ONE—
THE DOCTOR AND THE PLUMBER—
BUSTER & ZOOMER—
YOU MUST LOVE POETRY MORE

∽

I took the bus to Brewster to see the urologist, Paul McGovern. As soon as I stood in front of his office on Route 6A, I wished I had gone to the Drop-In Center. The road was lined with pristine antique shops, nurseries, taverns and restaurants. A yellow school bus deposited healthy children every hundred feet. It all seemed the opposite of my life.

One look told McGovern it was a venereal wart. He said he would have to do a cystoscopy and remove it at Cape Cod Hospital under general anesthesia. He told me to inform all of my recent partners. I waited for the bus on that road of privilege and splendor. I was lonely, diseased, impoverished inside and out. I went straight to Hester's though I didn't want to. She was on the Flagship's little lawn with Pepe who jumped to see me. I told her she should be checked. She thought I was accusing her and threw a fit in front of passing tourists.

"Who knows where else you've been poking your putrid pud," she said.

"I'm not blaming you," I said.

She dragged Pepe up the stairs so that his shoulder bounced off each tread. I had become weary of her sexual shenanigans, the last of which required me to strip-search her using a flashlight. The week before, she pulled cat masks from under the pillows.

Without Jeanne, and without evenings of treat-or-trick sex with Hester, I spent time at my desk. I quit the daytime Fo'c'sle crowd, so no one flagged me when I passed. Vince at the front table reminded me of a coyote nailed to a fence to discourage others.

Barkhausen learned CPR, joined the Rescue Squad and kept a walkie-talkie on his hip. He helped with injuries and seizures until medics arrived. He made a life in the life of the town. One afternoon I saw him sitting alone, scrawling on a big pad in the Fo'c'sle window. He told me the owner had installed a tiny grill at the end of the bar and he was writing the menu. A ham omelet was a Hamlet, and the stuffed tomato, The Ultimato. "I'm going for the jocular," he said. The bar served food for only a week because the owner didn't bother to get a license.

After a reading by John Hawkes, everyone went to the Fo'c'sle but when we arrived, the bartender had his leg on a stool, displaying deeply torn skin. A diving lobsterman by day, he had been attacked by a goosefish, whose enormous maw clamped on his leg as he rose from the ocean floor. He had bandaged it himself, but felt feverish and decided to see a doctor. He asked Barkhausen to take his place, and Artie immediately wrapped on an apron and wiped the sticky counter, startling the regulars back on their stools. His task would be simple. It was a shot and a beer place. No one ordered mixed drinks. We watched

Barkhausen flood the first few drafts from the tap with foam, but soon he drew them perfectly.

Porter dated Nonie, a pretty Provincetown native who had lost two husbands at sea. Vince referred to her as "The Kiss of Death." She liked the readings and was especially enthused about Hawkes's new novel whose narrator was driving his family at top speed into a stone wall. I sat with her, Porter and Vince while Jeanne gathered with the other fellows around Hawkes. I couldn't bear to be near Jeanne. I missed her thoughtfulness. It was painful to see her leaving the Bull Ring parking lot, carrying her copy of the *Boston Globe* to the common room for others to read, and worse when we faced each other—in a few seconds, we were laughing. I was thinking about this when Vince said, "I hope your friend knows what he's doing." Barkhausen was stirring a broom under an empty table, saying, "These ghost turds must have been here since Myles Standish."

"He's diligent, I'll give him that," Vince said. And then he added, "Hey Nonie, let's have some fun." He took a bill from his wallet. "Ask for a Donald Duck. But hesitate a moment and say, 'Straight up.'" Porter put his hand on her wrist but Nonie liked the joke and rushed off. Barkhausen was changing stations on the television, searching for the weather.

"A Donald Duck," she said. "Straight up." Barkhausen paused at her order. He liked Nonie, although he told me it seemed like it was always raining inside her head. Vince licked his lips. He was literally drooling over the gag. The guys sitting on each side of Nonie looked at her but kept quiet. Barkhausen filled a shaker with ice, and as he did, he squawked, a perfect imitation of Donald Duck, saying, "One Donald Duck, coming up!" He poured from several bottles, shook, drained the liquid into a rocks glass, jammed in a swizzle stick, and pronounced in the same voice, "One dollar, and you'll find no lip room on that drink!" Nonie walked toward our table cupping the rim of the overflowing glass as if it were a candle that might blow out. As she lifted it to her lips and drank, Barkhausen imitated Donald Duck having an orgasm, building little duck whimpers into full-throated squawks, climaxing in Donald yelling, "I'm coming! I'm coming!" causing Nonie to spew her mouthful onto Vince's yellow Banlon shirt.

"Must be some grenadine in that," Porter pronounced as Vince dabbed his chest with a handkerchief.

"I like it," Nonie said. Vince offered to buy her another. "I'd like to hear the duck get his rocks off again," he said.

"I always thought Daisy Duck had cute tail feathers," I said.

"You're sick," Vince said. "You're the sick one!" He went to the bar and ordered a Daisy, and Barkhausen said, "It's the same as a Donald, but without the swizzle stick."

As the anesthesia took effect, I heard Dr. McGovern telling me not to worry, saying, "I'm just a plumber, that's all I am, a plumber." I woke in a room between two other patients. Newspapers splashed with blood and urine covered the linoleum near our beds. A very old man passed gas with the sound of thunderclaps, yelling, "I'm letting terrible wind!" On the other side, a patient who had a kidney stone removed spent hours on the phone with his children, who lived with his divorced wife. He told them over and over that he was going to be all right, at the same time creating worrisome scenarios until I could tell they were crying. The old man swung out of bed toward me, lifted his johnnie and dripped a trickle of bloody urine onto the headlines. He continued to fart and the middle-aged man continued to torment his children. I had to be catheterized and when I thought things couldn't get any worse, Hester appeared with a bouquet of daisies.

"Why are there newspapers all over the floor?" she said.

"There are many accidents in the urology wing," I said. She put the flowers in the urinal. "I'm surprised to see you," I said.

"Porter told me. How are you?"

"A little numb," I said, "but okay." Dr. McGovern came in with a nurse and said I could leave the next day.

"Is this your doctor?" she asked.

"No," I said. "He's my plumber."

"That's what I am, a plumber," he said.

She whispered, "I need a doctor. That's what John tells me."

"Ask him if he's a doctor," I said.

"Call my office," he said to her, tapping the bed railing and assuring me the discomfort would fade.

Hester stared after his white coat as he left the room and exhaled dramatically. "It's not queer coincidence he arrived just as I did," she said in Stanley's voice.

I became drowsy and dreamt about plumbers and doctors, and Hester and the real doctor.

I did not seek out Hester when I recovered. I stayed in my room, celibate, sober and unhappy. Barkhausen dropped by one night with a bottle of Glen Flagler, a thank-you gift from a man whose life he helped save with CPR. I had been reading Rimbaud, and his theory of disengaging the senses gave me an excuse to drink, so we downed half the bottle and then left for the Old Colony. As soon as we got our drinks, Vince walked in, bragging about his new advice column for the *Advocate*, "Vincent's Two Cents." Two women in a corner, a dyed blonde in jeans, and a tall brunette in a giraffe print dress, whispered and gestured. The blonde kept rising to get more beer.

"Cookie's the blonde," Barkhausen said. "The other one's Valley. They act in local plays. I've driven them to Cape Cod Hospital a number of times." He twirled his index finger by his temple, making the cuckoo sign. When

I said they were kind of attractive, he called over, and they ignored him, murmuring again, head to head, but soon they languidly moved our way, as if they hated us. They switched to Scotch when Vince bought them a drink. Cookie's face was pitted from acne, and her painted-on, swooping eyebrows gave her a startled look. She went to the restroom and came back saying the toilet was so filthy she had to helicopter. Valley fluttered her dress to alleviate heat, which made the giraffes jump. The almost dignified look imparted by her high cheekbones was robbed by an overload of mascara. They argued over whether Paul Morrissey made Warhol's films, and were surprised I'd seen most of them. They leaned toward me, our knees touching. Vince kept buying drinks and I knew at last call we'd be facing a decision. The girls went to the ladies room a few times, more disoriented after each trip. Barkhausen mentioned the Glen Flagler and soon we were on the outside stairs to my place. Barkhausen told everyone to be quiet. He leaned over the railing toward the water and we heard a great whooshing sound. "A humpback," he said, and we listened again to the watery explosion. "It might be stranded." He ran onto the beach. "I'm telling Stormy Mayo," he called into the air and disappeared to find the head of the Center for Coastal Studies.

The girls sat on the couch and Vince and I took the wicker chairs around the coffee table. We drank the Scotch neat because I had no ice. In the lamplight, Cookie's ravaged face showed her acne was not all behind her. She was skinny, the denim jacket and jeans tight, revealing the build of a boy. When Valley shifted her broad shoulders, the giraffes stretched. Vince, in his khaki pants and banlon shirt, and me in my blue oxford shirt, paired poorly with our guests. Cookie rummaged into her big bag, pulled out an envelope of joints and lit up. Valley popped four beers from my refrigerator and set them next to the Scotch.

Valley offered Vince two fists. He tapped the left, and she exposed a red pill. "Zoomer!" she said. She opened the other and said, "You get Buster." I washed down Buster with a beer and Vince did the same with Zoomer. Cookie sneaked a second capsule into my hand, the way someone discreetly proffers a tip. She said it would add color, and I took that too. The girls were already zoomering and bustering and then they began giggling.

"Do you know your lines yet?" Valley asked Cookie.

"Don't ask me again," Cookie said.

"Request permission to ask you again, sir!" Valley said.

"I can't *hear* you!" Vince yelled. The two girls snapped their heads toward Vince.

"You know the play?" Valley asked.

"Say 'Yes, sir' or 'No, sir' when you address me," Vince said.

"*The Brig*," I said. I had seen it on public TV in high school and I remembered it because my mother turned it off.

"Maggot!" Vince said.

"We're doing it at the Universalist Church next week and Cookie doesn't know her part," Valley said. Cookie leaned over the table, lighting another joint and sneering.

"I directed it at the Berkshire House," Vince said. "Believe me, Cookie, with your looks, you can say anything you want."

"You're nice," Cookie said. Her grateful eyes had turned almost completely white, a half-moon of iris peeking above her lower lids.

"Out of the tomb we bring the flea market maven!" Those were my words though I didn't think I said them.

"Don't call me that!" Vince said.

Buster had kicked in, my senses disengaged. Cookie extended her legs under the coffee table, pointing the toes of her cowboy boots toward us. In one motion, Valley stroked Cookie from throat to groin where her hand lingered. She did it again as Cookie stretched like a cat before a fire. Valley motioned to Vince to do the same. Cookie buckled and popped under their simultaneous massage. Valley and Cookie kissed. When they separated, Cookie made a blubbering sound, sending spit bubbles my way. She looked out of her mask-like face, her mascara-streaked cheeks like a shattered windshield, and said, "Every insect has a secret." She collapsed awkwardly onto the cushions, her neck seeming broken.

I poured a glass of seltzer to revive Cookie. Valley bounced it under Cookie's nose. Cookie fixed on the bubbles and said, "Tiny igloos!" Then she jumped, knocking the drink to the floor and saying with a mad look, "And in each igloo, an eskimo with a spear!"

Valley lifted the giraffe dress over her head and onto the floor, stood in her bra and panties, and asked, "How many pairs in four?"

Attacked by the question and under the influence of Zoomer, Buster and Buster's colorful sidekick, Vince and I counted on our fingers, and our fingers multiplied. The giraffes left Valley's dress and loped across the rug.

"*Six*, maggots!" Valley said.

"Six in four?" I said.

Valley crossed her arms, pushing up her breasts, and said, "You and me. You and Cookie. Me and Vince. Me and Cookie. Cookie and Vince. You and Vince." While she spoke, Vince pointed to his chest and then to me and then to Cookie and then to Valley, then to me, to himself again and back to Cookie. Zoomer couldn't add.

"Everyone into the bedroom," Valley said. "I'm directing." We followed, trailed by giraffes. "Take off your clothes," Valley commanded.

Cookie's milky eyes opened wide and she said, "Request permission to undress."

"Too late, Cookie," Valley said. "You blew the part."

Vince dropped his shorts quickly, and we stood naked around the double bed. Valley fondled Vince's prick and said, "It's so Chihuahuan!"

Cookie pulled me onto the quilt, but when we kissed, I kissed two mouths. The lamp lit twice and the room fractured. I kissed four lips and four breasts among a thousand walls.

Vince said, "I'm married."

I turned from the bed. "You're married?"

It was as if I tangled with a spider with smooth arms and legs as I tried again to figure how six pairs were in four.

"And I have a little boy," he said.

"We're making a web!" Valley said, kicking a blanket high.

"I've got to go," Vince said.

The whimpers from Cookie never got louder, but kept at a plateau. Valley said to me, "Don't expect anything more," and she and Cookie fell asleep in each other's arms. Boosted by Buster, I cleaned the living room, alphabetized a shelf of books, wrote a hate letter to Hester illustrating it with color markers I found in the *Mad* magazine artist's desk, and went to sleep on the couch.

When I woke, Valley and Cookie had gone. I worried about another fern. I berated myself for having sex with them and for getting drawn into the Old Colony cesspool. I looked at my letter to Hester and it was nothing like Rimbaud. I went to the refrigerator for a soda, and found four tumblers of Scotch, an inch or so in each of them, which I had maniacally covered in plastic wrap, a rubber band around every rim. A label on the rug, torn from one of the girl's clothes, said, "Screamin' Mimi's."

I met with Stanley when he came to judge the applications. He said he heard I had a lot of girlfriends. I joked that I loved women.

"You must love poetry more," he said.

CHAPTER TWENTY-SIX

WORMS—A TEACHING JOB— DUNE PICNIC—LOST AT LAND AND LOST AT LAND'S END

In late spring, Provincetown's forsythia, daffodils, and crocuses came to life and I savored my remaining days by walking frequently from the Bull Ring to land's end. Getting into the shower one afternoon, I discovered two tiny worms writhing in my crotch. I immediately thought of Cookie and Valley. They had infected me with a disease that was eating me alive. I had turned into a maggot-eaten piece of decaying meat exactly like Maupassant. I didn't care that I knew the poetry-writing doctor and his nurse. I put the worms in a plastic bag and hurried to the Drop-In Center. I had to give my reason for the visit and I put "VD." I showed him the bag, and he knocked the worms onto a piece of paper. One had died, but the other moved hump-like across the page.

"These are inchworms," he said. "They're falling from the trees this time of year." He couldn't stop smiling. "They somehow got into your pants."

I dressed, relieved not to be being eaten by worms. When I paid the five dollars, the girl at the cashier bit her lip and the nurse came out and made a stupid face.

Ridge finished his year of teaching at McGuire, and the English Department, happy to have a National Book Award nominee, gave him the fall term off. He called one morning and told me I could replace him. Although I hadn't taught a day, I would be a visiting assistant professor at a salary of $6,250 for the fifteen weeks, an enormous sum compared to the Work Center stipend. He said that if I published a book, a permanent job might open up. He mentioned that with all the competition, a poet didn't only have to be good, he had to be lucky. I went to the Work Center to share my news. Stanley congratulated me, and Kurt shook my hand in the common room where he was posting the results of the second-year applications. The outside jurors had chosen Barkhausen.

"Not only will the Center be better off for his selection, the town will be as well," Stanley sang. And it was true. Barkhausen had knitted himself into the community, friends with firemen, cops, and shop owners. He had joined The Beachcombers, the male social club that met every Saturday when one member cooked dinner for all. The year before, I was invited by Vince, but declined because I didn't want to belong to a club that didn't allow women. We were in the Fo'c'sle when Vince asked me. Vince then turned to Dugan who said the same thing, but added, "I'm a feminist." Everyone laughed, thinking a man couldn't be a feminist, but when Dugan said it again, in that deadly voice, the table fell silent. A man could be a feminist.

Vince got a six-figure advance for his book on Pancho Villa and threw a party in the dunes. Cole Randle, a deaf-mute from Louisiana and the town's best chef, fashioned huge grills from oil drums for barbecuing. Cole was also the town's best drunk, once arrested for rubbing out a cigarette on a fire hydrant that turned out to be a sitting black dog. All the barflies in town came, along with bartenders and owners. Even a few tourists arrived which startled Vince, but after mixing a powerful punch, sampling it, adding brandy, sampling and adding, adding and sampling, he mellowed, wading into the surf toward Eddie Bonetti who had descended imaginary stairs into the ocean. His head floated above the waves, and he held a wine glass at each ear as he treaded water. Iron Man sat on the shore wearing a paper hat and spinning his top. He had just gotten out of jail for breaking the wrist of a con artist who sold him a potion that would make stolen objects invisible. Cole dragged a giant aluminum tub of punch between his two grills. Racks of ribs smoked on one; oysters fried in skillets on the other. Barkhausen and I sipped the heady drink and I asked where he was spending the summer. He said he had gotten a good deal from a writer in Truro, Phyllis Sherwood. I said I hoped he liked the work.

Vince rang a triangle and everyone lined up before Cole, who drank and laughed and spat as he slammed plates full of golden oysters and slabs of ribs. After a few bites, it was apparent that the oysters were inedible, mistakenly breaded in salt. Everyone went for the ribs, but Cole had doused the meat, not from the squirt bottles that housed his special barbecue sauce, but with cans of lighter fluid. No one could eat anything except the bags of pretzels and potato chips, which blew across the dunes, now chased by the hungry partygoers.

Barkhausen led the Rescue Squad against the artists and writers in a game of wiffle ball. Fielders lunged at grounders, stumbled around bases and stared at the sky. Some hungry players ate the salty oysters, which caused the punch barrel to be refilled over and over until most couldn't stand, and those who could soon fell. Women were tackled on the base paths. The centerfielder used his glove for a pillow. The pitcher couldn't reach the plate, so he moved almost on top of the batter, tossing the ball underhanded, as if to a child, and that child swung blindly, as if at a piñata.

The game ended with only a first baseman, a pitcher, and someone curled behind second in a fetal position. I decided to walk to town with Porter. At the top of the dune, we scanned the ravaged party's useless grills, empties, magical barrels of punch, torrent of loose napkins, and plastic and paper cups dotting the shoreline. Barkhausen was pitching, exhorting his lifeless crew. Post-Elliot swung hard, missing and corkscrewing into the ground, but he hit the next pitch high above the empty outfield. A white butterfly dipped toward it, following the ball to the sand where it hovered, believing it had found a mate, a lost thing like itself, fluttering over the dunes.

CHAPTER TWENTY-SEVEN

THE HARVARD OF THE SOUTHWEST— TOY AND FUN—NOWHERE MAN—THE IDEA OF AMERICA—A DINGE, A GUINEA, A KIKE— JACK DANIEL'S PEDAGOGY—THE EDUCATION OF LITTLE TREE—GOGOL

Everyone in the English Department at McGuire University in Dallas had been fired from Yale except for Jerry Morris, a novelist who raised palominos; the Texas literary historian Ron Tonald, and Grady Waycaster, a folklorist who had been Gene Autry's chauffeur. I was nervous because I had never taught. I was anxious because I had never been west of Iowa. And I was guilty because I didn't deserve the job.

Ridge sent me a letter with a scanty map on a napkin. Lemmon Avenue was jotted between two parallel lines, followed by an arrow with the words "Into Area." This sketch led me to central expressway and its automated billboard tracking the Dow Jones. Where Lemmon crossed Mockingbird, I rented a furnished place from a widow named Toy. I declined weekly maid service offered by Fun, her Asian companion. When I left the grocery store on my first day, a pretty girl in sunglasses leaned against the plate-glass window and asked if I wanted a date. I walked across the street for the *New York Times*, but the shop contained only a few magazines and a back room offering sex toys and pornography. The Tabu Lounge, a strip club next door, upset the local wives, so as a community service, the local paper published the license plate numbers of cars parked there each evening. I had moved into the red light district.

I went to the department secretary for my schedule and stood by Betty's door, afraid to disturb the elderly woman who was writing, head close to the page, tongue curling from her mouth, almost licking the paper. When she finally looked up, she told me she had just finished printing Hopkins's poem, "God's Grandeur," backward, and was about to check her progress with a mirror.

A memo in my mailbox summoned me to a "post-placement interview luncheon" by the search committee. The formal tone, the McGuire seal on the stationery, the name of the chair of the committee, Worthington Ramsey, all reminded me there had been no search. Unqualified for the job, I was grieved at soul. Ramsey escorted me to the dining hall wearing a bowler and twirling an umbrella bound with rubber bands. He asked where I had been teaching. I said I hadn't. He said he came from Yale, a colleague of Erich Segal, author of *Love Story*. He chuckled that maybe I recognized him as "The Nowhere Man" in *The Yellow Submarine* where Segal portrayed him as "Jeremy Boob, PhD, a man who lives in the Sea of Nothing." He pronounced this description with pride. I didn't connect him to the Beatles movie, but I did recognize him from Ridge's mentioning the medievalist who spoke as if he had swallowed a monocle. We joined Megan, a composition specialist, the only other committee member. She asked where I had been teaching.

The home economics classes held a fashion show amid the tables of tomato soup and hot dogs. Each time I tried to answer a question, I was interrupted by female students turning and dipping, showing feathery shawls, sundresses and ruffled gowns. At the end of lunch, Megan pointed to the old man who had taken our meal cards with trembling hands. He'd been an air traffic controller at O'Hare for fifty years, had just moved to Dallas and gone back to school. She asked if I could handle such a student, but before I could respond, a huge football player banged his thigh against our table, showing off his handmade kilt.

Jack Myers ate lunch with me every day at Kuby's delicatessen. A poet, Jack was married with two young boys. Ridge's offer of a tenure-track position freed Jack from his job selling roofs in Boston. Jack and I traded poems—his about his unhappy marriage, and mine about my unhappy loneliness. At the end of two weeks, he returned to his brown-bag sandwiches. I realized lunch at a restaurant was something he could ill afford, but he was generously orienting me to the alien culture.

Along with my poetry workshop was a composition course called The Idea of America. Fraternity boys in blazers and coiffed, manicured sorority girls comprised the class. They saw me for what I was: the English teacher who alternated two sport coats. Brad Oberding, a football player, wrote a paper arguing that he didn't plan to see any black people after graduation, so why should he see any now. Ted Shaver said he wanted to graduate to get a Lincoln Mark IV, which had been his brother's reward. Jorge Garza, a rare minority student, came from a fine local prep school where he had been completely neglected. No one had bothered to teach him to capitalize the days of the week. Two girls wrote about the difficulty of hiring trustworthy domestic help. Imran Manzoor, from Iran, was also rich but isolated by his dark skin.

The text contained a section of bad poetry. One piece described cuddling on a winter night, and used the phrase "the spoon position." The class turned to me for an explanation. I said "It's not necessarily sexual. . . . But the two people are holding each other. . . . One grasping the other from behind. . . ." Finally, I went to the board and, to their delight, I drew a reclining couple, back to belly.

We read an excerpt from Dos Passos's "The Body of an American," an account of the remains of John Doe killed in France. Dos Passos had written:

> Make sure he aint a dinge, boys,
> make sure he aint a guinea or a kike.

No one understood it, so I defined the ethnic slurs, and after class, I sat in my office asking myself what I had done.

In the Advanced Poetry Workshop, I kept confusing Anne with Brenda, and Brenda with Anne. After the second week of repeatedly calling on the wrong girl, the students rolled their eyes at my mixing up the two blondes whose large breasts promenaded above the seminar table. I found I could recite hundreds of lines, which I knew by heart without realizing it. I urged the class to read great books, quoting Stephen Spender's "I Think Continually of Those who were Truly Great":

> The names of those who in their lives fought
>   for life,
> Who wore at their hearts the fire's center.
> Born of the sun, they traveled a short while
>   towards the sun,
> And left the vivid air signed with their honor.

A student raised his hand and asked, "Who's Spender?"

The two best poets were bitter rivals. Gary Beattie's father made a fortune selling handmade cowboy boots.

Gary was wiry and frenetic. When a poem of his was praised, he spun from his chair, crossed his arms, squatted and spurted into a Russian dance, showing off boots of ostrich or elephant skin. Jim Miller, handsome and staid, came from a family of Arkansas farmers. He had no money, but he got the girls. One night we critiqued Jim's sonnet about making love during a heat wave. Gary mocked it mercilessly, laughing and blaming his uncontrollable hysteria on the poem. His final, breathless verdict was, "It just *sucks!*" Jim, stone-faced, said, "No, *you* suck!" Gary replied that Jim sucked and as Jim reaffirmed his opinion of Gary, the class wondered what I would do, something I was wondering myself. I ordered them to my office. They followed me through the hall and down the stairs. When I told them to sit, they looked around. There were only two chairs: mine behind the desk, which Gary took, and one for a visitor. Gary faced Jim while I, displaced, leaned against the wall, my elbow on the file cabinet. That I did not deserve the job was roundly apparent and, as they looked at me, I wished I had stayed on the Cape working with Phyllis Sherwood. I wished I were walking around New York. I wished I had taught somewhere before so I would know what to do. I wished for class to be over so I could have a drink. At this last wish I remembered a fifth of Jack Daniel's in my desk drawer, and I handed it to Gary.

"Take a swig," I said.

Gary gulped and made a face. I gave the bottle to Jim who also drank. I took the bottle and held it, gazing at them authoritatively, as if this were a significant component of a wise pedagogy. While they stared at each other, I downed as much as I could. We walked back in silence, the three of us chastened and confused.

Holding office hours on Friday afternoon was Ridge's idea. He said no one would come by. He was right, but I would have welcomed the company. When I left for the weekend, I didn't speak again until Monday. Occasionally, I went for a beer with Jack, but his family life consumed him. I spent those Friday afternoons playing checkers with Betty and, several weeks into the term, she asked me to join her at a Wellesley Book Club luncheon featuring Forrest Carter and Barbara Tuchman. Colonel Rutherford, a retired literature teacher, bought the tickets, but didn't eat lunch, just drank Enfamil baby formula. Forrest Carter took the stage drunk and referred to his autobiography *The Education of Little Tree*, about his Native American upbringing, as "a kind of *Roots* thing for Indians." He called Barbara Tuchman a "good ol' Jew girl," which made her laugh, and he invited everyone to his ranch, giving extended directions. I asked the colonel if he could help me find the ranch, but he said Carter was not a worthy associate. He was right. Years later it turned out that Little Tree's real name was Asa Carter, a member of the Ku Klux Klan. When Carter's true identity was discovered, his book jumped from the *Times'* nonfiction best-seller list to the fiction. I drove Betty home, and she told me she was retiring. Over the years she had occasionally taught composition, until displaced entirely by those from Yale. She stared glassy-eyed out the window and quoted Gogol on his stint as a university professor with words that scorched themselves into my brain—"Unrecognized I mounted the rostrum, and unrecognized I descended from it."

CHAPTER TWENTY-EIGHT

MERNEY, NERNEY, NU—MAPLE SHERROD—
YADDO—SIGHT TO INSIGHT—THE POETRY
GUESSING GAME—WHY AM I LOST?—
AN EXCITABLE DOG

A middle-aged businessman stopped by my office to talk about poetry. I had just collated the student poems for the following week and when he asked to see them, I had no hesitation in handing them over. He put on his glasses, turned page after page thoughtfully, then flung the manuscript across my desk so hard it almost landed in my lap.

"I'm after something deeper than that," he said.

He opened his briefcase, removed a piece of thick bond and read his poem aloud.

THE UNSETTLED STATE OF AFFAIRS TODAY

The time has come when few must host the many.
When love and friendship merney, nerney, nu.
When the family life of the living loses its turny,
    burny, fu,
And freedom and liberty for autobotta slu.

But with the birth of liberty and autobotta slu,
A whole new world was open for mendla,
    kendla, tu.
For man became his own masterdoner wu,
And freedom and liberty for autobotta slu.

Ah yes merney nerney nu, turny burny fu,
For autobotta slu and mendla, kendla tu,
With masterdoner wu because,
The time has come when few must host the many.

"Would you call me after you've spent some time with it?" he asked, and gave me the poem and his card. Lincoln Jenkins was a lobbyist for Shell Oil with addresses in Dallas and Washington, DC.

Something about his interest in poetry in this poetry vacuum touched me, and I escorted him out as if he were an esteemed guest or maybe a discharged patient. He had parked in the handicapped spot in front of the building and a note on his windshield excoriated his thoughtlessness. It said, "Because of you, I'll have to wheel all across campus and be late for my exam."

"I didn't think I'd be here this long," he said, looking at the paper. Crushed by the anger of the writer and by his own inconsideration, he got into his car without saying good-bye. As he drove off, I noticed a sign in magic marker taped to his bumper: "My mother raised me to be a faggot."

I returned to my office where Jack Myers waited with Maple Sherrod, an undergraduate and daughter of an oilman. Jack's poems mentioned divorce and, though he was not yet separated, this was the evidence. We went to four bars, all owned by a friend of Maple's, where drinks were on the house. Obsessed with Lily Langtry, the owner had named each after her—Lily Langtry's, The Jersey

Lily, and the anagrams, Really Tingle and Illegal Entry. I became friends with Maple, and went to her father's mansion for Thanksgiving dinner, which was attended by more than a hundred people. I overheard one of her uncles say, "What's Maple doing with the professor?" After dinner, we met Jack at The Texas Teahouse where the band played behind chicken wire. Jack said that when I was in the men's room, one of the cowboys asked Maple, "What're you doing with the bookworm?" She answered, "He's a professor of poetry at the university." The cowboy said, "I coulda guessed that!" Maple traveled the world and I did not see her again, but she called me from a Joe Cocker concert in London, saying she would fly me over to meet the singer. Another time she phoned from Peter Sellers's Rolls in Paris saying they were hunting for a rare wine.

Stanley Kunitz recommended me to Yaddo, the artist colony in Saratoga Springs, and I was accepted for the month of August. I called Stanley to thank him, and he said he had been there, but only for one night. A tapping noise on the window of his room in the mansion's tower kept him awake. When he switched on the lamp, it stopped. When he turned the light off, the ticking began again, with such intensity he thought the glass would break. He was sure it was the ghost of one of the two Trask children who died in the room where he now slept. They had contracted diphtheria from their mother, whose family founded the art colony. He left the next morning.

I spent the term providing hundreds of pages of handouts to my students, overdoing it in fear of not doing enough. I wrote in the early mornings and spent the evenings watching *The Porter Wagoner Show* and *Marty Robbins Spotlight* on a tiny black and white TV. Toward the end of the semester, Betty urged me to a Friday afternoon soiree at Norbert Lane's. I pleaded my office hours but she insisted. I knew his name, the author of *Sight to Insight*, a best-selling poetry primer. Jack had told me department members got drunk sitting around an old Victrola while Norbert conducted a guessing game: name the poet on the record. Jack said Norbert had called on him again and again, and he did so poorly that his reputation with his colleagues suffered, something he feared would hurt his case for tenure. He warned me not to go, but I couldn't deny Betty.

Lane's enormous house was built on *Sight to Insight.* Acres of lawn tended by Chicano gardeners surrounded the massive stucco adobe. Four faculty members held glasses in the living room. I recognized Binky Spillane, a heavy woman who taught modernism. And Wes Glazer, the Victorian. Granville Bonner, in his eighties, the most debonair man in the department, wore a straw hat and seersucker suit. He had been a dean, but was demoted in a scandal involving a sorority girl, from which he recovered by marrying a Dallas dowager. He never attended department meetings, refused to serve on committees, gave every student an A, and zipped around campus in a pink Cadillac. I was glad to see Ricky Marsden, a fiction writer, the only person my age.

Lane, a small man with a kind face, whose hands shook from Parkinson's, sat next to the couch in a tiny chair of wood and straw. This made him both large and small— like a child, yet perched on this miniature seat, he seemed huge. His wife brought me a glass of sherry. Granville, very much at home, dashed into the kitchen, yelling over his shoulder, "I'm making a martini, if anyone's interested." Out of the corner of my eye, I saw the Victrola.

"How's your wife, Ricky?" Lane asked. Lane petted a big German shepherd named Browning.

"She wished she could make it, Norbert, but she's giving lessons." Ricky explained that his wife was a violinist who wanted to be a conductor, but she couldn't practice because she didn't have an orchestra. I sat on the couch next to Binky.

"Why are *you* here?" she said. "You don't have to be, you know."

"Betty invited me," I said, and Binky shrugged. In the kitchen, Granville held a stemmed glass to the sun.

"I'm coming up for promotion," Binky said. "If I get it, you'll never see me here again."

When everyone was settled, Norbert said, "Although he has just a few weeks left, let's welcome John!" And the group chimed in with greetings.

"I'm sure you'll put us all to shame," Norbert added.

Glazer said, "You know, I read something the other day I hadn't realized—*all* poetry was once *contemporary* poetry." "Poetry" left his lips with a hefty plosive, so he lauded the word and spat it at the same time. Betty was quickly tipsy from her second sherry and joined Binky and me on the couch. She said, "I wish you'd stay here instead of that egomaniac Ridge!"

"Come, come, Betty," Norbert said. "Ridge knows poetry. He does know his poetry." When he said "poetry," it sounded so much like "putri," that for a moment I wasn't sure what he meant.

"Yes, Ridge knows the field," I said. The old Victrola grew larger each time poetry was mentioned.

Mrs. Lane went around the room with a tray, showing us her husband's bonsai plants, their roots bound with wire. Granville was stirring a steel shaker in the kitchen. Betty retrieved the crystal decanter, refilling glasses, and helping herself liberally. Ricky suddenly spoke to Norbert, but so loud that everyone heard. "The truth is that Fran and I split up. When I came home the other day, she was in the kitchen with this guy in our building. She told me she was helping him balance his checkbook."

"I'm sorry to hear that," Norbert said.

Ricky recovered and said to me, "Hey, you're single. Come over to my place sometime. I'll invite a few girl-friends of Fran's, get a bottle of wine and take out my guitar. Bring one of those bundles of wood they sell at Piggly Wiggly, and we can have a fire."

"Thanks," I said. "I'll have to see."

"Oh go ahead, that sounds like fun!" Betty said, fully enthused and starting to slur.

"The heart breaks and breaks and lives by breaking," Norbert crooned from his little chair. "Do you know who wrote that?"

"Stanley Kunitz," I said. I had heard Stanley read the line in Provincetown the year before.

Norbert smiled. "Stanley *Jasspon* Kunitz," he said.

"Not bad," Binky said. "You're a lot better than Myers. Maybe you should be here instead of Jack."

Norbert rolled the Victrola to the center of the room and placed his little chair next to it. Betty refilled her glass from the sideboard. My third glass of sherry made me feel worse. In the kitchen, Granville leaned over the counter, paging through the newspaper and feeding treats to Browning. Norbert's shaky hands removed a record from a built-in bookshelf holding what seemed like thousands. He pulled the disk from its sleeve and placed it on the turntable. A voice retched from the speaker:

For three years out of key with his time.

Glazer's hand leapt, and he yelled, "Pound! Old Ez!"

"Right you are," Lane said, "but that was an easy one." He played more of the poem, and mentioned he had a recording of Pound at Harvard banging a drum. Betty's eyes closed and she listed to one side, leaning on my shoulder. I nudged her gently, but couldn't wake her. Mrs. Lane came around with a bowl of peanuts and Wheat Chex. None of us guessed the next voice, which turned out to be Eliot reading from "The Four Quartets." When Norbert gave us the answer, he tilted his head and rubbed the tips of his index fingers at me. I gave Betty a good shove, which woke her so she jumped to her feet, extending her right hand and yelling, "We've been introduced before!" Then she crumpled into the couch.

I had no idea who the next reader was, but Betty perked up and named the poet, Dame Edith Sitwell.

"She always rises to her favorite," Mrs. Lane said.

"And also to her brother Osbert," Glazer added.

Betty opened her eyes, but stared at the floor, repeating Dame Edith's words exactly as they had shuddered from the record:

> Why did the cock crow,
> Why am I lost,
> Down the endless road to Infinity toss'd?

Binky asked me if I knew Betty's past. "Her only son shot himself on Mother's Day, and Betty found him in a chair with a pair of her white gloves in his lap." It was as if another poem had been played and I was absorbing it when I realized Norbert was calling my name.

"Your turn," he said, though there had been no taking of turns. It was Archibald MacLeish saying a poem should not mean but be.

"Isn't that Cary Grant's real name?" Binky asked.

Although I got MacLeish right, Lane said to me, "Try again." This time I had no idea whose voice was on the record.

"It's Tolkien!" Norbert said. "The first chapter of The Sil-mar-ill-ion. Aren't you familiar with The Legend-ar-ium?"

"A paean to the imagination!" Glazer seconded.

"Unfair!" Binky said in my defense. "That's not poetry!" In the silence that followed, we noticed that Ricky had retreated to a corner where he could be heard weeping.

"Poetry can do this," Norbert said.

Binky whispered to me, "And so can finding your wife balancing another guy's checkbook," and she started to laugh, shaking her big shoulders.

"Let's call it a day," Norbert said.

As we got up to go, I saw Granville struggling to leave the kitchen. I thought he must have been really blasted from the gin, dragging himself with difficulty out of the doorway, but then I saw that Browning had attached himself to Granville's shin and was humping away. The dapper professor could not shake him, so they entered the living room together, Lane rising from his seat to swat the excited dog from his colleague's leg.

CHAPTER TWENTY-NINE

A THANK YOU CAKE—PENDEMONIUM—
TUTORING ALEX—MY OWN MONT
BLANC—TELEPATHY—WEE MARIE—
A MOCKINGBIRD SHOWS THE WAY

At our final department meeting of the year, Dr. Ramsey asked, "What do we do with someone like Pope?" His question was answered with a familiar question. "Is Pope an age or a man?"

I handed in my grades in mid-December, my appointment over. If I ever got another job, I could name a place I'd taught. With nowhere to go, and my lease running through the summer, I decided to stay in Dallas, reading and writing, until August when I'd leave for Yaddo.

In late spring I sat in my apartment ordering my poems into a book, surprised at just noticing most were love poems, or really, anti-love poems, as forced as Holly's anti-jingle bells—they protested too much. I went into despair, the despair of being blind to my longings and shortcomings as well as recognizing its "Johnny One Note" quality. I looked into the courtyard at the magnolia tree that stayed green all winter, thinking I should throw out the manu-script and start over. A loud siren pierced the walls and windows. I opened my door and saw an extension cord running from the door of the apartment across the hall and down the stairs to the outside. I guessed the racket was caused by my neighbor attaching a powerful vacuum to his car. To get away from my book, I went for a drive. Lemmon Avenue was empty, the sky a greenish dark. A cruiser pulled next to me at a stoplight and the police-man yelled out his window, asking why I was ignoring the sirens, a tornado warning, and he ordered me home. I sat at my desk, feeling like neither a man nor an age, waiting for a tornado that never reached ground.

On one of my walks through the city, I found a statio-nery store called Pendemonium. Behind the counter was Mary Murray, a student from my Idea of America class, whose parents owned the shop. She was an atypical McGuire undergraduate, apart from privilege and preju-dice. On the last day of class, I was presented with a sheet cake, and I felt she was behind the gift. It said, "Thanks for the knowledge, especially about slurs and spoons." Two things I had successfully taught: ethnic derision and a coupling act. Mary introduced me to her mother and father and, since I didn't want to leave empty-handed, I bought a padded envelope and a notebook, the cheapest things in the shop. The next day Mary's mother called. She needed help for her son, Alex, a high school junior at risk of dropping out. He wrote poems and songs, but was disillusioned with school. She asked me to tutor him, and said she would pay the going rate.

Alex came to my apartment, his long hair flowing over a baseball jersey on which he had scrawled the name "Dock Ellis," a pitcher famous for throwing a no-hitter under the influence of LSD. He handed me a dozen envelopes. We sat in my living room and we talked about Ellis. I had gotten a kick out of Ellis's recent shenanigans—he had worn hair curlers in the locker room—and Alex seemed pleased that I knew he had just been traded to the Texas Rangers. He read me a poem and a song. He told me that he liked literature but that everything else in school was irrelevant. I told him he was probably right, that most everything was irrelevant. I suggested he do what he loved and live with the rest. Alex came every Sunday for an hour. I refused payment and looked forward to the meetings. He was angry at his school because he had been impeached as class vice president for forgetting to string leprechauns across the basketball court for the Saint Patrick's Day dance. He didn't plan to go to college, his mother's concern. I said that since he was writing poems anyway, why not hand them in and get credit. Since he was reading, why not write about it. I told him he would meet some boring teachers, but some great ones too, and we both laughed at the question of whether Shakespeare was an age or a man.

We went to a Ranger game and Alex spotted Dock Ellis leaning over the bullpen railing, talking to a girl in the stands, and spitting long streams of tobacco juice onto the field. The girl's date kept winding around her to get in on the conversation, but Ellis looked straight ahead, talking and spitting. The boyfriend began spitting onto the field as well, but without tobacco, the poor guy strained to muster any juice.

"They're dogs marking territory," Alex said.

"Aristotle believed the sign of a poet is the ability to make metaphors," I said.

"Then maybe I'm a poet," he said.

I told him I was sure of it.

The week before I left, at the end of July, Mrs. Murray called and thanked me, saying that Alex seemed happier, and had decided to go to college. She said, "No one ever told him school is really bullshit."

"Is that what I said?"

"Yes!" she laughed, "and now that he knows, he can deal with it."

A few days later, I received a package from Mrs. Murray. The box contained a giant black fountain pen, a Mont Blanc 149, just like the one Jay Hankard displayed in the Fo'c'sle.

Mont Blanc. I pronounced it out loud. It was hard to say the name without honking like a goose. *Mont Blanc.*

I packed my few belongings, discarding student poems, handouts and syllabi, and found the poem by the lobbyist. I had brought it home and forgotten it. I sat on the couch and read, *The time has come when few must host the many* . . . The lines seemed meaningful, all the more because I had let him down. I was reading the poem again when the phone rang.

It was him, it was Lincoln Jenkins.

"I'm sorry to bother you," he said, "but someone just phoned and hung up and it sounded like your voice."

I said it wasn't me and we said goodnight. Some telepathy had taken place, which Stanley once told me was the real beginning of poetry. I felt not only guilty, but convicted by his call. I had not been the host he needed.

I mopped the floors and was wiping the counters when the phone rang again. I answered with a whisper. It was Jack saying he had a feeling I was alone and wanted company. We went to Lily Langtree's where I told him about Lincoln.

"That's weird because I had an intuition about you too," Jack said. "That's why I called. You're sending out signals of some kind." He said he wished he could make the trip with me to New York, especially because I was stopping by Iowa City.

When the bar closed, I said good-bye to Jack and made the unwise decision to leave town immediately instead of waiting for morning. I carried my suitcase, boxes and typewriter to the car and drove off. After a few blocks, I felt the car tilting to the left, as if I had gotten two flats on the driver's side. I stopped and saw I had been driving with my two right tires on the curb. I couldn't find Mockingbird Lane, my route to the highway. I blared the radio to the *Open Road Show* where Bill Mack played an hour of Ernest Tubb. His sidekick, Wee Marie, spoke in squeaky, almost inaudible monosyllables. Straining to hear her kept me awake. A squirrel cut in front of my car, attacked by a mockingbird, and followed the center of the road, followed by the bird, followed by me, driving very slowly, listening for Wee Marie. The squirrel turned left onto Mockingbird Lane and the bird and I followed him out of town.

I spent the night in Lawrence, Kansas, at the Navajo Motel where the shower ran into a hole in the floor and the worn sheets were thin as tissue. I ate breakfast at the counter of the diner next door. The middle-aged waitress asked me where I was going and I said Iowa City. She said that many poets lived there, and I said that was true. She asked if I knew William Stafford.

"I don't know him," I said, "but I've heard him read."

"He was born here, you know, in Lawrence."

I said I knew.

"He's a pacifist," she said. She leaned over, looking at me, her hand on her chin.

"Yes," I said. "I like his poems."

"He went out with my girlfriend," she said. "For a long time."

She left to get more coffee for another customer. When she came back, she said, "Yeah, he went out with her for a long time. Never married her though."

I couldn't tell if she was hurt for her girlfriend, or had been interested in Stafford herself. She said she guessed he loved poetry more. Although she did not sing the sentence in Stanley's lilt, I heard his voice.

CHAPTER THIRTY

GOLD STARS AND BUTTERBALLS—M'EDITOR—
A COUNTDOWN AT EIGHTY—THE NEXT
HEAVYWEIGHT CHAMPION OF THE WORLD—
A RUMP MAN MEETS A COCK WOMAN—
A BAT COMES TO THE PARTY—
SARAH LAWRENCE—BOOK NEWS—
GOOD-BYE TO YADDO

I drove through Yaddo's tall iron gates and onto the four hundred acre estate once owned by the Trask family. I passed the mansion and arrived at the office. A staff member showed me to West House, formerly servant quarters. I had a bedroom with two desks, and a study with two more desks. He told me quiet hours were from nine to four, and overnight guests forbidden. On my way to dinner that evening, I met an old man tending a patch of tuberous begonias. George Vincent, the retired gardener, had worked at Yaddo all his life. He walked me toward the mansion, and described Elizabeth Ames, the first director, praising her sense of decorum. She wouldn't allow politics to be discussed at dinner after James T. Farrell had started so many arguments forty years ago. George was devoted to Yaddo as well as to Mrs. Trask.

"When Miss Ames died," he said, "I was the only one who knew where she wanted to be buried."

I asked where that was.

"Ten feet from the madam," he said. He pointed in the direction of their graves and said good-bye.

Everyone entered the dining room from having cocktails on the terrace. I stood in line for a napkin ring labeled with my name, along with a glass of iced tea and fresh mint. I took a tall-backed chair between the composer, Ned Rorem, and Tobias Schneebaum, a writer. Three visual artists joined us. We were served roast chicken, new potatoes and string beans while Rorem conducted the conversation as if it were a salon. He asked me what I wrote about, as he passed me a bowl of small grooved yellow globes.

"I have a hard time answering that question," I said, wondering at the little balls before handing them to the artist next to me.

"Then," he nodded, "you should *learn* to answer."

Turning to a sculptor, Rorem asked, "What are *your* subjects?"

"Love and death," he said, biting a drumstick. He had learned to answer.

Schneebaum said, "I hope everyone will come to my studio tonight. I'm showing slides about both." He took a piece of bread, dabbed his knife into the mysterious bowl and spread one of the balls of butter across the crust.

When melon was served for dessert, Rorem said, "I'm going to lodge a complaint." He stared at the pale slice. "Fruit every night. I need a dark pleasure like chocolate. I have no lover. I don't use foul language. I don't drink or smoke. I wait all day for dessert and then it's melon."

"Yes, and I hear these can play the devil with your foreskin," Schneebaum said.

After dinner, the composers took turns at the piano in the chapel, while Rorem walked up and down the hallway on his hands. He was a trim fifty-year-old, his full head of dark hair giving him the look of a much younger man.

That night I went to Schneebaum's studio. His thick eyebrows pointed down like two deep diacritical marks accentuating a big twisted nose, large eyes and ears. He had made a name for himself as an unconventional anthropologist for his book about living with cannibals, *Keep the River on Your Right.*

When everyone was seated, Tobias showed slides of the headhunters in the Amazon whom he met as he walked naked through the jungle. He hinted he had sex with several of the men and also ate human flesh, including heart. He described tribesmen carving a canoe in a hut, scoring the likenesses of their ancestors into the bark. When they finished, he said, four men held each side of the craft, but, as they moved toward the door, the canoe made a great whooshing sound, a sound like a strong wind, and it pushed them back. This happened several times, until they finally rushed it out with a noise like a slamming wave. Tobias spoke gently as he told his stories, and we left in awe of our adventurous colleague who seemed anything but the adventurer in appearance and manner.

As I lay in bed that night, I heard a strange sound, a constant hum. I peered into the West House yard, which was brightened by floodlights. Bats circled the treetops. The noise continued and I recalled the windowpane of Stanley's room, and Tobias's canoe, and I tried to ignore both by reading Ned Rorem's *The Later Diaries*, borrowed from the mansion library. To my horror, I found he had rated his Yaddo dinner companions. He gave "silver stars" to Donald Justice and Mark Strand, and a "gold star" to David Del Tredici, one of the composers who played after dinner. The sound grew louder and I traced it to the hall, to the half-open door of Larry Dalton, the artist with whom I shared a bath. Four hairdryers, clamped on the backs of chairs, were aimed at a girl in a bikini made of something

resembling seaweed, who stood before a large paper fan shaped like a clamshell. Her hair was flat from the heat. I recognized the waitress who served us at dinner. Dalton was taking photos, and comparing her to Venus.

Back in bed, I opened Rorem's diaries and found a portrait of Frank O'Hara, written three weeks after his death. I admired the line, "Frank O'Hara died in the middle of a sentence," and fell asleep.

The next morning I learned the breakfast routine: walk through the dining room, open the door to the kitchen, and state your order.

"Two poached, Beverly," the woman in front of me said. Beverly, dressed in white, sat at a table, which held a tub of butter. She placed a spoonful in a bowl of ice water, then molded it into a sphere. She rolled it between two grooved paddles, making the "butterballs" which had confounded me the night before.

I joined a table but when I introduced myself, everyone burrowed deeper into their books and papers. This was the "silent table." But because no one spoke, no one told me.

On my way out, I passed a guest and said good morning.

"I don't talk before breakfast," he said.

Mail delivery was the highlight of the day, everyone surrounding the letters, packages and cards on a desk in the lounge. I had received several envelopes from my mother containing rejections of my book, A Little Faith. I had resigned myself to the fact that I'd written a collection of love poems, and the editors complained about the book's small orbit. One asked, "Isn't sincerity the biggest con of all?" Porter sent On the Cod, his book of barroom monologues. His letter said he had walked nervously into the Fo'c'sle, terrified of meeting his contributors. He had quoted their binges, betrayals and thefts. To Porter's astonishment, no one recognized himself. He guessed they had been either too drunk or lying. He mentioned that

Vince's publisher rejected the draft of his Pancho Villa book and he owed a chunk of the advance. He took an advertising job in Boston, but after a month he returned to the Fo'c'sle, fired for his copy for a jewelry store that said, "We'll give you the ring, if you give us the finger." A postscript said that Barkhausen won a contest for his first book, *The Birthday Suit*. I loved that poem, an account of his father presenting him with a three-piece on his thirteenth birthday, but had advised against using it for the book since it also meant to be naked. Still, I preferred it to his original title, *Eating Out the Angel of Death*. Barkhausen's neologisms began to make sense. As cockeyed and impetuous as they were in conversation, they charged his poetry with an askew and often mad language. My teachers had seen it, Stanley saw it, and I came to believe in it—it was poetry—the thing that no one could define, the thing about which it could be said that no one really knows what it is.

There were readings and slide shows every week and an eighty-three-year-old poet with a long gray beard, Henry Chapin, read one night with Spear, a San Francisco poet. She performed her poems, flinging her arms in the air, snorting, growling and inhaling gruffly between phrases like the musician Roland Kirk. She introduced her final piece saying, "This summer, I fulfilled one of my lifelong dreams. I did something I always wanted to do." She paused. "I went to my favorite Chinese restaurant and tried something from everyone's plate."

The crowd laughed.

"It's not funny," she said. "I'll tell you when it's funny."

Her poem began as an homage to the delicacies and their origins and then veered into a litany of the injustices endured by those who brought them to our tables. With the final line about the fiery rashes of those who peel shrimp, she stormed off the stage and rickety Henry

ascended, using a cane. He wore a heavy tweed jacket despite the heat.

"Spear," he said, "I feel you've thrown a lot of confetti into the air and it's still coming down."

"Those are serious issues, Henry," Spear yelled back. Henry said he was sure they were, and then introduced himself. He had gone to Princeton with Edmund Wilson, whom he called "Bunny." He said Bunny hated his poetry. Many years later he contacted Wilson, saying, "You were right to avoid my poetry when we were young, because I was a very bad poet, but now I'm a very good poet and would like to give you my books." Wilson was famous for the postcard he sent to those who made requests from him. Henry had one with him and read it:

> "Edmund Wilson regrets that it is impossible
> for him to: Read manuscripts, write articles or
> books to order, write forewords or introductions,
> make statements for publicity purposes, do any
> kind of editorial work, judge literary contests,
> give interviews, take part in writers' conferences,
> answer questionnaires, contribute to or take part
> in symposiums or 'panels' of any kind, contribute
> manuscripts for sales, donate copies of his books
> to libraries, autograph works for strangers, allow
> his name to be used on letterheads, supply personal
> information about himself, or supply opinions on
> literary or other subjects."

Henry then showed the card, with Wilson's answer to his letter scrawled over it in big black letters, "NO! NO! NO! NO! NO!"

He read from his book, *A Countdown at Eighty*, and then "A Narrative Poem of the Norse Discoveries of America." Spear cheered him on from the front row, calling him "brother." Next to her, the poet Sally Elgin, wrapped in scarves and appearing much older than her sixty years, drank from a flask.

Rorem stopped me on the way out and said, "You look like a man who's been waiting a long time for a bus." I could feel he was getting ready to give me a bad grade.

Lewis Abolia, known for his sonnets, invited everyone to his room at the top of the mansion to toast the poets with port. Dalton, who liked Henry, brought several blueberry pies, with help from his girl in the kitchen, and everyone held slices on sagging paper plates. After a glass of wine, Henry fell asleep in a rocking chair, the pie on his lap, his chin lost in his beard, looking like one of the Norsemen he described. Sally whirled through the room, commending the blueberries at the top of her lungs so loudly that even Spear shuddered. I talked with a woman in her late twenties, a fiction writer, who told me she had published stories in the *New Yorker*. Her name was Melissa Owen, and I thought we were hitting it off when she excused herself, saying she had to make a call. And yet she stayed. And mentioned again that she had to make a call. There was only one phone in the mansion, and a line usually formed to use it. I finally realized she was trying to get me to ask who she was calling.

"Your boyfriend?"

"No," she whispered, "M'editor."

"Who?"

She said it again, a breathy word I couldn't understand.

"M'editor." She closed her eyes when she spoke it. "M'editor at the *New Yorker*."

"Oh," I laughed, "Your *editor*!"

"We have to discuss changes."

Sally had overheard us, and pointed a finger at Melissa, shouting, "I must make a call myself!" She asked Dalton to put another piece of pie on her plate and unsteadily rushed out the door. Melissa did not seem to care that she would have to wait.

"He thinks it's the best thing I've done."

We were interrupted by Abolia yelling at two other poets, "I'm not bitter! I am *not bitter!*" Leaded windows surrounded Abolia's bed, and I recognized the room as Stanley's, the room in the tower he had told me about. Henry opened his eyes and asked if I would escort him to West House. I said I would, and waited while he lectured the young poets for five minutes on contemporary poetry's neglect of the amulet as a fecund image.

Dalton told me the kitchen girl asked him for a reference to art school. Melissa repeated, "m'editor," to a leftist novelist from the village, who turned away, saying, *"New Yorker, New Schmorker!"*

When I thought Henry had run out of steam, he pulled a piece of paper from his overstuffed wallet and read a poem clipped from the take-out menu of Hattie's Chicken Shack in downtown Saratoga. The room quieted. "It's called 'Woman,'" he said, and read:

> She's an angel in truth, a demon in fiction.
> A woman's the greatest of all contradiction.
> She'll scream at a cockroach and faint at a mouse,
> then tackle a husband as big as a house.
> She'll take him for better, she'll take him for worse.
> She'll split his head open, and then be his nurse.
> And when he is well and can get out of bed,
> she'll pick up a teapot to throw at his head.
> You fancy she's this, but you find that she's that
> for she plays like a kitten and fights like a cat.
> In the evenings she will, in the mornings she won't
> and you're always expecting that she does when
> she don't.

Some women in the room began to hiss at the third line, but Henry persisted until the end, which had Abolia applauding and Spear puzzled.

"Let's go, Henry," I said, and we went down the staircase arm in arm.

Melissa was waiting for the phone, stamping her red shoes. She said, "You're not supposed to stay on that long. Sally knows that!"

I leaned Henry against the wall and tapped the solid oak door of the booth.

"Maybe it's empty," I said, listening.

"No, she's in there," Melissa said. "I heard her."

When there was no sound, I knocked loudly, wondering if Sally might be hard of hearing.

"Let me take a look," I said, and when I turned the knob, Sally, who had fallen asleep against the door, tumbled out and crashed her plate, pie and fork onto my feet, yelling, "This isn't my stop!"

Melissa and I picked her up and Melissa guided her to her room.

Henry said, "She has nice legs."

As we crossed the grounds, he said he didn't want to be boastful in public, but he had received letters from two well-known poets in response to *A Countdown at Eighty.*

"Here they are," he said, handing me a flashlight and paper strips from his wallet. "Read the underlinings."

I focused the beam. *You've outdone yourself, Henry.*

"Nice, isn't it?"

"Very nice," I said.

"Someday I'll tell you who they are. Read the other."

I found the sentence circled in blue ink. *I always know a poem by Henry Chapin!*

"I didn't want to brag," he said.

Two poets, Sandro Brezini and James Dorwin, invited me for a drink downtown. Dorwin was a gaunt Midwesterner who had the odd habit of scratching his head with the hand opposite to the itch, so his right fingers circled over his head and above his left ear in a simian gesture. His grandfather invented Shredded Wheat, which, he said, changed the way Americans ate breakfast in the morning. Brezini was powerfully built, but dainty. After Del Tredici played the piano after dinner, he called, "Oh David, how I love to watch your fingers fly!" He began a series of poems, a dialogue between the black and white keys on the piano.

The bar, The Neutral Corner, was outside Saratoga proper, in the woods behind the Grand Union, far from the touristy Triple Crown, Winner's Circle, and Thoroughbred's. Dorwin said that famous boxers used to hang out there, and that the place was filled with autographed photos. Brezini asked what the name meant and Dorwin explained that when you floor an opponent, you have to retreat to the farthest neutral corner before the referee can start his count.

As we were getting into the car, the English critic Malcolm Bradbury leapt from a hydrangea. Since he didn't have transportation, he hung around the parking lot, hitching rides. Bradbury had founded a renowned creative writing program at the University of East Anglia. He smoked a pipe and his wiry long hair sprung from his head in all directions. We drove through the main streets of Saratoga, past the supermarket and onto a dirt road that led to the bar.

"How'd you find this place?" I asked.

"The bartender at the Winner's Circle said his brother owned it," Dorwin said.

"I also got the feeling his brother was a loser," Brezini added.

The bar was packed with tradesmen in work clothes who looked us over. We paraded past them in our khaki pants and white button downs and sat in a booth in the back room, which had a pool table. The waitress took our drink order and also gave us menus of Chinese food. The

Neutral Corner was both bar and a Chinese restaurant. I went to see the photos. Jack Dempsey, Joe Louis, Rocky Marciano—all signed to Bill. I guessed Saratoga drew them here in its prime, and then I noticed each name was scrawled in the same handwriting. I told Dorwin about the fake autographs and he picked up a cue, walked into the bar and darted it toward several photos.

"You got a problem?" the bartender said.

"These are all signed by the same person."

"Asshole!" the bartender said, pumping glasses into the soapy sink.

We were explaining the ruse to Bradbury and Brezini when a young woman entered through a rear door. She wore a tight blouse, short skirt and high heels and approached a three-foot square platform. A table of her friends cheered and one played "Midnight at the Oasis" on the jukebox. The Neutral Corner was a bar, a Chinese restaurant, and a strip club. The girl danced very awkwardly and self-consciously. She removed her blouse, all elbows and forearms. Then she swiveled out of her skirt and fought it off, as if she were undressing in her apartment, solitary and sorrowful. A minute into the song, she stepped from the little square, put her hands to her face, and ran from the room. Two women from her table followed with her clothes.

"I feel sorry for her," Dorwin said, "but it was erotic."

"You call a little girl from the sticks standing on a pallet in a cheap bar-cum-Chinese restaurant *erotic*?" Bradbury asked, puffing hard on his pipe.

The bartender had left his station and stood by our table, looking down at Dorwin.

"You think you know something about boxing, wise guy? I'll tell you something, and you can bet on this." He pointed his finger at Dorwin who listened with his mouth open.

"Next heavyweight champion of the world," and he paused so we could grasp the enormity of the information. "Beau Williford!"

We had another round, and Brezini asked the waitress what happened to the dancer.

"She's new," the waitress said. "She didn't do too bad."

We were enthusiastically agreeing when the dancer, fully dressed, returned and sat at the table with her friends.

Brezini said, "We should tell her she was good."

Dorwin added, "Should we tell her we're poets?" When no one answered, he asked again, "Shall we tell her we're poets?" He was grinning uncontrollably at the thought that the dancer would be impressed with the quality of her audience. We managed to curb his notion but when we left, Dorwin couldn't help himself from approaching the would-be dancer's table as a professional dancer gyrated. Outside, he said, "I told her to keep at it, that it was an art, like ours. Like poetry."

Barkhausen wrote me from The Institute of Living, a mental hospital in Hartford, where he had checked himself in. Many sentences of his ten-page letter were missing prepositions and conjunctions and I wondered if Artie was on medication. He said he needed to stay calm because he had been seeing everything from the window of a train traveling a million miles an hour. He spent his days reading, but the books he asked for were not delivered. He wanted Marguerite Duras and got Alexandre Dumas's *The Man in the Irony Mask*. Was the "irony" intentional? He wanted *Black Sun*, the life of Harry Crosby, but got *The Black Son*, about a boy whose father was a slave and mother a plantation owner. He was working on a novel and said he might use a "Guy de Plume."

Melissa was in a great mood. Her agent sold her book of stories and she had fallen in love with William Still, a conceptual artist who signed his work "B. Still." They walked the grounds hand in hand, drove around Saratoga, ate together. By now, many guests had bonded and, when the door for dinner opened, friends claimed tables by setting their drinks next to their plates and then retrieving their napkins from the sideboard. I sat mostly with the poets, Jean Valentine my favorite. She had a quiet demeanor, hushed voice, and a smoky laugh that filled the room. Melissa approached each new arrival, introducing herself and saying, "You'll do great work here. I have. My book is coming out next year." Then she nodded, whispering, *Simon and Schuster.* Her words were perfectly timed to the bowing of her head, just as the nuns in my grammar school had taught us to do at the name of Jesus. At the name of her publisher, all the muscles in Melissa's neck went limp. Melissa and Bill had decided to live together, but there was a stumbling block—she had a dog and he a cat, and they wondered how the pets would get along. They planned to drive to Brooklyn to introduce them. Melissa would forgo her stay at the Virginia Center for the Arts to be with Bill. "I've already had a long year of colony-hopping," she said.

The composer Giorgio Visconti stood at the front of the dining room, tapped his glass with a spoon and announced that everyone was invited to his composer's tower for a bash on Thursday. It was a celebration for a performance of his latest piano concerto at Amherst College and he was leaving for it the following day. Henry asked if I would escort him to the party. His back was hurting him and he had a harder time getting in and out of his chair. I said I would, as the tower was a long walk from West House. Dalton said he'd seen Giorgio earlier that afternoon with a woman driving a silver Jaguar, the girlfriend who was taking him to Amherst.

"She's beautiful, dark hair, black dress, very New York," he said.

"Big boobs?" Henry asked.

"She was pretty, Henry. I really didn't check her out that much," Dalton said.

"Well, it doesn't matter. I'm a *rump* man myself," Henry grinned.

"I'm a *cock* woman myself!" screamed a feminist artist at our table, famous for her sculpture of Emma Goldman made of tampon applicators she found on Jones Beach.

Henry blushed and said, "What a lovely girl."

It was time for dessert, and everyone rose to the sideboard. As I got up, Henry gave me a pained look and asked, "John, would you bring me a black coffee and a piece of cake? My spine feels like broken glass."

The artist stared when I placed the plate and cup in front of Henry. He thanked me, saying, "Serving those who cannot serve themselves is humanity at its best," looking at everyone, so it seemed we formed a brotherhood, a bond, between two rump men.

The night of the party I found Henry in his room reading *Death Starts in the Colon*. We made our way out of West House and down the pine-needle path. A little moat surrounded the tower. We crossed a rickety bridge, about ten feet long, with rope handrails and I held Henry tightly. The planks swayed. We were talking about Giorgio's music, which we had heard in the chapel after dinner.

"It sounded like God having a nervous breakdown," Henry said.

The cock woman was leaning against the tower entrance, smoking with a friend, and she smirked when we approached. We did seem a strange pair. Henry, out of another time, with his beard, long gray hair and woolen coat, and me holding him, his preppie nephew. We continued talking about Giorgio, but just as we got in front of the two women, Henry said loudly, "I like his chamber music, but I'm particularly fond of his SYMPHONY IN G—SPOT!" And then he laughed, twisting away from me and prancing into the tower, balletic and youthful.

The artist glared at me and said, "You're such an asshole!"

"What did I do?" I said. I could see Henry in the tower, waving his cane at the wine, asking someone to get him a glass of red.

The round tower was three stories tall and made of brick. A boom box played and everyone drank from the full bar. Giorgio wore a Hawaiian shirt and introduced his girlfriend. She was as pretty as Dalton had reported, all in black. Most of the guests brought guests of their own, so it was crowded and noisy. I got in the spirit and drank shots of Old Grand-Dad with beer chasers. Dalton told me the girl from the kitchen had broken up with him as soon as he submitted his reference. Henry joined us, his gray beard stained with burgundy. Dalton brought the bottle of bourbon from the bar and filled my glass again. When I told him I had already had enough, Henry held out his wine glass for a taste and said, "Each stage of the rocket needs fuel!" He began a discourse on varieties of zinfandel and Dalton sneaked off.

I excused myself from Henry to talk to Jean Valentine. I tried to tell her how much I liked her poems, but my sincere feelings seemed like tipsy flattery. Jean asked how my own work went. I meant to say I felt fortunate to be here, even though I might be poor, but the word *portunate* came out which evoked her long hearty laugh before she quit me for a cigarette. I had another bourbon, leaned against the wall and watched Dalton dancing with the cock woman. She was a great dancer, and I suddenly noticed how attractive she was. I couldn't stop myself from watching her slim body zip around the floor. My drunken scrutiny led me to observe a yellow stain, a smudge, but heavier, something three-dimensional on the back pocket of her jeans. I kept staring as she spun this way and that.

Jean returned and said, "She's quite a dancer," raising her eyebrows.

"Yes, she is," I whispered, "but she has a stain or something on the seat of her pants."

"You've been paying close attention."

"Look!" I said, pointing.

The song ended and, as the artist walked away from Dalton, I followed. I saw it close up. The blotch was sticky and familiar—I was certain it was, yes, it was a butterball!

I tapped her shoulder, and she turned, surprised.

I decided it would be gentlemanly to whisper for the sake of discretion, but when I began to speak, I found myself yelling to be heard above the music.

"I think you sat on a butterball."

"What?" she said.

I repeated it, but she shook her head.

I turned her by the shoulder and pointed to the smudge. She twisted her neck, saw it, and said, "You are one fucking jerk."

I walked back to Jean. "I thought she should know," I said. "I would like to know if I sat on one of those butterballs!" Jean just stroked my elbow.

Dalton pointed to the ceiling where a bat dipped and soared.

Henry said, "They'll go right for your hair!" and many women ran out to the bridge, covering their heads. Giorgio took off his Hawaiian shirt and flailed at the diving bat, circling the circumference of the room, jumping and flinging it against the wall. We all huddled in the middle of the floor as Giorgio and the bat went round and round.

Giorgio swatted the bat when it landed on a protruding brick. The bat and the shirt fell together and the guests moved into a tighter circle. Dalton and I tried to help Giorgio, who bent over the pile of color. Instead of grabbing the bat through the shirt, he inexplicably put his bare hand under it and grabbed its neck between his thumb and forefinger. When he carried it through the crowd, all we could see were two big ears as it went by, squeaking.

A scream came from the doorway. The bat had bitten Giorgio just before he threw it into the night sky. Bradbury ran over, took a handkerchief from his pocket and stanched the blood's flow. The women returned from the bridge and Giorgio walked around with his girlfriend on his arm, holding a beer in his wrapped hand, telling everyone he was fine.

Henry called Brezini's favorite poet, James Merrill, "a toe-dancer." Brezini replied, "Your bits of knowledge came to you like change dropped through a boardwalk. You gathered a dime here, a nickel there . . ."

Henry pointed his cane at Brezini, and said, "You haven't the brains to understand the epic."

People started to leave. It was dark, and difficult to see over the bridge, so Giorgio grabbed a lantern and escorted his guests across the moat. Someone walked a drunken Henry to the mansion because I was too drunk. Giorgio asked me to take over the boom box and I fumbled with the tapes, inserting the wrong sides and pressing the wrong buttons. A song finally played just as there was a big fuss at the door because Giorgio had fallen off the bridge. Dalton, Bradbury and I ran out and pulled Giorgio from the moat. He had hurt his ankle and lost the lantern.

Giorgio sat next to his girlfriend, both of them devastated. He had told Dalton that he was looking forward to a big romantic time at the Adolphus Hotel since he had been without sex for the past month, but now his swollen foot rested in an ice bucket and a bloody kerchief covered his hand.

The next night at dinner everyone dressed in white, at the forceful command of a conceptual artist, who wanted to document it. I had forgotten her notion announced earlier in the week, and walked toward the balcony in my blue shirt and jeans. The crowd looked more like a cloud, a gathering of souls, wash on the clothesline, figures from the heavens. Melissa announced to the room that Giorgio had broken his ankle and was in the hospital.

"He missed his *nuit d'amour* and he'll also miss the performance," Melissa told us.

During my last week, vitreous floaters danced on the white wall above my desk and my corneal erosion returned. My throat clicked when I swallowed. I thought about making an appointment with an eye doctor and throat doctor. Paramecium-shaped figures in paisley patterns slid across my updated résumé. One image particularly troubled me. It looked like a question mark, and I kept following it across the page, trying to get a better look and, as I did, I swallowed, and my throat clicked. I was closing one eye and then the other when Jean Valentine knocked. She sat on the bed and asked if I wanted to replace her colleague at Sarah Lawrence, Jane Cooper, who had fallen ill. Classes started in a week. Jean and I left the next day for my interview.

The quarter-acre campus was set on a hill. Some students had already arrived, and one stood under a tree wearing a beret and dabbing at a French easel. I met with the advisory council in the office of its chair, pianist Kenneth Newman, who was discussing his standing order for Birkenstocks. Cold autumn light burnished the pine paneling, illuminating the teapot into which Newman scooped chamomile. Bill Park and Bob Wagner of literature joined us, along with Verna Serrini-Smith, a darkly beautiful historian with an Italian accent and a crimson scarf around her forehead. I recognized Bill Park as the editor of my college poetry text. He said that in the year of its publication, he took his family to France, but then a devastating thing happened. He looked to the sky, and said, "The Norton," referring to the *Norton Anthology of Modern Poetry,* which replaced all others.

We sat in armchairs around a dank fireplace and Newman filled our cups. He wore a beard with no mustache and as he lighted his pipe in front of a porthole-shaped window, I felt I was on a ship.

I handed out my vita, but they put it aside and asked about my favorite poets, what I was reading, what part of my education I thought lacking. We discussed the use of slang in Auden and the influence of Auden on Ashbery. The hour flew by and ended with Ken telling me there was no rank at the college, all teachers were equal members of the writing faculty. As we stood, Verna casually asked about my outside interests as she undid her scarf and shook out her raven hair. I didn't have any, and I knew I was supposed to. I used to watch the Friday night fights on television with my father, so I said, "Boxing." Everyone turned, looking again at their poet turned pugilist. When I added, "On TV," the room relaxed, except for Verna, who squinted.

Jean brought me into the office of Dean Ilya Wachs, who had combed his long white hair over his bald spot, but the unwilling lock fell in the other direction, a scythe-like flip. He smoked and talked about his specialty, Flaubert, and about French poetry. Afterward, I waited for Jean in the snack bar, surrounded by posters advertising coming lectures: *Is There Rape in the Animal Kingdom?* and *Problems Facing Women Rabbis.* Jean walked in and said I got the job.

On the drive back, she mentioned that if I were to publish a book, my appointment could be renewed. And if I taught well, it could be renewed again and again. She warned how hard it was to publish a book, with all the competition from students in writing programs, and repeated what Ridge had told me, that you needed luck.

We arrived in Saratoga Springs just before dinner and on the mail table I found a letter from Barkhausen and a note to call the editor of Midwestern University Press. Jean went into the dining room while I phoned. He was effusive about my manuscript. Unlike other editors, he said the love poems got to him, that some really broke him up. I kept thanking him although I found it hard to thank someone who was complimenting me for making him weep. He said again and again, "This is my book. This is my book." After a silence, I asked what he meant.

"Don't you know?" he said. "My wife died six months ago of pancreatic cancer. This is *my* book." He shouted the words.

Jean had saved me a seat and put her arm around my shoulder when I told her the news. That night I called Ridge. He said, "I told you. You need luck. If his wife hadn't died . . ."

Barkhausen's letter contained poems and the news that he would succeed Kurt as Chair of the Work Center's Writing Committee.

Dalton left, others arrived, and Melissa and Bill returned from Brooklyn. At dinner, Bill explained that his cat, Purr-Mew, was terrified of Melissa's rat terrier, Pal, and he felt they would never get along. He had devised a test: they would put the animals in the car and drive around the block. Melissa's dog was in the back, and she drove while Bill held Purr-Mew, but Pal kept barking and climbing over the seat, and the cat scratched Bill badly. He showed the marks on his wrists and arms.

"We've decided to let them know each other a little better before we make a move," he said.

Melissa rose from the table and said, "It goes deeper than that!" She threw down her napkin ring and ran from the dining room.

My stay and Henry's ended on the same Saturday. I took a last walk through the rose garden, the only part of Yaddo open to the public, and passed a young woman holding a baby. She stepped in front of me.

"Are you a guest?" she asked. I said I was.

"I was born in Saratoga," she said. "My husband and I used to walk here. He wanted to be a writer. He dreamed of staying in the mansion. That was his goal, but he died last year in a car crash."

I said I was sorry.

"We have a tradition in my family," she said. "We come here when someone dies, and remember them in this rose garden, but I never thought I'd be remembering my husband." She rocked the child in her arms and said she hoped he'd be able to be a guest one day.

"I hope he will too," I said, and I left her on that path shouldered with roses.

I loaded my car and drove by the mansion for the last time. I saw Henry and Melissa talking, so I pulled over. Henry stood in front of his ancient Volvo. As I approached, I could hear Melissa ticking off the places she was giving readings over the winter.

"How do you arrange such things?" Henry asked.

Melissa whispered her answer. "M'agent," she said.

She told us that she was leaving early, a week ahead of time, because she couldn't bear being around Bill. They had broken up.

"I was hoping to have a normal life," she said. "Anyway, I just got into MacDowell!" She clapped her hands and lifted herself on her toes. "I guess I'll go on living grant-to-mouth!"

We said good-bye, and Henry put on leather driving gloves and settled behind the wooden steering wheel. I got in my car and waited for him, but the Volvo sputtered. He tried again and again, but the empty groans continued. I walked over.

"Luckily we're on a hill," he said. "Just give me a shove."

I pushed hard on the bumper and the car began to roll. Henry furiously turned the key and finally the engine caught. He waved his arm out the window in thanks and a few moments later I followed him through the stately gates.

EPILOGUE

We were hell-bent to become poets. Many dodged hell, others were singed by its flames, and a few went up in them. The extracurricular activities at poetry's finishing school had long-term effects: Alcoholics Anonymous, Sex Addicts Anonymous, loss of life and limb. Some counted the hours without a drink and some the days without accosting strangers or the partners of friends. I recalled my abstemious Iowa classmate, Denise Graves, saying, "After Thanksgiving, everyone in my workshop had taken up with the person on his left." To counter that atmosphere, she threw a party, her invitation on the bulletin board proclaiming "No Booze! No Smoking! No Dope!" McPeak whipped out his pen and wrote, "No Fun!"

Frank Ridge's flourishing career featured appearances in the *New Yorker*, a reading at the Library of Congress, and a Yale appointment. Within a year, sexual harassment charges brought by several students forced him to resign. He said this ultimately saved his life, as he joined SAA, became a sponsor and wrote a memoir about his addiction and recovery. I hadn't thought of his past as problematic. That his girlfriends far outnumbered mine I attributed to his doggedness and good fortune. Now I remembered the many times he leered at an overweight clerk or dowdy cashier, referring to each as a "sex goddess." And that he had often said with great assurance that a woman we passed in a supermarket or hallway was flirting with him. I used to think he was lucky. Now I knew, as he did, that he had been out of his mind.

Pryor and Wendy bought a house near the Alamo and Pryor started a journal called *Cards that Fell from the Deck*. His mission was to right the wrongs of the publishing industry, and his editorial standard demanded that all submissions be rejected by at least a dozen magazines. Belinda Schaeffer taught comparative literature at Vassar and married a French diplomat, spending half the year in Paris. She turned from poetry to criticism and then vanished into theory. Monique and Falcon Namiki married and moved to Tokyo. *Newsweek* featured an article on the couple, doing business as Namique, whose entrepreneurial skills had made them wealthy. The caption under their photograph read, "They Brought the Croissant to Japan." Despite running every day of his life and carrying that big .45, Abe Gubegna was murdered in 1986 by Haile Selassie's men, as he predicted.

Joe Cleary and loudmouth Trotta were banned from The Deadwood after one too many brawls. They divided their time between the Lazy Leopard Lounge and The Depot, two bars by the railroad tracks at the city's edge. After last call, they continued drinking near the Rock Island Line's mesmerizing stream of boxcars. One night, a train hit them both. Cleary lost an arm and Trotta a leg.

They could be seen downtown afterward, holding brown bags on benches, like victims of an Islamic punishment.

Dan Cook never went to NYU. Upon getting the call to interview, he separated in his mind from Nora and they began to bicker. He insisted she make an independent life for herself instead of being a wife and mother, and urged her to learn photography. By day, she was seen focusing her Nikon on the swing sets and monkey bars of playgrounds; in the evening, at nighthawks dive-bombing the Capitol building. A few months later, someone did move into that river stone apartment, just as Cook planned, but Nora did not fall in love with him. In fact, she fell wholly out of love with her husband, who became her new tenant, banned from their house and her bed. Cook railed that someone at NYU torpedoed him, someone sandbagged him, and now Nora had exiled him to the cell of his own making.

Mike McPeak got up from a table in a Chicago restaurant after a large Italian dinner and died of a heart attack that followed a weeklong binge. His wife sent me a poem she found among his papers:

DEAR JOHN SKOYLES

You and I are not unlike
The morning and evening stars—
Apart by space and time, we never meet.

It's raining here.
All the rivers are rising again.
I read letters you wrote years ago.

And what are you feeling, my friend?
Since I saw you last,
I've not been able to drink like a man.

What was I feeling? I missed my friend. The simile, "like a man," always seemed to come at the end of sentences dealing with violence. McPeak had given that phrase a new dimension. I recalled the night a state trooper stopped us, when we were drunk and speeding on Interstate 80, McPeak's greasy hands on the wheel and boxes of Howard Johnson's fried clams in our laps. The trooper asked him if he'd been drinking, and the question and the clarity bestowed by the beam from his flashlight made me notice that one lens of my friend's cockeyed glasses was nowhere near his eye.

"To tell you the truth, officer," he said. "I have had a couple of beers."

"Okay," the trooper said. "I want you to park by the side of the road for an hour, then take it easy going home." As soon as the cruiser's taillights faded, McPeak floored the gas pedal and we were quickly on our way, and that way had an end, and he had come to it.

Hester returned to New Orleans for her mother's funeral, but when she arrived, her mother had come back to life. A nurse, Elppa, claimed credit, saying she had unhexed the corpse through voodoo. Hester not only fell under Elppa's spell, but started calling her poems "charms," and worked in the nurse's shop selling statues, potions and oils. Elppa promised to give Hester a juju name over time, just as Elppa's was Apple in reverse.

Jeanne and Wayne stayed together, a stake and a tetherball. Jeanne continued to manage the Bull Ring and Wayne invented ways to make money during tourist season. I received an invitation from him to subscribe to his wine cooler newsletter. At Jeanne's insistence, Wayne limited his dope smoking to Herring Cove at sundown, but even then, on his walk home one evening, he wound up receiving stitches at the Drop-In Center from gashing his forehead on a stop sign.

Stanley Kunitz devoted himself to giving poets the chances he never had. He founded Poet's House, affording space to writers and showcasing every volume of poetry published each year.

My editor asked me to provide a blurb for my book, and I wrote to Dugan, unaware he was undergoing major eye surgery. Nevertheless, he fought to read the manuscript, and Judy mailed his paragraph printed in huge block letters on a fourteen-by-seventeen-inch sketchpad. Dugan, following the example of William Blake, looked through his eye and not with it.

Mitchell Lawson sent me a form letter, saying he was guest-editing an issue of the *Iowa Review* and asking to include one of my poems. He began cordially, saying he remembered the piece and wanted to print it. Out of hundreds of pages of student work, this one had made an impression, and the issue would contain only twenty choices. I should send the poem and permission agreement within the week. I should not send any other poems. He wanted only this one. Any others would not be considered. In fact, if I sent any additional work, or substituted another poem, he would not publish anything at all. I should follow the rules of publication and editorial etiquette, and he failed to see why that was so difficult. He hoped to be able to use my contribution, but if not, he had a second tier of poets just as accomplished. He concluded with the hope that I would be as pleased to be invited, as he was pleased to include me. ML.

McPeak, roused from the grave by this letter, pulled out his pen and wrote on the bottom, "No!"

Out of respect for the dead, I didn't send the poem.

I moved back to Queens, living with my parents and commuting to Sarah Lawrence, happy with the job and its $8,600 salary. Jean Valentine did not have to take me to lunch during my first weeks because every Tuesday we laughed through the noon hour in the faculty dining room with Grace Paley, Allan Gurganus and Tom Lux. We were often joined by classicist Sam Seigle, whose overstuffed shopping bags spilled small volumes of Hesiod and Theocritus in a breadcrumb-like trail to his office.

Among my students was seventeen-year-old freshman Lucy Grealy who, at our first conference, kept her head down, her blonde hair covering her face. She hardly spoke, which made me babble and joke until she finally looked at me. She was missing most of her jaw, the result of multiple surgeries for cancer. We became close, regularly eating dinners of Chinese takeout in my office. She told me Halloween was her favorite day, the only time she looked like everyone else. Her memoir, *Autobiography of a Face,* would recount her struggle with the disease. Then there was Becca Schwan, who shaved half her head and wrote poems about Boy George and Fendi furs, and who wore hose clamps on her wrists and biceps. She was well-read, with a great imagination—when I asked her why she had missed an appointment, she said, "My twin fell off a high wire." One day in my office she kept wriggling in her chair. She eventually opened her shirt and pulled out a white rat named Andy Warhol. At lunch afterward, I told my colleagues. Grace wondered how I responded.

I said, "Put it back in your blouse."

"The voice of experience," she said.

And there was a lot of experience in the faculty dining room. Grace, almost always in a house dress, argued for Paul Goodman's fiction over Cheever's with Doug Bose whose every pastel sport coat was festooned with so much spilled ink you could almost read it. Harold Axe, the piano teacher, fought a losing battle with the turned-up points of the collar, which poked his neck, swatting at them as if attacked by invisible forces. Someone kidded Ike Burke about his belfry office seeming an ivory tower, and he looked over his glasses and said, "The most common ivory tower is the average person's passivity toward experience." Hefty Nino Lo Presti, who boasted being born with a wooden spoon in his mouth, rejoiced when the college hired a gourmet chef. He looked at his plate of linguini and clams and sighed, "Lady luck has lifted her slip." Gilbert Goulet, a novelist and Iowa graduate, asked at lunch one day if I knew Daniel Cook. Gil also taught at NYU and said that Dan's disastrous interview had become legendary. Dan had tried to flatter Galway Kinnell by saying, "We have to stop our students from writing like you," and he said, "You're the best we have," to two different novelists. The chair of the search committee complained to Cook about a celebrated English short story writer they had rejected for the post. Dan, impressed with the quality of his vanquished competition, asked why, and the chairman said, "Because I heard he referred to me as 'a no-good Jewish cocksucker!'" Cook thought for a second and said, "I didn't know you were Jewish." Glamour flashed from the theatre people, as when a whirlwind of scarves and sleeves blew past the table with the actress Viveca Lindfors somewhere in its midst. Many were eccentric, some were slightly mad, but all were thoroughly human.

I had a second residency at Yaddo over Christmas break when a composer's mother died and, because of my proximity, I was offered a portion of his stay. Unlike summer's large season, the mansion was closed. Twelve of us lived in West House and ate dinner above the tack room. Jerre Mangione had replaced Director Curtis Harnack who was on leave. We took walks together in the afternoon and, passing the composer's tower one day, I mentioned the party. He stopped abruptly on the path and said the insurance company threatened to drop coverage because of the incident. He asked me to testify as to what happened that night.

Jerre scheduled a call with Yaddo's lawyer in his office, and was on the phone with him when I arrived. He pointed to a chair and I listened as he said I was filling a sudden vacancy, that I had been at the party, saw the bat bite Giorgio, and helped drag him from the moat. He told the lawyer I was a poet, the first time someone referred to me that way, and I took the receiver anxiously. The lawyer asked if I knew the conversation was being taped. Yes. Did I agree to it being taped? I did. Where was I on the night of August 15? At Yaddo. Did I see the bat bite Giorgio? Yes. Was he hurt? His hand was swollen. Was I present when Giorgio fell off the moat? I was. Did I help him? I tried. Had I seen him afterward? Yes. Was he hurt? It seemed so, his ankle was immersed in ice. Did I see him dancing after the fall? I couldn't remember. Had Giorgio been drinking? Yes. Did you see what he was drinking? Beer. Are you sure? Yes, I brought him one when I got one for myself. Was he drunk? He didn't seem so. Were you drinking beer? Yes. How many? Eight or nine. Were you drinking anything else? Bourbon. How many? Five, maybe six—I lost count.

"Thank you, Mr. Skoyles," he said. "I'll let you get back to your poetry."

My contract was renewed and, when our enrollment demanded another teacher, I suggested Barkhausen. Jean liked his work and invited him for an interview. He took the bus from Provincetown.

Ken Newman convened the advisory committee and included me for the occasion. Ken served the chamomile, and Barkhausen handled himself well except for pausing at Verna Serrini-Smith's question about teaching a student body mostly female. Artie seemed flummoxed for a moment and I knew why. It was not only Verna's beauty, but he was haunted by Dugan's poem about teaching at Sarah Lawrence:

> . . . a Sophomore (female)
> got down on her knees
> before me by my desk
> and tried to pull me
> over her with the door
> to my office OPEN. I said,
> "You don't want to be a slave,"
> and she answered, "Are you
> kidding?"

His brain swirling, Artie finally answered that women poets were among his favorites, listing Emily Dickinson, Marianne Moore and Louise Bogan. No one questioned him further. When enthused, as he was often during the interview, he couldn't halt the ends of his sentences, but only I seemed to notice his referring to the New York publisher as "Little, Brown Jug."

Artie left the room and Newman praised his "rambunctious erudition," and the others agreed. Ken asked what we thought of Lawson's recommendation which touted Barkhausen's work but called him, "a man of rough manners personally." Ken accepted my explanation of Artie's impetuousness, sipped his tea and said he would recommend the appointment.

I accompanied Artie to Provincetown for the weekend. Ronnie drove the Bonanza bus out of Port Authority as he had all these years. We moved to the rear after sitting behind a couple who had just returned from Botswana. They were describing in loud detail to passengers across the aisle how elephants had bowed to them because they sensed their power as healers. Their neighbors in turn told about a crow funeral they had witnessed at the Race Point parking lot, conducted by a chief crow, at the head of a circle of mourning crows around a dead crow. We took seats near the man I recognized from my first night in town, the one I stumbled against at the Fo'c'sle, the one who lost his voice when his wife left him. Artie sat by the window, and we shared the sack of favorite books he had hoped to display at the interview. He filled me in on things in Provincetown, saying he had become good friends with Dugan and Judy, often going to their house for dinner. He loved Dugan's poems all the more and read aloud:

> When I woke up with my head in the fireplace
> I saw the sky up the chimney. "No clouds,"
> I thought. "Good god day, what did I do
> last night to wake up in these ashes fortunately
>   cold?"

"Only Dugan could see the world from the bottom of a chimney, taking the point of view of a burnt log," I said.

"And still optimistic about the weather," Artie said.

At the rest stop in Providence we bought Cokes and tossed crackers to pigeons bobbing around the bus. One dragged a wing, and couldn't nab any tidbits no matter how accurately we aimed his way. I mentioned Stanley's "Robin Redbreast," about a hurt bird he tries to help into the air, and I recited the final lines:

> But when I held him high,
> fear clutched my hand
> for through the hole in his head
> cut whistle-clean . . .
> through the old dried wound
> between his eyes
> where the hunter's brand
> had tunneled out his wits . . .
> I caught the cold flash of the blue
> unappeasable sky.

A few hours later, we approached the Sagamore Bridge, with its sign, "Depressed? Call the Samaritans," and climbed thirteen stories above the Cape Cod Canal into clouds we saw from neither a bed of ash nor through an open wound—a sky of our own—and below, the surface of the water like slate, far down.

ACKNOWLEDGMENTS

Portions of this book have appeared in the *Boston Globe* and *Five Points: A Journal of Literature and Art*, in slightly different form. I have quoted passages from various poets, most of whom are cited, but include Weldon Kees, to whom I owe the book's ending phrase. A sabbatical leave from Emerson College was instrumental in my writing of this book.